LAYS AND LEGENDS OF THE
FOREST OF ESSEX

FOREWORDS

Essex, perhaps the least known but the best abused of English counties, is, yet, full of interest, not to say charm, for those who have eyes to see, and mind to enjoy Dame Nature, in her quietest, but not necessarily her least attractive aspects.

For such there are wide tracts of woodland; breezy hills and watered valleys; time-old cottages under shadowing oaks and elms; with sequestered homesteads amid woods and fields, more than enough to fill an artist's portfolio, and all within a score of miles—I had almost said within sight—of Paul's tall dome.

The philologist, too, willing to lay aside his town-bred reserve and academic 'stand off for I am better than thou' and consort with keeper, farmer or labourer on terms of equal manhood and good fellowship, may hear words and encounter modes of speech, current in the days of Chaucer or Gower, but long since obsolete elsewhere.

Antique legend, burden ballad, or gruesome tale, with quaint songs and sayings he may also hear, at the cost of a glass or two of ale, moderate but necessary largesse, wherewith to moisten the throat of his rustic entertainer.

And are not its woods and fields, as in the days of Ray, full of wealth for the botanist—very parterres of wildings, in places, unrivalled for size and beauty. Myself, did I not gather a cowslip of fifty bells open and unopened, not a stone's throw from the *Woodman* at Sewardstone; primroses big as a crown piece at Theydon; with wood hyacinths creamy white, and violets innumerable, fragrant as the breath of Cytherea herself, almost within the shadow of the lonely little Norman church at Lambourne?

For him, too, that follows the bent of good old Stukeley, ruined abbeys and priories, moated granges and farmsteads, crumbling halls and earthworks, are they not in plenty, with churches a-many, some large, some small, but all of them old, old almost as the county itself, and one of them, at least, of the forest logs that formed it nearly a thousand years ago? While joy of joy to the pedestrian, far and wide may he ramble, without being pulled up at every corner, except perhaps in the vicinage of some busy town, by that particularly irritating and especially Kentish nota bene—abundant there as mushrooms —'Trespassers will be——.'

With respect to the legends themselves, it may be objected that a certain sameness of thought runs through them all. O Reader! I am not careful to answer thee in this matter, seeing that here, as elsewhere, the bucolic mind, outside the things of farm and field, dwells mainly upon two others, the relation-

ship of the sexes, and the supernatural. Especially
is this so in the more wooded districts, where the
people are few, few also, till of late, the opportu-
nities of external intercourse; while Nature is everywhere present in her most seductive and perhaps
least ethereal mood.

But granting the objection, in what respect do the
smock-coated labourers of our woodland villages
differ from their fustian-jacketed brethren of the
towns? Yet further one might go and ask, What
novel takes with the reading public, or what drama
' catches on ' with the playgoing, unless based upon
passion with a goodly spicing of the marvellous?

Be this as it may, to the inhabitants of the forest
county I have known and loved from boyhood—
to them first of all—then to those of our civic brethren
who delight in field and copse and shaw—and finally
to all those to whom a wood is something more than
a ' chance medley ' of trees and bents and bushes,
but who believe with Wordsworth, that—

> One impulse from a vernal wood
> May teach us more of man,
> Of moral evil and of good
> Than all the sages can.

—I offer these Lays and Legends of the once great
forest of Essex.

CONTENTS

PROLOGUE

THE western sky with crimsoned gold aflame,
Day's royal lord profuse of parting light,
To Harold's bridge in Waltham mead I came,
My walk at end at bid of nearing Night.
Ablaze with gold and purpling shade the stream
Lapped murmurous by, while rush or pensive reed
Bent down asighing o'er the watery gleam
That kist each droop resemblance. Calm the mead
And still, save now that out the minster tower
The call to prayer pulsed slowly o'er the crest
Of cot, and town whose stir the dark'ning hour
Constraining softly, drew at length to rest.

Here sat I somewhile, till o'erhead a star
Looked forth, but doubtful sought again the haze;
As cottage maid, her casement pane ajar,
Peeps forth, and seen, draws back in shy amaze.
Now too the wind that lurked within the wood,
Made bold of gloom, soft stealing forth began
To roam the field and wake the willowy brood
That girt the stream which now more darkly ran.
These making murmur-answer, soon the sedge
'Gan sighing low like hunted Syrinx, worn

Of flight and fear; while o'er the forest edge
The pale moon, climbing, hung her crescent horn.
Sweet! eve's reposeful charm! But most of all
To me, short space befreed from civic toil,
Its harass tumult, and its gold-greed thrall
With all its sordid soul-debasing moil.
So sat I long, my gaze upon the fane
By royal Harry havocked, crumbling nigh,
Till—'Wait you, sir, for ghost of Lilian Lane?'
One asked, who unperceived had come me by.

At this I rose. A grey-haired cotter, bent
With stress of years, field-toil and penury,
Stood smiling by. 'Your pardon, sir, I meant
You no offence; 'tis but you bar for me
My way to Waltham.'

       'Nay good friend, no need,
To make excuse,' I answered, 'Mine the fault
To block the path at eve in open mead.
I crave your pardon, but yon ruined vault
And crumbling gate allured me. I too go
To Waltham where I sometime stay, so now
Relate the tale of Lilian Lane, if so
You deem it worth the telling.'

       'Sir, I trow
The tale to most were trifling,—olden tale
And one of many such my grandther told
Me trembling on his knee, of bluff King Hal
Who robbed the Abbey in the days of old;

Like city squires who buy some worn demesne,
And then ride roughshod over all at will;
Rob us poor folk of wayside patches green,
And make life doubly hard, where best is ill!
In sooth the tale is naught, but there's my cot!
An' you would hear the legend, share my meal,
A crust with ale and rasher—poor man's lot
But wholesome! Come, and I'll the tale reveal.

I followed where the cotter led. Beside
The convent gate, whose thorntopt turret hoar
Bethreats ere long to dam the miller tide
That careless chafes and mines its scragged floor,—
The cottage stood, its door wide ope that scent
Of pink and thyme and gilliflower might fill
Its parlour small, that harboured yet content,
Rich guest whose pinions, peace-plumed, banish ill!
Here, set between the cotter and his girls,
I learned the legend sad of Lilian Lane—
Of Thoydon Roland, slain for tire of pearls,
And Agnes Leigh, sweet maid of Fairmead plain.
Then Nasing's demon stag—then monken ghost
Behaunting Loughton wood; with many more
Not here set down; till night and morning met,
When I in haste resought my hostel door,
First court'sies paid, with gift for comely Kate,
Who ruled the cot in lieu of turf-laid dame,
And eke to grandchild Joan, who oped the gate
And kissed the stranger guest, devoid of blame.

WALTHAM

WALTHAM, instinct with memories of Harold Infelix, and of another, not less celebrated, if less warlike king, Bluff Hal of noisome renown, lies, now, fully a couple of miles away from the Wald whence it got its name. But just beyond the cemetery in Seward-stone Street, on the outskirts of the town, is a pleasant uphill field-path leading to a charming forest ridge, High Beech, whose church spire can be seen all the way from Waltham overtopping the trees of the surrounding woodland.

Of course the great feature of Waltham is the remaining portion of its once noble abbey. Central tower and transepts, with its choir extending more than a hundred feet eastward of its present ending, are, unfortunately, gone. They were undermined and blown up soon after the dissolution, one or two entries in the churchwarden's account books referring to the sacrilege.

'Imprimis. For coals to undermine a piece of the steeple, two shillings.'—'Item. To labourers which did undermine the wall (of the choir) forty-five shillings and ninepence.'

But the nave is left and is a grand specimen of early Norman work, while the Ladie chapel—for many a year used as a schoolroom—is a fine building. It stands over a crypt of chalk, 'the fairest I ever saw' says Fuller, which, as there is nothing parti-cularly fair about it, would seem to imply that the worthy historian had seen but few vaults constructed of this durable but somewhat unusual material.

Fuller, the historian, who was vicar of Waltham from 1648 to 1658 or thereabouts, must not be confounded with Robert Fuller, the last abbot—the Fuller of the legend—who, under compulsion, surrendered the monastery to the king's commissioners, Cromwell, Lee and others.

Harold's tomb (he was buried here after the removal of his body from the seashore at Hastings) was destroyed at the demolition of the choir, with a score of other tombs, and numerous abbatial brasses. But his battle-axe, rusted away to a fragment, is still preserved in the abbey vestry, with some seals and parchments of the ancient foundation, not to mention sundry gruesome memorials of crossroad interments, etc. The great walled garden of some twelve acres still exists; but the famous crusader tulip-tree, that flowered in June and July, and brought visitors to it from far and near, has long since perished. Perished also by this time must have most of the chests and coffers, settles and tables that were made out of it after it had been cut down.

Gone, too, is the snow-tree of the churchyard, that every year when its Eastern brother was gay with bloom, whitened the graves beneath it with its feathery down. But the gateway to the abbey precincts survives, though the great house of the Dennys has followed the Refectory and Dormitory which it supplanted.

Also, hard by the silted-up fishponds, where mint and

iris, moneywort and pennyroyal flaunt gaily enough in
their season, is Harold's Bridge. A couple or more
of its strong ribs still span the miller stream ; and
here the antiquarian rambler can throw himself
down and moralize, happy if cotter or townsman will
break into his dreaming with an hospitable call to
supper.

Romeland, too, but a stone's throw from the abbey
gate, must not be forgotten. It derives its name
from the fact that here, as at St. Albans and elsewhere,
the tolls taken from the market held within its enclosure
went to Rome to help maintain the Italian shavelings,
who then, as now, were the keenest of worshippers of
the Mammon that perisheth. It was here that Bluff
Hal had the little house to which he retired when on
pleasure bent, whether to hunt the dappled deer of
the woodland in the words of the old song—

> The hunt is up, the hunt is up,
>   And it is well-nigh daye ;
> And Harry, our King, has gone hunting,
>   To bring his deer to baye.

—or the fairer deer of the township, as in the case of
poor Lilian Lane.

Romeland, too, is otherwise famous, for it was
here, while Harry was in his 'little house,' that
Cranmer gave his celebrated opinion as to the King's
contemplated divorce from Queen Catharine, and to
use the royal phrase ' got the right sow by the ear.'
An opinion, by the way, that had much to do with
the Reformation that so shortly followed ; and after-

ward with the death of the opinionist at the stake by the justly offended daughter of the divorced queen.

But Hal's doings in Romeland are not altogether savoury memories. Sweeter by far is it to hear in imagination the music pealing from the abbey organ under the hands of the abbot, or the yet more skilful fingers of Thomas Tallis,—sometime organist till the surrender of the abbey—afterward gentleman of the Chapel Royal, composer of the extraordinary forty-part song, and of Church music that will be sung so long as English cathedrals, abbeys, and 'quires and places where they sing,' severally deck and delight the land.

Two other names connected with Waltham and its Abbey are worthy of mention. The learned and pure-souled Joseph Hall, sometime Bishop of Exeter, and afterward of Norwich till dispossessed by the Puritans in 1643, was vicar here for many years, and here, it is believed, wrote his 'Contemplations.'

Fox, the martyrologist, was also an occasional resident, and a garret in an old house in the churchyard by the market-place is still pointed out as the place in which he compiled his terrible record. His son Samuel was an inhabitant, and his commonplace book records the birth of a daughter Sarah who lived till she was eight years old and 'lies buried at Waltham Church by my puedore.'

LILIAN LANE

I

Slow swept o'er Waltham's convent pile the chime;
  'Twas call to Mass for Harold, erewhile slain,
With all his warrior brethren in their prime,
  On Senlac's fatal, blood empurpled plain:
When Fortune flown, and victory denied,
Unconquered still, the Saxon fought and died.

For him betrayed of Fortune, what so well
  Became as death with rest within the fane
His largess founded? Oft the woful knell
  Slow rung of monken hand, should wake again
In patriot breast the warrior flame, and chide
Lethargic hate that brooked tyrannic pride.

'Twas dawn, and weird within the minster fair
  Loomed chauntry, aisle, and chancel, dimly seen
By gleam of shrine set taper, or the flare
  Of cresset swung the transept arch between:
O'er all a glamour lay, with laborous light
O'erhead from boss or gilted corbel bright!

For gloom prevailed, for all the Eastern gate
  Stood ope unlatched at blithe Aurora's call;
For all through pane of servile Flemish state
  The purpled radiance softly 'gan to fall
O'er shrine and tomb and costly parquet pave
And prayerful slab o'er crosiered abbot's grave.

Through pillared nave, and broad triforium span
  By sculptured stall and rood of Bethlehem,
Rich gift of angel hand, the pleading ran
  ' Eternam ei dona requiem '
With retinue of echo whose refrain
Renewed the plaint again and yet again.

Sonorous now, as when the slumbering sea
  Rageful awakes—storm-lashed—to tempest feud ;
Now plaintive, low, as when some moorland tree
  Sighs forth at eve lament of solitude,
The Mass went on till all the sentient air
Of pain grown voiceful, piteous, swelled the prayer.

Now paled the taper's futile ray, the while
  The blazoned casement overhead grew bright
With beam of day. Within the lowbrowed aisle
  Night sullen lingered, till prevailing Light
Renewed the war, and drave him thence for all
Sustent of pier and portal, vault and wall.

His Mass at end, the monk, arising, closed
  His missal limned within and out with gold ;
Then slowly turned him where the king reposed
  In tomb of porph'ry, richly wrought of old,
'Neath vaulting slight with rib and pendant fair
So cunning carved, they seemed to hang in air.

' Infelix Harold ! ' murmured he, his gaze
  Upon the legend, simple, gleaming red
On scroll of gold, that shone amid the blaze
  Of kindling light which all the shrine o'erspread

From nearer casement, where the glowing pane
Portrayed the king in conflict with the Dane.

'Infelix? No! Unhappy he that spoils
   God's Church on earth, pretending hate of crimes
So like his own, they seem but counterfoils
   Of his own royal passions. Evil times
Were thine indeed, O warrior earl, but still
Thou diedst a king, nor brooked tyrannic will

'In self or other. Thine the nobler meed—
   A warrior's death—than his, whom foul disgrace
Pursues, the while he thinks to cover greed
   With fierce rebuke of ill in lesser place;
Whose vices grow, till victims hourly plead
O'erpatient Heaven for judgment on his head.'

So sighed the monk. Yet while he mournful spake,
   Upon his brow day's first full radiance fell.
'Twas healing touch. His face grew calm. 'So
      break,'
   He softly said, 'God's morrowings after spell
Of darkness and disfavour. I will trust
Him though He slay, for all His ways are just.

'His ways are just. He chastens to reform
   Alone, and metes but scanty meed of wrath.
His Church shall show the fairer for the storm,
   Though trembling now as reed in tiger path;
Not yet the dirge of sacred truth is sung,
Not yet her knell by hands unholy rung.'

Now thoughtful turning where the organ stood,
  But waiting touch of skilful master hand
To fill the fane with sweet harmonic brood
  Of music tuneful as seraphic band,
Here sat he down to lose in restful strain
Distractive thought and sting of viper pain.

Awhile he played; then sudden at his side
  Brake forth a song surpassing rich and clear;
He mournful smiled, alone such tuneful tide
  Could flow, he knew, from him that warbled near—
A youth, a lad of lofty look, and hair
Of gold, that streaming fringed his surplice fair.

Like lark uplift on humid wing, and lost
  In flood of song, and cloud of morning gold,
The lad sang on from placid heart, untost
  By wave of tempest passion, or the cold
Recoil of stern repression. Sweeter song
Ne'er swept the minster's columned aisle along.

'Twas ancient hymn, oft sung with bated breath
  In cave and catacomb by trembling tongue,
While Death stood listening by, and fiery wreath
  Of martyrdom already overhung
The singers' heads, with spirit hands unseen
Outstretched to bless, or cheer, or intervene.

And playing on, yet softly, till the song
  Was done, and all the echoing aisles were still,
The monk beheld in visioned bliss the throng
  Of white-robed witnesses that life and will

Laid at their Master's feet;—beheld, and smiled
To think how pain a while had him beguiled,

Of faith and hope, their comrade, yet, of earth,
　Like them foredoomed to sorrow, trial, loss.
Himself again, thrice blessed prayer had birth :
　'My God, like Thee, so may I bear the cross
And flaunting reed, else never victor palm ;
Know stripes and thorns, else never heavenly balm.'

So prayed the monk, his head upon his breast,
　His eyes o'ercast by sorrow's filmy frieze ;
Till song at end, the chorister caressed
　The tear-stained hand that idly grasped the keys ;
And 'Father Abbot, why thus sad ? ' he said ;
'Why weep you thus, and droop your holy head ?

'The morn is fair—how fair ! the minster gay
　With newborn radiance ; all without is bright
And careless, glad at coming of Dan Day.
　See how yon tapers blink amid the light !
Their pigmy glory lost amid the flood ︿
Of flame old Titan pours o'er screen and rood.

'Within the cloister, hark the tuneful din !
　My song has stirred to emulance of skill
The fleet-winged brood, that often venture in
　The church at prime or vespers, ling'ring still
To learn, methinks, some inkling of the strain
We sing, to sing it to their mates again.'

The abbot smiled, a weary smile; then slow
    And mournful spake, his hand upon the bright
And clustering curls that decked his scholar's brow :
    'Can that be fair, dear lad, that turns to night
Day's golden hope, and scatters fear and gloom
O'er all the land, with swift and cruel doom

'Of death to those too faithful to accept
    A tyrant's will in place of holy trust ?
And all, forsooth, that sin and wrong have crept
    Betimes among us, as they will and must
While men are men, else wherefore watchful pray'r,
Or priest, or Mass, or instant Christian care ?

Firm stand these walls, in pride of strength severe,
    Yon burnished panes diffuse effulgent ray.
Yon roof shows fair, as beauty naught need fear
    At wanton hand. Ah, me ! Ah woeful day !
A little while and all shall havocked be
All doleful lie in shapeless misery.

E'en now the king's commissioners set forth,
    And I must yield them strict accompt of all
I have in charge of great or lesser worth,
    Nor dare refuse for dread of bloody fall.
Woe's me ! that fear should fetter godward will
And Heav'n so near, earth lure to bondage still !

'So am I sad, dear child; yet not that I
    No more shall sit in seat of godly men,
Or mitred rule. An old worn man, I fly
    Distractive parley for the quiet pen,

And calm of cloistral cell. Enough for me
God-given scope for Christian charity !

'Yet sing again.   Nor, Francis, e'er forget
    Old Abbot Fuller, how he taught thee well
To use thy gift of song; nor e'er regret
    Forsaken bed at call of convent-bell.
Sing yet again, before the doomstroke fall,
And voiceless ruin brood in choir and stall !

'Thou canst not, child, thy soul so disarrayed,
    And voice and speech suffused in guileless tears ?
Then be it so!   Together we have prayed—
    Our morrowing task at end, with all thy fears—
Full oft at yonder shrine. So kneel again
And holy Mary grant surcease of pain ! '

Oh, fleet-winged prayer, celestial courier,
    Outspacing space, impassioned pursuivant
Of weary man to tireless Arbiter
    Of all, enshrined in sevenfold firmament !
Be mine to pray when care and grief oppress,
Or summer joys entice with loveliness !

Be mine to pray when morning's pinions cleave
    Resistless way through night's disparting veil;
And mine to pray what time reposeful eve
    Her peaceful mantle casts o'er crest and dale,
In hopeful youth, proud prime, and av'rous age,
Be mine to pray all through life's pilgrimage !

II

Where laggard Lea disparts her pleasant stream,
 And wraps the Waltham meads in soft embrace,
Young Francis strayed ; and, as in mocking dream
 Oft exiles see the roof-tree of their race,
So gazed the lad with sad and wistful eyes
Beyond the stream, where church and convent rise.

The crime complete, already spoiler hands
 Mad havoc wrought within the sacred fane ;
Already, slave to callous greed's commands,
 Unlettered violence won unhallowed gain ;
While sledges smote incessant, and the clang
Of pick and bar through crypt and cloister rang.

Down all ! down all ! Down choir magnifical,
 With shrine and tomb, and matchless sculptor dream,
Firm set in stone ! Down shaft and capital !
 When tides are full, what boots to dam the stream ?
What profits skill, in scale with miser gain ?
While greed triumphant, beauty pleads in vain.

The lad went on, and o'er, by Harold's bridge,
 The limpid stream that placid flowed around
The meads unmoved by ruin. Slow the sedge
 Waved restless in the wind. The snakeweed wound
Its slimy folds. The broad-ribbed arch beheld
Its shade within the water as of eld.

Beyond, deep set within the minster wall,
 There stood unlatched a broad and studded gate

Thence bordered paths, o'erhung with bushes tall,
   Went in and out the pleasaunce desolate;
Untended now, all in disorder lay,
Unkempt the lawn, untrimmed the border bay.

The Provence rose for lack of trainer hand
   Ungraceful drooped; the snow-flecked jessamine
In tangling clusters hung; her chaliced wand
   Queen lily lifted doubtful; bindweed twine
Ran over all unchecked; while pansies mild,
By ruder growth obscured, dejected smiled.

Above a porch, deep carved within the grit
   A pedant monk belaboured cogging boys,
With 'Disce, doce, aut discede' writ
   Beneath for legend. Often simple joys
Refreshen skill, and thus in sportive vein
The sculptor monk entabled learning's pain.

Alas for pity! Windows wrecked and bare,
   Walls grimed by fierce explosive, since no force
Of sinewy arm or iron sledge could tear
   The bonded mass asunder, or the course
Of ruin run till fiery flame had set
Its scathing seal on wall and parapet.

Ah me! How oft at foot of teacher monk
   The youngling here had hearkened legend old
Of saint or martyr, while weak childhood shrunk
   Aghast from tale of horror, trembling told
By some, ordained themselves ere long to know
Attaint of ill and chastening of woe!

Nor seldom, too, would Abbot Robert come
  Among them gracious, with uplifted hand
Bestowing blessing, while all knelt, and some,
  Thereafter bold, oft-granted boon demand
Of grace from task, with leave awhile to rove
Through garden, maze, or nearer woodland grove.

So nevermore! Yet as he stood there rang
  Serene and clear the soft-toned sanctus-bell.
He started, doubtful. Whence the silenced clang
  That filled his ear, like throb of funeral knell?
What impious hand dare mime at awful cost
The solemn lifting of the atoning Host?

The choir indeed was but a wreck—the roof
  Agape and robbed of rafter joist, and lead;
Yet worse within, where pillaged tombs gave proof
  How sharp-set greed could spoil the very dead,
And Christian nobles scatter saintly bones,
And grope for gold in graves and charnel stones.

Amid the wreck a workman stood and tolled
  For sport the bell, while others jested nigh.
By righteous rage inspired, of horror bold,
  The lad stood forth, with loud and wrathful cry:
'What do ye, madmen? Doubly mad to tempt
Your outraged God to punish base contempt!'

They drave him thence with laughter, floutings, blows.
  ''Tis but the shavelings' minion come again.
Goodlack! how loud the monken fledgling crows,
  The oldsters gone from out their' goodly den!'

L.L.   C

So laughed they, scornful, mating evil speech
With stripes from aught that lay to hand or reach.

With bursting heart the lad escaped beyond
    The convent precincts. In the hither mead
He threw him down against the Lenten pond,
    Whose finny tenants, wont to welcome tread
And call, drew near, but rose and plashed in vain;
The hands that fed should feed them ne'er again.

There lay the lad devoured by bitter thought,
    Till in his dream there mingled chiding voice,
Whose tones were music, sweet as lark's untaught
    Of bars and cage, whose gladsome notes rejoice
The wayworn trav'ler, lonely, longing sore
For joys of home, scarce counted joys before.

Beside the boy there knelt a maiden, meet
    For poet's song or painter's mimic pen;
Full like the lad that grovelled at her feet,
    But older, fairer, cynosure of men;
Like Francis crowned with chevelure of gold,
That falling met her kirtle's swelling fold.

And 'Francis, cease, dear brother, cease to grieve,'
    She gently said, and kissed his angry brow;
' 'Tis idle sorrow,—when comes ne'er reprieve,
    All things to storm do wisely bend and bow.
The king himself decreed the thing should be;
Who, then, can thwart or let his high decree ? '

'The king!' he cried in angry scorn; 'his King
  Decrees him traitor to his kingly trust.
Last night, in dream, I saw an angel wing
  His way to earth, while abject in the dust
Lay king and council. Down they grovelling fell
Abashed—aghast as fiends at holy spell.'

'Hush, hush, dear Francis! Did knee-crooking knave
  But hear your madness, we were both undone.
Recall the reed that Abbot Robert gave
  Us both at parting. Patient hope in One,
In whom all things do centre, right or wrong;
By whom are warriors weak, and striplings strong.'

'And striplings strong!' the lad exclaimed; 'would I
  Were man to meet him in his royal place—
Foretell his fate, as when I saw him lie
  All terror-struck before the archangel's face;
Denounce his crimes——' But here a stern voice bade
The boy be silent, and alarmed the maid,

Who rose dismayed. Against a neighbouring tree
  He frowning stood, whose aspect chilled her blood.
Appalled she knelt, and whispering, 'It is he!'
  Embraced her brother. 'Now, by holy rood,
No help have we, dear lad, but in the Lord—
The king himself has heard our every word!'

The boy sprang up with flashing eye, but all
  His courage failed in face of tiger wrath.
So torrent flood and noisy mountain fall
  Are lost in sea. Across the grassy path

The despot strode, his cruel face aflame,
And bade the boy declare his place and name.

But he was silent, fear, with rage at fear,
  Restraining speech. Again the tyrant cried,
The while his minions noiseless gathered near.
  Ungentle they, nor slow to serve his pride,
Yet some were moved to pity, when the maid
A sheltering clasp about her brother laid.

And meaning looks they cast. Too sweet and fair
  Was she by far to meet the greedy look
Of him who yet was never known to spare
  Or maid or wife; whose pride could never brook
Resistance in a subject; whose fell mood,
Once roused, abated but with cloy of blood.

Now outspake one, yet careful : ' These, my lord,
  Are gentle children, but betimes the boy
Is fay-possessed. They dwell against the ford;
  Your highness may remember old Mountjoy
There pulled down quarry yester-eve. 'Tis said
There's fairy seal upon the youngster's head.'

' So! Is it so ? ' the king replied, his brow
  Relaxing at the fable. ' By the Mass!
The wench is comely. Let the losel go.
  Nay, now, good Denny; I would speak the lass.
Soft there, my sweeting, leave yon lout awhile;
The king, methinks, may claim of right a smile.'

Our lord the king! what subject dare gainsay
  His word or will! Her angel face she raised
With pleading look, her bosom's trem'lous play
  Betraying fear. With greedy eye he gazed
Again and yet again, while plain to view
Unhallowed longing in his gazing grew.

Beneath his look she trembled like to fawn
  Wolf-charmed, that fears, yet harmless knows not
      why
Or what the danger, all its nature drawn
  To instinct dread. So looked she modest, shy,
Her soft eyes full of mild entreaty, while
His answered madly, full of pride and guile.

'So! that is better. Sooth, I never knew
  Our Waltham woods contained such goodly deer;
His chase in sight, the hunter must pursue.
  Sweet wench, a kiss. Nay, ne'er show sluttish fear.
Well, hark away, chaste quarry, yet that lip,
So ruddy ripe, enticeth lover sip.'

He now made sign that spake the king; the maid
  With low obeisance quickly drew aside,
And with her drew her brother, as afraid
  He yet might wake the vengeful tyrant's pride;
With evil smile the king beheld them go,
Then strode away with dark and knitted brow.

III

Within the wood, removed a little way
  From town and convent, nigh a saucy brook
That, dancing into being, laughed at day,
  Then joyous fled by thymy knoll and nook,
There stood a grange, age-bowed, with girdling stream
That flowed around with dark and sullen gleam.

Yet lilies grew, and spread within the pool,
  Their snow cups floating large amid their leaves ;
And mouse-ear near the bank, with parsley fool ;
  And loosestrife tall, with gladwyn's golden sheaves,
And mint that matted all the bank ; and weed
Obscure a host, that gained but little heed.

And over all a bridge with massy piers,
  And slender arch scarce lift above the moat
In lieu of drawbridge, long removed, that years
  Of peace made irksome. Nigh the bridge a boat
That floated idly where the lilies lay,
And in it Lilian, pure and chaste as they.

Her little hands, among the snow cups set,
  Drew slowly to her side the blossoms fair ;
Some few she chose by way of coronet,
  First kissed, then wound the wildings in her hair,
Her fair face kindling, and her azure eyes,
Love's mirrors, full of tender sympathies.

And 'Holy Mary, how the world is bright ! '
  She thoughtful said ; ' what love her blessed Son

Must carry earth, to fashion such delight
　For careless eyes and hearts so hardly won!
I' faith, sith earth doth show such braggart wise,
How wondrous fair His own bright paradise!'

Through forest rift the sun, with ruddy glare,
　Shone full and low; it kissed her virgin cheek
To summer glow, and dyed her glossy hair
　To deeper gold. No longer maiden meek,
But vestal priestess, robed with hallowing flame,
She seemed, and pure beyond attaint of shame.

So he confessed that stood beside the stream
　With clouded brow, and marked her guileless play
With leaf and lily. Not yet maiden dream
　Of love indulged, with mild complaisant sway
O'er manly hearts; each impulse of her breast
Calm, chaste, and clear as babe's in cratchet nest.

'Twas he who friended Francis other while.
　Now stepping forth, he called the girl by name;
She startling heard, then turned with sunny smile
　Her glowing face that way the summons came,
And merry laughed: 'Sir godsire, will you wear
My badge to-day, a lily light as air!'

A bloom she plucked, and cast it lightly o'er
　The wat'ry marge; he raised it to his lips,
Then, as recalled to purpose pressing sore
　For quick solution, answered gravely, 'Quips
Are folly now, so, Lilian, lay them by.
When fowlers snare, the turtle needs must fly.

' Ay, cease to toy with simples! There is one,
  My child, would toy in otherwise with thee.
'Tis deathly pastime, therefore get thee gone
  Ere night, and keep thee close at Nazing Lea!
Hist, girl, more near! This very night the king
Intends thee aught but harmless visiting.

' So get thee gone with Francis, ere the night
  Garbs evil thought with opportune of gloom.
But keep my counsel. Mine were sorry plight—
  Perchance unheaded shoulders, bloody tomb—
Did Henry wot I sped forestalling bolt.
And warned his quarry out of Waltham holt!"

So whispered he. With shame and fear she heard,
  Yet nothing answered; only in her eyes
He read resolve, that needed never word
  For full expression—steadfast will that dies
Alone with dying. Never tyrant's slave
Were Lilian Lane, while earth had stainless grave.

' Bestir thee, Lilian! Show thy father's child!
  Ill fell the hap that took him yestermorn
To shire assize, yet worse that I beguiled
  The king to linger. Never's rose but thorn!
Would God the manor lay beneath the sea,
Ere harm, dear heart, should light on thee by me!

' And now farewell! Keep close! The danger past,
  I'll send thee word when thou mayst safe return.'
He kissed her cheek, she faintly smiled; at last
  Came faltering speech : ' Fear not, good friend, I
    spurn

Unholy wooing! Yet 'twere best to flee
Unharmed, than prove King Henry's courtesy.'

Her godsire gone, she hastened in, and soon
  Prepared for flight, stood eager by the gate;
Why came not Francis? He at close of noon
  Had sought the woodland. Now 'twas growing
     late,
The western sky o'erspread with crimson light,
And purple eve forerunning sable night.

She waited long, her breast aglow with shame,
  Her heart fast beating, while encroaching fear
Thrilled every nerve. Would God that Francis
     came!
Now Hesper flamed, and danger drawing near
Tongued every leaf, and voiced each brook and rill
To wake in her, sweet child! responsive thrill.

Made bold of gloom, the owl with dismal hoot
  Alarmed the wood; the night-hawk weirdly chirred;
From out the pool, disturbed, the timid coot
  Flew darkling upward. Sure the forest stirred
With step of stranger! Cold and pale of fright,
She, trembling, fled for refuge in the night.

Unfollowed, soon her courage came again;
  'Twas like that Francis loitered by the brook
That lapped the minster. Now a laden wain
  Slow creaking by, she, grateful, comfort took
From honest presence; close within the sound
She kept, yet fearful, often gazing round.

The convent wall now rose to view. She sighed :
   ' Alas ! were Abbot Robert but within,
How gladly would the holy father hide
   His whilom charge from pursuance of sin !
Distressful change ! Now royal might is right ;
No convent aid awaits unhappy wight ! '

No sound arose but distant roister shout
   From roadside inn or township hostelry,
With swir of ash that lithely tossed about
   Its yellowing tufts in aimless revelry.
Not far away the ruined minster stood—
Dark, lifeless, dull, fit home for ghostly brood.

With hasty hand she made the holy sign
   On breast and brow, then stealthy made her way
Toward the ruins. Shapes unseen, benign,
   Guard now her harmless footsteps. Sanct array
Befriend her, helpless ! Hark ! what descant rude.
Assails her ear, and shocks night's solitude ?

See, torches flame ! Amid their fumy glare
   There treads the causey merry-making crew ;
And in their midst—alas ! what did he there ?—
   Her brother guarded ! Spellbound, full in view
She stood, nor further thought of self or flight,
In fear for him and his untoward plight.

Too soon perceived of all, loud laughter broke
   Anew the night. Then over all a cry
Rang sharply out, and Francis wildly spoke :
   ' Fly, Lilian, fly ! Think not of me, but fly !

There's harm against thee.' Fearless as to cost,
Thus much he cried, with more in clamour lost.

Now came the king, and did the trembling maid
   Half mocking reverence—' Marry, then, fair quest,
You save some seeking.' So he blandly said
   With careless smile, then haughty bade the rest
Halt by the stream, which done, a space apart
He drew the maid, with base and villain heart,

And sought to kiss her lips. But with a cry
   She brake away, through grant of helpful strength
From angel guard. Enraged he saw her fly
   Tow'rds Harold's bridge, and followed scarce a
      length
Behind ; but fleet as startled bird on wing
Of fear she fled, and soon outran the king.

She gained the bridge, but looking back to know
   Herself escaped, her foot slipped and she fell.
By dread aroused, though blinded with the blow,
   She stagg'ring rose. Ah me ! what tongue shall tell
The power that led the fainting girl so near
The starlit stream that washed the flinty pier.

Again a fall—a cry—the waters close,
   And, weirdly murmuring, tell no further tale ;
But, horror-stricken, well the tyrant knows
   What bleeding lies beneath their gleamy veil.
' Ho ! lights and men ! Quick, knaves ! your heads
      shall pay
For laggard help or ill-conceived delay.'

They drew her forth—a lily on her brow,
  Self-twined—sweet Lilian, loveliest flower of all,
Her tresses dank and tangled, living glow
  Gone evermore! Ah, sad yet welcome pall!
And stream more kind than stony heart, that bade
Death's gate unbar to guard the gentle maid.

IV

Escaped, the stag regains the thorny brake,
  And panting lies, concealed in ferny bed;
The hounds, athirst, their baffled fever slake
  At rushy spring; the jaded hunters spread
Their evening meal, with glaive and staff and horn
Laid idle by at foot of beech and thorn.

Alone, apart, from ardour of the chase,
  From hounds and men, the king at length drew rein
Beside an oak of mighty growth, whose base
  Usurped the hill, and overeyed the plain,
Where, red-roofed, dim, 'neath evening's purple crown,
Mid stream and tree, reposed the quiet town.

He wound his horn, but scarce the cheerful call
  Had roused the woodland echoes out of sleep,
To make reply all dreamily, and fall
  Again to rest, than out the welkin steep
Fierce lightning leaping, cleft low-hanging cloud,
And shook the holt with thundering long and loud.

'Twas lightning such the wood was all ablaze
  With flood of fire, and shivering shrank from flame

That living leaped. Earth plainly shook. By craze
  Of terror moved, one wildly loud acclaim
Uprose from bird and beast, then silence fell
Profound as death o'er plain and crest and dell.

Again the bolt leaped out its lurid crown,
  And scarce the king could curb his steed for awe.
Heart smitten now, a neighbouring oak came down
  With rend and rush and crash that shook the shaw ;
Supreme in ruin as in girth profound,
The falling giant spread destruction round.

The king's gaze set upon the tree, there came
  Unseen a youth from out the nearer wood.
'Twas Francis, madness in his look, and flame
  Of frenzy in his bearing. Full he stood
Before the king, and fearless bade him hear
Malefic doom and retribute severe.

' Accurst of all, and callous as the sea,
  That aye devours and yet is never full ;
And never worn of wanton cruelty,
  But brooding ill while waves and winds are dull ;
Here would I slay thee, strong in righteous hate,
Did not thy God decree severer fate.

 · ' So live thou on, earth's malison ! Fulfil
  Thy course unclean, like pestilential star
That banes in flight, and, failing, darkens still
  Men's lives in dying. Tyrant ! better far
Thy bloody axe and dungeon grave forlorn,
Than lifelong hate and unborn ages' scorn.

' Ay, frown at will ! Hark yonder thunder roll,
   That shuddering earth repeats in hollow tone !
Thou know'st it well, for, monster, in thy soul
   Thou hear'st again thine ordnance' murd'rous groan
That told thee Boleyn died, her guiltless head
Laid low to smooth adult'rous bridal bed !

' Mark, too, yon flame, o'erleaping Waltham tower,
   Where, snatched from thee, thy latest victim lies.
All powerful thou, and soulless in thy power,
   What friend but death dare thwart thy tyrannies ?
Thine, tyrant, thine, to bid sweet Lilian die ;
Thine, fiend, the curse that fired her glazing eye !

' Fulfil thy fate, thou scourge of earth and bane
   Of all things good. In lust and blood and crime
Fulfil it ; then find Herod's doom. Attain
   To death in life ; and, noisome in thy prime,
Call death in vain, while demons shrink aghast
To know hell pain by mortal pang surpast.

' Then die to glad thy people by thy death,
   And lift a load from off a nation's heart,
Thy name recalled with loathing, bated breath,
   And curse in utterance. Tyrant ! thine the part
To show that earth can rival hell in ill,
And demons vile, yet kings be viler still.'

The lightning sprang, the thunder shook the roof
   Of listening heaven. The lad with gesture wild
Exulted loudly : ' Murd'rer ! 'tis approof
   Of Lilian's curse. Now live, thy soul beguiled

From ill to ill, till, all thy crimes complete,
Thou goest hence to retribution meet.'

He turned and fled. The tyrant, sore amazed,
  Nor sought nor thought to intercept his flight,
But haggard smiled. ' In sooth the lout is crazed ! '
  He muttered fearful, then from lowering night
And fury-storm turned homeward, evermore
His stricken soul a prey to torments sore.

        *   *   *   *   *

Beyond the sea in quiet cloister fane,
  Unhavocked yet by royal spoilers' hand,
A little while there lingered Francis Lane,
  To die ere manhood, far from home and land.
Too large his heart to bear life's sterner cross
Of blighted hopes, sharp grief, and bitter loss.

Soon Abbot Fuller died, his convent home
  Become a mine whence all men quarried stones ;
Contented still through faith in Him whence come
  Both good and ill, he calmly slept, his bones
Laid reverent to their rest, where priests still lift
To prayerful lips love's last benignant gift.

But oft of night within the chapel old—
  Our Lady's, spoiled of all its ancient show—
A tonsured priest and lad with looks of gold
  Are seen absorbed in converse sad and low,
While dirge-like, soft, unearthly numbers rise,
And fill the church with wailful symphonies.

And Lilian oft beside the murmuring stream
   Is seen what time the stars give misty light,
And mead and tree show ghostly in the gleam
   The crescent moon affords the new-throned Night—
To Harold's bridge will come, then fearful look
In haste behind, and vanish in the brook.

And still at night, when winter blast and gale
   Entice to warmth within the hostel's glow,
The din of song and laughter hushed, the tale
   Of Lilian Lane is told in accents low;
While honest rage each rustic bosom fires
To scorn of greed and hate of base desires.

NAZING

NAZING, one of the manors with which Harold endowed his Waltham foundation, to use a homely phrase, ' lies high and dry and five miles from everywhere.'

Possibly this is the reason why Nazing is still a village, and its common, one of the finest in the county, still unenclosed.

But delightfully out of the world as it is, the pedestrian can reach it comfortably enough by a walk of five miles or thereabouts from Broxbourne, by river and meadow and lane right away to the knoll on which the village and churchyard stand. And

Nazing church, overlooking as it does mile upon mile of the fertile land to the west, to say nothing of its antiquity, is a joy to the artistic tramp, while the ordinary wayfarer is more than repaid for his hour and half's walk by his rest amid its picturesque seclusion, and his enjoyment of the far-stretching prospect at his feet as he bestraddles the stile of the tree-shaded churchyard. From Epping, too, it is accessible, and the walk is more than a pretty one, taking on one's way the old church on its hillock quite a couple of miles away from the thirsty old town, where nearly every third house in the High Street is an Inn or ' Licensed to sell Beer by retail to be drunk on the Premises.'

Epping old church is a feature in the landscape still, its tall tower of red brick showing occasionally through a gap in its surrounding trees, or its parapet above the crests of the lowest of its leafy companions. For peaceful solitude, too, it is not to be surpassed by anything at an equal distance from the ' wen,' as outspoken Cobbett somewhat irreverently called our modern Babylon. The rectory adjoins it, while the *Chequers Inn* is opposite the further gate of the churchyard. In addition to these there are a couple of farms within a few minutes walk of it and—*voila tout.*

But alas ! and alas ! for the poor old church itself. Some few years back there arose a Pharaoh who knew not Joseph, in the shape of a Rector with a craze for restoration, and the quaintly beautiful old building with its alterations and accretions of centuries, was rigidly restored to what the sapient newcomer thought the building must have been when it left the hands of architect and builder some seven hundred years before. I had been away for years, and coming back to the spot shortly after the restoration, and remembering the age-old edifice as it was, when as a boy I sat in the churchyard seat—gone of course —beneath one of its irregular Tudor windows, through which one could catch a glimpse of hatchment and hangings, I could have wept to see what it had become under the tasteful hands of its Vandal restorer.

But I did not, only I cursed with cursings 'not loud but deep'—remembering I stood upon consecrated ground—Rector, faculty granting Chancellor, architect, workmen, all who had a hand in the miserable business.

A wretched barrel-roof, cold and bare walls, pierced with deeply splayed lancet windows, encaustic tiles in lieu of the stones and brasses—memorials all of them of some good old family of the parish or vicinage (some of the torn up brasses are now stuck up on end in the belfry)—pine benches, already, I have no doubt, *à la façon de ces gens la*, stricken with dry rot, everything spick and span, new, smug and tasty —behold Epping old church after *restoration*.

Parting from these ' 'twixt anger, shame and fear,' as Denham says, because the philistine parson being by no means extinct—would to heaven he were !— the same fate may yet overtake many a venerable Essex heirloom—a short walk over the fields to the left of the *Chequers Inn* brings us to the pond, the pump and the *Travellers' Rest Inn* on Epping Long Green. Here, crossing the road and field by the inn, the great Nazing common spreads out before and beneath us, and beyond it, hidden away in trees and coppice, is its picturesque village with its hall and church.

Nazing Hall was long the seat of the Palmers. One of them, Lieut.-Colonel George was the last of the Verderers under the ancient régime.

Long will his name be had in remembrance, for, like a fine old English gentleman as he was, he did his best to preserve the forest, and many a surreptitious enclosure did he ' throw out ' single-handed as he was at the last, when forest courts had come to an end, and the rolls, charters and documents of centuries had been hidden away or destroyed at the instigation, so the story runs, of the disreputable Lord Warden of the forest, Long Tylney Wellesley Long Pole, as Horace Smith calls him, and the greedy gentry ycleped lords of the manors of the various villages in or about the forest.

Honour to whom honour and blame to whom blame, and in justice to these greedy ones it must not be forgotten that their earth-hunger was quickened and their teeth sharpened by the unscrupulous action of the then Commissioners of Woods and Forests, who from about 1817 to 1863 virtually connived at the encroachments, if even they did not instigate and urge them, for the sake of the paltry sums, some £15,593 in all, paid into the Exchequer in extinguishment of the Crown rights. To these same sapient Commissioners we owe also the disafforesting and destruction, in the space of about six weeks, of that noble piece of woodland, Hainault Forest.

Only to think of it! What an unspeakable boon to the thousand upon thousand of toilers in Stratford and Barking and Ham, not to say of Ilford and Romford, it would be to have as a breathing place, and not far from their doors, that grand stretch of royal woodland almost in a ring fence and some five or six miles round. If but a few of the stones that are hurled at the heads of 'the great unpaid' could be diverted in their flight to those of 'the great overpaid' what a satisfaction it would be to many of us, especially as withal there would be exceeding small scattering of brains.

N.B.—Since this was written, and some fifty years after its disafforesting, a small portion of the land has been acquired by public subscription, aided by a grant from the Corporation of the City of London, for the benefit of the people, mainly through the exertions of Mr. Edward North Buxton of Knighton, Woodford.

THE DEMON STAG

A LEGEND OF NAZING

At morn, Sir Ralph with troubled brow
  Awakes from visioned sleep;
His face is stern, his looks foreshow
  Resolve, relentless, deep!

'Now shrive me clean, sir priest, I pray,
  Absolve from every sin!
And I would foil the fiend to-day,
  No taint may lurk within!'

'My son, and dare you seek the dell,
  Meet warlock, fiend and fay?'
'I dare full well, though brood of hell,
  Rise up to bar my way!

'Have I not fought for Christ, His land,
  In blood, disaster, pain?
Thrice paynim host, with spear and brand,
  Flung back on Judah's plain?

'And shall I fear to meet a foe
  Hellborn, accurst of heaven?
By God's sweet wounds, sir priest, not so,
  And by his wordies seven!

'So shrive me clean from soil and slough;
  Then make with holy hand
The sacred sign on breast and brow,
  On ring and rood and brand!

II

'Unleash ! unleash ! good woodward mine ;
  Up ! Up ! unleash I say !
How fair the field with gleam and shine !
  How bright the morrowing ray !'

'Sir Ralph forbear ! Bethink you well
  A year 'tis but to-day,
And brave Sir Guy, by warlock spell
  Betorn and lifeless lay !'

'Peace, churl, and do my bidding free !
  And if my son were slain
Of fiends, must harm then happen me ?
  Unleash I say, amain !'

'Yet, master dear, last night in blood,
  The dull sun wallowing set ;
The moon rose red, loud rang the wood,
  With wail that fears me yet !

'The demon stag was out, and she
  That haunts the shadowy dell ;
The death mort rang o'er hurst and lea,
  The chase was chase of hell.

'And well I ween, when these are seen,
  There's deathly dolour nigh !
Who lies that warlock's breasts between
  Ere night must surely die !'

'Peace, knave, I'll hunt whate'er befall!
  Nor were-wolf, ghost, nor fend
Uprist of hell, can e'er appal
  Whom Christ His Saints attend.

'And I have that of Beth'lem nun
  Will bring me aid at need!—
Hark! hark! yon horn, the hunt's begun
  Bring out my good roan steed.'

III

Halloo! Halloo! By bush and brake
  The stag flies. Swift behind,
Come hounds and men, the woodlands shake,
  And shoutings shrill the wind!

By spur and hand and voice sustained,
  How fleet the bonny roan!
None other near—the dell attained,
  Sir Ralph he rides alone.

But see, brave sight, a maiden bright,
  With eyes as woodbell blue,
Gold tressed, she glides with step as light
  As fay o'er pearly dew.

With smile and song she trips along
  The dell path fair and free,
Or culls, to twine her locks among,
  A bloom on bended knee.

'So, ho! fair maid, what dost thou here,
    In grassy dell so green?
Hast never fear? Hast lover near?
    Sweet maid of maids the queen!'

'I cull, Sir Knight, the simples bright
    That guerdon bush and lea,
And if thou wilt, a garland light,
    I'll weave, Sir Knight, for thee.'

'No more, fair maid, I garlands wear,
    Sith my dear son was slain;
Uncomely falls my tangled hair
    O'er haubert, corslet, chain!'

'Of maids and am I then the queen,
    Then sit thee down by me,
Thou knight so dour, and stern of mien,
    And scant of courtesy.'

'Oh, yes, I'll sit me down by thee,
    Thou maid of maids the queen!
But see my ring of porphyry.
    Has paled its purple sheen!'

'Put by thy ring, Sir Knight, or lay
    The bauble on my breast;
That done I'll charm thy cares away,
    And kiss thy griefs to rest!'

'My ring I may not give to thee;
    'Twas laid on holy shrine,

What time I kneeled upon my knee
  In far off Palestine!

'And aye when danger threats, or ill
  Would life or soul pursue,
My faithful ring gives warning still;
  As now by change of hue!'

'Lay by thy ring, uncourteous Knight,
  Dismount thy restive roan!
See yonder bank! would'st not 'twere night
  Or telltale daylight gone?'

Her arms about the knight, so bold
  She flung, and showed the hill—
'Thy kiss 'tis cold as charnel-mould
  Thy lips as corpse-lips chill!

'And see yon stag, that draws so nigh
  His full eyes flaming hell!
Had I not charms at hand I'd fly
  Fair maid thy beauty's spell.'

'Sir Knight, 'tis nought but hart, outrun
  The hunter's crafty snare.
The chase is done, why kisses shun
  Or fear love's bliss to share?

'Yet charms! so tell them o'er to me,
  Sir Knight, that I may prove,
Sustent at need, when wandering free
  In dell, or dene, or grove.'

'Oh, yes, I'll tell those charms to thee!
　See then this bloodstained wood;
'Tis relic brought from Calvary,
　The dear Christ's holy rood.

'But why dost tremble so at name
　All Christian folk revere?
Why shrinkest so? Shame, maiden, shame!
　Shouldst hold thy Lord more dear!

'And he that bears this blessed wood,
　On him nor ban nor charm
Can work, for ever spirits good
　Are near to guard from harm.

'And once 'tis set on changeling brow,
　Then he true form must take,
While demons foul their lord avow,
　And fiends with terror quake.

'Why move thy lips, thou winsome maid,
　Yet make nor speech nor sound?
Why beck yon stag from out the glade
　And trembling clutch the ground?

'But yet another charm I bear,
　Dost see this bugle horn?
'Twas brought from Christ His sepulchre
　First wound when Christ was born.

'And when 'tis wound, a spirit host
　Speed forth to aid the right.

Shalt find it now no idle boast
   Thou fiend, as maiden dight.

'Ah me! a year this very morn,
   Beneath yon hawthorn tree,
My brave first-born lay demon torn,
   Of warlock treachery;

'That lured to sin and doom and death.
   With clasp and kiss and sigh;
And panting drew his boyish breath,
   And mocking bade him die.

'And so I bring these charms to thee,
   Thou hag in maiden dress,
Against thy lips the sacred tree
   Thus once, twice, thrice compress.'

*   *   *

A shriek that shook the very dale,
   A yell that shocked the air,
No maiden frail—but beldam pale,
   That shape so wondrous fair.

A hag deformed, she stood, confest,
   Despoiled of spells and charms;
Nor more should tempt to guilty rest
   Within her deadly arms.

One blast upon the bugle horn—
   The stag had turned to flee—
One blast, and lo! beneath the thorn,
   A wondrous company

THE DEMON STAG

Of spirit horsemen, pallid, rent—
  'Ho! Ho! the debt is due!
Chase, brethren, chase! His course is spent,
  Give chase! Pursue! Pursue!'

Full fleet the fiend, but fleeter still
  That ghastly ghostly crew;
They seized him ere he gained the hill,
  His leman yet in view.

They tore him limb from limb, his gore
  Bescorching bush and tree.
'Farewell, Sir Knight! Thou'llt need no more
  Our spirit company.'

The hell-hag dragged beneath the thorn—
  For ruth she cried in vain—
With good sword blessed at early morn
  He clave her skull in twain.

*   *   *

'Now speed thee home, my bonny roan,
  By woodland, moor and lea;
Can mass and moan for sin atone
  I'll save yon company!'

LOUGHTON

LOUGHTON, Lucton or Luketon is another of the
manors bestowed by Harold upon his Abbey at
Waltham.

Fifty years ago it was as pretty a village as one
could find in a day's march. A village upon seven
hills it was and is, witness, York Hill, Traps Hill,
Church Hill, Staples Hill, Baldwins Hill, Goldings
Hill, Albion Hill. Fine views are to be had from
each, even now, though some of them in place of
oaks and elms, groan under unsightly growths of
brick and mortar. Also the sweet rich smell of the
bonny burning logs within the ingle of cottage and
homestead no longer delights the nostrils of the
wayfarer ; fumes of coal and gas filling the air instead.
Nowadays Loughton is as typical an example of the
modern suburban paradise as any within an hour's
ride of London. It is full, to use auctioneer's English,
of ' choice residential properties ' and ' villas replete
with every modern convenience.'

Oh for the days before the railway invaded the
woodland! When the London coach ran through
the village to the *Cock* in Epping, and fifty cottages,
a dozen homesteads, and the squire's wide hall by the
ancient church of St. Nicholas made up the village !
In addition there were the inns,—what village would
be complete without them ?—the *Bag o' Nails*, the
King's Head, and the *Crown*, wherein, ' the summer

being hot and dry' a glass of ale went down like nectar, or in winter—

> When the soundless earth was muffled,
> And the caked snow was shuffled
> From the ploughboy's heavy shoon,

—a seat by the roaring wood fire of either hostelry was a thing not lightly to be despised. Then everybody in Loughton knew everybody else—while a good-natured geniality was the order of the day generally, and life, emphatically, worth living. But now, he, of the choice suburban residence of eighty pounds a year, thinks small beer of him who pays sixty; while he of sixty turns up his nose at his neighbour of forty; who in turn thinks himself a king compared with the cottager of ten or twenty, who very likely, taking manhood as a standard, is a better fellow all round than any of the 'city men' above him.

Here at Loughton it was that that ubiquitous rascal and prince of highwaymen Dick Turpin had his cave in the hollow beneath the camp at High Beech. Here, too, he perpetrated his 'burning joke' of setting an old woman on her kitchen fire. She lived in a solitary farmhouse upon Traps Hill, and was said to have money hidden away in the building. Unused coin being of a truth but worthless dross, Dick resolved to turn it to account. So he made his way, with a couple of companions, into the house; but as no threats could induce the brave old lady to reveal the whereabouts of her store, Dick, losing patience, bethought him of the original and historical example

of Reginald Front de Bœuf, and forcing the poor
creature down upon the burning hearth, held her
there till she purchased her freedom with the whole
of her hard-earned money. For which ungallant
violation of the 'humanities' Richard Turpin, Esq,
must do penance, according to the greybeards, by
riding down the hill thrice in the year on his famous
Black Bess. As he approaches the farmhouse, he is
said to quicken his pace and cast many a fearful
look behind, the old lady waiting by the lime tree
at the gate, ready to spring upon the crupper of his
flying mare, and share his midnight ride, presumably
in quest of the stolen gold.

Loughton is a storehouse of good stories. One
that often goes round still, is how the sturdy village
folk frustrated the evil intentions of a generous
minded lord of the manor of King Charles's time.

It seems that a brother lord of Waltham, by giving
a grand supper and 'drunk,' as the forest folk still
call it, to the loppers on the night of the eleventh of
November—the night when at midnight, according to
the royal charter, lopping must commence or the
privilege be lost—contrived to make everybody so
drunk that no lopping was attempted, and the right
was lost.

But he of Loughton had no such good fortune. He
provided the supper, a right bountiful one, and his
tables were well furnished with guests—everybody
came indeed—and the consumption of good things
was great, exceeding great. But the knowing ones
of the party had their axes with them, hidden away

under their smocks; and as midnight drew near,
these knowing ones rose up and made for the door.
But the door was shut! Yet more it was fast barred
and bolted! Alas for that manorial door! Out
came the axes! Splinters and chips were soon almost
as plentiful as the execrations of the lord and his
friends who, held back in their seats by the remainder
of the guests, could only look on and curse lustily
and loudly, while the gorged but unthankful ones
smote down door and bar and rushed out whooping
and yelling, to hack away merrily as of yore, at
the stroke of twelve!'

So 'drunks' being thrown away upon them, the
Loughton loppers maintained their right to cut
winter fuel, down to our own days, when the forest
question finally settled by Sir George Jessel—righteous
Jew judge having no sympathy with them that
remove their neighbour's landmarks—some compensation was given the loppers in lieu of their rights
—and lopping ceased. And truly one cannot regret
its ceasing. For wherever this lopping privilege
existed, there, with the exception of the crab-trees,
always exempted on account of the deer who make
much of the fallen fruit ruddy and golden among the
russet leaves in the winter—not a tree above five
and twenty or thirty feet could be found, and this
over miles of otherwise beautiful woodland.

With regard to this lopping business, there is a name
in Loughton that will long be had in remembrance,
and deservedly, that of Willingale.

Of course, after the sale of the Crown rights by the

aforesaid Commissioners of Woods and Forests—
vide Nazing—Loughton forest was soon enclosed.
In this case we will not be too hard upon the squire,
a truly worthy gentleman, for he acted upon the
advice of a respectable firm of solicitors, and more
than liberally compensated freeholders and copy-
holders for any loss they might sustain by the
enclosure. But the loppers were overlooked, and
though most of them had long ceased to exercise
their right, finding it cheaper to buy coal than to
spend a week at their own expense in the woodland
cutting wood, yet the remainder naturally enough
refused to give up their rights, and the Willingales,
father and son, brave as their Saxon forefathers,
right manfully maintained their cause against squire
and keepers.

So being haled before sundry sapient Justices of
the Peace, these worthy gentry in solemn conclave
assembled, pronounced them guilty of trespass with
damage, and the sturdy pair refusing either to submit
to the judgment, or pay the fine, went to jail.

The case made a sensation. London presently
came to the rescue. A great fight was fought and
won. The forest was declared the heritage of the
commoners and every enclosure illegal.

Oh, to have seen the faces of those worthy J.P.'s
after the delivery of the judgment!

Granting, of charity, that the 'fellow feeling
that maketh wondrous kind, had nothing to do with
their committal of the Willingales, then as each
bethinking himself of his great prototype Dogberry,

ejaculated slowly and solemnly—'write me down
ass'—their faces must surely have been a study
worth a journey from London and back to see.

In pace requiescant. By this time they are nearly
all dead and gone and their names have perished,
but that of Willingale is still a household word in
Loughton. They come, too, of a good old Essex stock,
taking their name as they do from a village a dozen
miles further in the county than Loughton. For is
it not written in the chronicles that the taking of
names from town and village ceased, at the least,
some six hundred years ago.

The Hollow of the legend, a wild secluded spot,
lies a little way down the old bridleway to Abridge,
on its right hand side. This ancient way begins a
stone's throw from Loughton Hall—not the Public, or
Robber's Hall, as the villagers call it, seeing it was
built out of a portion of the compensation fund, which
rightly or wrongly they say should all have gone to
themselves—but that of the squire adjoining the
sequestered churchyard of St. Nicholas in Chigwell
Lane.

The bridle way is closed by a five-barred gate, and
half a mile down has been cut through by the railway
to Epping, but there is a right of way by the
Home Farm, and over field and railway into that
portion of it which runs into the lane to Abridge from
Theydon Bois by Pigott's Farm.

KATE OF THE HOLLOW
A LEGEND OF LOUGHTON

WHO lingers so late in the hollow, by night,
In shadow and shade, and the mistladen light
  Of star and the cloud-cradled moon?
With footsteps as soundless as fall o' the flake,
And visage as pallid as lily in lake
  Or maiden in death seeming swoon?

Her raven black ringlets fall down to her waist—
She loiters—she lingers—she listens—in haste
  She seeks now the sedge-hidden rill.
Her eyes they are flaming as fire o' the fell,
Her thin hands are clasping her bosom,—the bell
  Slow booming o'er graveyard and hill.

The shriek owl he hooteth, deep hid in the wood,
The hollow wind moaneth o'er marish and flood,
  The sedge hurtles eerie in fen.
The balefire glides onward, malefic in mist,
The gibbet-chained outlaws swing loathsome and
      twist,
  The cling-clang alarming the glen.

Now hearken! Deep down in the depths of the dell
The wail of a babe above soughing and swell
  Of storm, and the stormbeaten trees.
Why startleth that maiden? Why trembleth she now?
Why weepeth she bitterly, clasping her brow?
  Why falleth she low on her knees?

Now rising she tracketh the wail to its lair—
The bantling lies famish'd—lies perish'd and bare,
  Bewailing with hungerly cry.
She stoopeth, she snatcheth the babe to her breast,
Its cold lips she kisses—by colder carest—
  And murmurs a mad lullaby.

Ah, baby! ah, baby! my shame and despight,
Cease, darling, thy wailing, thy pain is but slight
  To that which thy mother must bear!
Dost hunger so sorely? My daughter thy smart
Is naught to the vulture that gnaweth my heart
  With fang of a quenchless despair!

He swore that more faithful than lodestar to pole
Or ocean to breaker, his soul to my soul
  For ever unchanging would cling.
Woe's me! I believed, and believing was lost,
Naught dreamed I—love's plaything—of waking and
      cost,
    Betrayed, of grief's viperous sting.

Ah, Edward! ah, traitor! to leave me forlorn,
To battle with hunger, reproaching and scorn,
  And outcast, to die of distress!
Oh, Father of mercies, what crime have I done
Against Thee or Nature, that womankind shun
  E'en graze of my dew-draggled dress?

Am I then less woman because I have bowed
In womanly worship to lover-lord—proud
  If only his shadow beneath?
I love him!—I love him! and loving would do

Again, of devotion, the deed that I rue,
  Whose guerdon is misery—death!

Hush! hush thee, poor bantling, thy passionless cry;
Vain! vain is thy plaining! My bosom is dry!
  Nor food now, nor shelter I know!
Here where he first met me I bring thee to-night,
Together, ere morning, our spirits shall slight
  Earth's cruelty, hardness and woe!

Wherein have I trespassed, my father, that thou
Who gavest me being, should malison now
  Thine offspring, outcast in thy scorn?
My mother! my mother! my sin is thine own
If sin then it be, for in thee was it shown
  By bearing as I have but borne!

Are vows then unholy when whispered to Him
The Lord of Night's temple, when blazeful or dim
  His starworlds encircle the pole?
Is marriage more sacred for priest-sprinkled bed,
Or wealth-purchased virgins less venal though wed
  By priestling in surplice and stole?

Dost sleep now, poor infant?—Ah, God, it is death!
My baby!—My baby!—Kiss, kiss me!—Thy breath
  It trembles,—it flutters,—'tis gone!
Ah, Edward! ah, husband! Great God of the sky,
Forgive him! I love him! Forgive me, I die!
  May death for my weakness atone!

Out! out! where the water shone glassy and cold
She sprang, her dead daughter clutch'd fast to the
    fold
  Of her panting and grief-stricken breast.
A struggle—a sigh—and untroubled she lay
Asleep in the haven of measureless day,
    Laid calmly and surely at rest.

II

In Alderton Hall, on the Eve of Cecile,
There's roister and revel, with drinking at will
    And clinking of tankard and glass.
The master uprises—'Now pledge me, my friends,
The bride whose rare beauty shall make me amends
    For all that with marriage must pass.'

Each pours him a bumper, all rise to their feet,
One strikes a few notes on the harpsichord sweet,
    'So pledge me fair Alice Lorraine!'
Hurrah and hurrah now! With three times and three,
With shoutings and laughter and half drunken glee
    They drink it again and again.

The master what ails him? His glass he sets down
Untasted, and, startling, looks round with a frown,—
    'Who whisper'd that ill-omened name?'
They marvel, but jocund, reck little of mood.
There's ever distemper in fever-fed blood
    And folly in wine-kindled flame.

For fearful he hears in the depths of his soul
That death cry distressful; the sad accents roll
  Like thunder through bosom and brain.
And ' Edward !   Ah traitor ! ' rings loud in his ears,
A face too he sees that is clouded with tears,
  Like lily in curtain of rain.

With effort he conquers emotion.—' A song !
A song now from Kendrick !   Hereafter for long
  We meet not in Alderton Hall.
Who's mated gives hostage to Fortune and wife ;
Fresh paged and fresh lettered the scroll of his life ;
  He's freeman no longer, but thrall.'

With thrilling and throbbing the music again
Makes prelude, the singer breaks forth into strain
  Of love and the crimson-winged boy ;
Whose arrows fate mingled, to this one are death—
To this one dishonour—to this willow wreath—
  To this one bliss void of alloy.

Well sung and well sung !   But the master is mute,
Nor e'en had applauded though Sappho her lute
  Had struck for his pleasure alone.
For ever he heard through the ditty the cry—
' Forgive him !—I love him !—Forgive me, I die !
  May death for my weakness atone ! '

All marvell'd.   One whisper'd—' Of bride-stolen kiss
Sir Edward is dreaming, foreshadow of bliss
  Takes edge from the joy of to-day.'
Then loudly—' The health of the bridegroom to be !

Our host, for the best of good fellows is he !
  Long life with his ladylove gay ! '

Charge, charge now your glasses—' Our comrade and
        host ! '
Not one but with clamour doth honour the toast,
  He rises perforce in his place.
Yet nothing of purpose can frame in reply
For evermore hearing that pitiful cry,
  And seeing that death-stricken face.

The revel is over. Sir Edward till light
Lies restless and troubled.—Most welcome the sight
  Of morn with the flushing of day.
He rises. By meadow and hedgerow he'll go ;
The balm of the morning may freshen his brow,
  Calm nature bid harass away.

And aimlessly going—is't hazard or fate ?—
Unconscious of purpose he comes to the gate
  And follows the path to the dell.
Great God, and what is it !—A dead woman's face !
A cry of despair and he flees from the place
  Distracted—his bosom a hell.

        *   *   *   *   *

'Tis over. Sir Edward is wedded—his bride
Sits blushing beside him, as swiftly they ride
  Away for their honeymoon tour.
And loudly the ringers break out overhead,
O'er bridegroom and bride—and the girl that is dead
  And the babe that is stiffen'd and stour !

Sir Edward thereafter he goeth his way,
Good husband and father, no tongue but will say
 His honour is kindness to all.
But none know the sorrow that scorcheth his heart
And none know the terror that ne'er will depart—
 The dread of the vengeance to fall.

And often when hamlet and village are still,
By night in the churchyard that crowneth the hill,
 He stands by a grass-hidden grave;
And mournful will whisper—'I cannot atone!
Forgive me!'—while ever with murmur and moan
 The cypresses gloomily wave.

III

Oh, joyous the Spring-time, when Flora awakes!
When hourly the breezes blow sweeter—the brakes
 Upcurling 'mid orchid and bell.
When daisies with silver bespangle the lea,
When wood-doves are cooing in coppice and tree,
 The missel-thrush voicing the dell!

And down in the hollow the sward by the stream
Is golden with celandine—violets gleam
 Dew-glister'd through covert of green;
While primroses peep through the leaves by the pond,
And pearlcups bewhiten the waters beyond,
 With marybuds flaunting between.

And thither came Roland—Sir Edward's boy-heir.
'The water is deadly! Beware then, beware!

He dies who its poison should drink!'
His nurse thus, pursuing her chargeling with speed,
Who laughing runs forward, nor ever will heed,
  But plucks at the bents by the brink.

His eager hands full of the blossoms, he tries
To grasp yet another more distant, his eyes
  But only intent on the bloom.
See! See what arises asudden to sight
From out the still waters!—The maid in affright
  Leaves, spellbound, her charge to his doom.

A weed-tangled infant!—Young Roland holds forth
His child-hands to help her—no longer of worth
  The wildings full quickly let fall.
'Tis shade of his sister, behaunting for long
The pool where she perished, till falsehood and wrong
  No longer for punishment call.

The baby-hands meet.   He is drawn from the shore—
He sinks in the waters—his brief day is o'er—
  The pearlcups close over his head!
They find him thereafter, a smile on his face,
With never of pain or of sorrow a trace,
  Asleep—but the sleep of the dead.

          *   *   *   *   *

Sir Edward! Sir Edward! Though vengeance delay,
The threat-sword hangs ever; it waits but the day
  When Nemesis seeketh her own.
He felt it, heart-stricken, his soul in the dust;
And murmured repentant—'Oh, Father, the Just!
  Let death of my darling atone!'

CLAVERING

CLAVERING has for many a year been quite outside
the boundaries of the forest, all of which to the north
of Bishops Stortford was disafforested in the reign of
John. But though thus disafforested by royal
charter, it retained much of its original woodland
character long time thereafter.

The village lies on the borders of the county some
seven or eight miles beyond Stortford and close to
the much prettier villages of the Pelhams in Hertford-
shire. But for all its distance from the forest as we now
know it, the stirring legend, with its groundwork of
truth attached to it, seemed far too interesting to be
omitted. I have retained the name of Hugh, as it
came to me, though Morant and others call the con-
science-stricken Constable Henry.

Hugh, then, of Essex was a man of note, Constable of
England and lord of Clavering and a score of other
manors. The story as it is here given affords a
probable explanation of his otherwise unaccountable
cowardice in the affair of the Welch Marches.

Except for the earthworks of the earl's stronghold,
which are extensive, the village itself is not particularly
interesting. All the masonry of the castle above
ground has disappeared, but the configuration of the
keep can still be traced. As with the neighbouring
hold of Anstey, built by Eustace of Boulogne, some
of the stones have gone to the building of the church
which stands a little beyond the donjon mound and

its rapidly silting-up moat.   But where are the rest ?
Elsewhere in the vicinage of castle or abbey I have
seen grottos and rockwork in a score of cottage
gardens, formed out of the fallen stones, with corbels
of angels, or demons, or donors staring stolidly out of
ferns or houseleek, almost, as it were, with a look
of supreme contempt for their soulless despoilers.
Vaulting springers turned into mounting-blocks for
inn and homestead have I also seen, with bridges
whose chiselled and sculptured stonework plainly
spake of ecclesiastical quarry-heaps not far removed.

But here at Clavering, as at Anstey, there is no
river to be bridged over ; cottagers and farmers
reck not of rockwork or grotto ; no hall, no farmhouse, knows of them for foundation or walls—where,
then, are the stones ?

Ask the question aloud as, after an hour's profitable
meditation upon the fate of the strong and the great,
you descend the castle mound ; and the walls of the
old church, if they answer at all, will send you back
the Irishman's echo, ' Ah where ? '

HUGH OF ESSEX

A LEGEND OF CLAVERING

BLITHE the morrowing's golden beams,
  Oh, that sweet May morning !
Startling woke a monk from dreams,
  Cell and convent scorning !

Woke and wept through stress of grief,
   Vainly weeping, praying,
' Mary mother ! send relief
   Death so long delaying ! '

Cheerly sang in beech and oak
   Nightingale and linnet.
Untold lays uprising woke
   Wood and haye and spinnet.
Sparkling leaped the brook along,
   Bank and margent spurning ;
Joyous, all its course a song,
   Seaward, home returning.

' Oh, the bright and blissful beam,
   Oh, the gladsome morning,
Oh, the fleet and sparkling stream
   Mead and slade adorning !
Oh, the linnet, lark and thrush,
   Oh, the breezes blowing,
Oh, the lay from tree and bush
   Thrilling, overflowing ! '

Thus a youth of lofty mien
   In the convent garden,
'Neath the boughs so goodly green
   And the blossom'd warden ;
Gathering lilies—maiden fair
   What more sweet could fancy ?
Marigolds for breast and hair
   Cullumbine and pansy.

'Song is sweeter far than gold,
  But my love is sweeter!
Coy is she, yet never cold,
  Leaps my heart to meet her!
Kisses soft her lips invite
  Red as Provence roses,
Pearls her teeth, her tresses bright,
  Gold as kingcup posies.

'Oh, so dainty is my queen
  Oh, so fair and slender!
Never yet her mate was seen
  Angel sweet and tender.
Soon the King shall dub me knight,
  Golden spurrel gaining,
Then I'll seek my lady bright,
  All my suit attaining.'

'Ah! the wretch that wakes to weep;
  Ah! the heart that's breaking;
Ah! the bliss of mindless sleep;
  But the woe of waking!
Ah! the drag of day to day
  Anguish aye encumbered,
Hell pangs, naught can e'er allay
  Mass, nor pray'rs unnumbered.'

Thus the monk with bitter moan
  Heark'ning boyish ditty;
Head bowed down and hands outthrown,
  Ah, the woe, the pity!

'Jesu, Jesu, on Thy rood,
  Droop with pain and anguish,
Pity me! Ye angel brood,
  Wing ye, where I languish!'

Through the open casement flying
    Came a bird,
    All unheard
Whirr of wing, for sob and sighing.
  Was it real? Was it fancy?
  Miracle or necromancy?
Yet as soft the carol ran,
    Did he hear
    Silver clear,
Song of bird, as speech of man?

All his ruddy plumage swelling,
  Perched the while upon the rood,
Sang the robin, proudly telling
  Tale of ruth in scene of blood.

'I am he that wrest the bramble
  Out the brow of Christ the Lord;
What time he like lamb to shamble
  Guiltless, driv'n with rod and cord,
Dying hung 'twixt earth and heaven
Till the fall of sorrowing even.
    Evermore
    Holy gore
On my breast for sweet reward.

Out His blood-suffused eyes,
  Piteous bent on murd'rous men,
Looked he on my sad emprise
  Mournful smiling, blest me then;
Gave me pow'r each year to show,
Penance pathway out of woe,
Him who prone at Christ His cross
Mourns repentant, Christian loss!'

    All amazing
    He upgazing
Saw the bird upon the rood:
  And in wonder, losing sorrow,
  'Blessed Jesu may I borrow
Help from bird of kindly brood?'
    Thus he sighing
    Swift replying
Sang the bird in joyous mood—
'If repentant, thou wouldst pray
  Heartwhole, eased of torment sorrow,
If at close of holyday
  Sleep with hope of peaceful morrow,
    Lay aside
    Cloke of pride
Hellwove, seamed with seam of hate.
Lost thy name, with wealth and station;
Thrill him with the weird narration
Tell of Pride and Lust and Fate.
    Told of all,
    Bid him fall

Low before the rood and pray.
  Noble is he, yet doth evil
  Lurk his path, a traitor devil,
Satan set to tempt and slay.'

So sang he, then out the casement
  Flying sought the cloister-green ;
While the monk in sore amazement—
  'Christ! What may this portent mean ?
Is it sooth, or am I dreaming
Sottish made of devil scheming ? '

Soon his resolution taken
Cell and pallet swift forsaken,
  Followed he th' expectant bird.
'Son, with you a word in warning.'
'Certes, father ! ' He part scorning,
  Part attentive as he heard.

Then the monk in tones of sorrow,
Soul-struck chords that naught need borrow
  Or of rhetoric or art ;
Hand uplifted, eye bright blazing,
Spake he now, the youth amazing,
  Spellbound, loth to stay or part.

'Son, give ear! I pray thee, hear me !
Would my words were fire to sere thee,
  Burn the demon out thy soul !
Demon-passion, once thy master,
Mocking, fast to fell disaster
  Driving, void of all control.'

II

Hugh of Essex! Hugh of Essex!
  England's greatest noblest he.
Wide his manors, strong his castles,
  Vast and proud and fair to see;
Valiant, comely, wealthy, great,
What should shake his high estate?

Hugh of Essex! Hugh of Essex!
  Standard bearer of his King,
Sleepless tost him in his chamber
  Of his hold at Clavering;
Rose at length, or yea or nay
Mine is she ere break of day!

Varlets, waken! Morn advances,
Waken, bowmen, waken, lances,
  Saddle ye without delay!
Swift they sprang to do his bidding,
First at call is never nidding,
  Last for feud or fray.

Ah, the stars they brightly glitter'd,
In their nests the fledglings twitter'd
  As the meiney rode along.
Yet, no star, oh God! to stay him,
Meteor flame nor flash to slay him,
  Kindly, ere he did the wrong!

'Neath the grange's low-hung thatching
Slept Adele, sweet maiden snatching

Short repose from vigil-prayer.
In the Holy Land her father
Battling linger'd—Ah, that rather
  Here had warder'd daughter fair!

She for him, unheedful patrons
Ceaseless praying; laughing matrons
  Babe-claspt, bade her rather wed.
He will ne'er return! 'Tis duty,
Virgin smiles and virgin beauty
  Bless the quick and not the dead.

But she faithful—'Lover never
Will I, while the sea shall sever
  Warrior sire from daughter dear.
Shame to me, love's soft caressing,
He his Lord's affront redressing,
  Wan and worn, with brand and spear.'

So she said, nor e'er gave over
Fast and prayer for friend or lover,
  Faithful ever to her vow.
Vainly Hugh of Essex wooed her,
  Vain with prayer and gift pursued her,
  Guerdon ne'er his suit might know.

Now resolve unholy taken,
Honour, fame, and faith forsaken,
  Reckless rode he through the night.
Grisly phantoms eager aiding,
Demon tempters aye persuading,
  Deed of darkness, lifelong blight!

Soon the lonely grange surrounded,
Soon its scanty few confounded,
    Enters in, proud Clavering's lord.
'Lady! long I've sought thee, prayed thee,
Yield thee, none are nigh to aid thee,
    Mine henceforth by cross and sword!'

Rudely waked from virgin sleeping
Left she now her maidens weeping,
    Borne to horse and borne away,
Chaste as angel left she Hayden,
Yet at morn no longer maiden,
    Hapless shamed ere dawn of day.

But his felon passion sated,
Soon his weeping prey he hated,
    Mocked her, helpless, in her woe.
Then she rose and taught of heaven,
Flamed with fire of sacred seven,
    Bann'd him coward, evermoe.

'Hugh of Essex! Hugh of Essex!
    Great in pride and proud of state,
Learn of me thy weeping victim,
    What thy doom and what thy fate.
Mighty, greater tyrant he,
Using might remorselessly!

'Coward! See thy master's standard
    Cast at foot of scoffing foe!
See! thou tight'nest rein and turnest,
    First the path of shame to show.

See ! forsook, thy squadrons broken,
See, they flee ! Thy doom is spoken.

'Constable, thy staff is taken
   Out thy once resistless hand,
See ! they lead thee forth to judgment,
   Thee whose word o'erawed a land.
Trembling right of battle claimest,
Ere the king thee traitor namest.

'Conquer'd ! see in monkish cloister,
   Life spared of thy master's scorn,
'Mid unseemly jest and laughter,
   Thee, henceforth a shaveling, shorn.
Manhood gone with name and station,
Live to curse thy day and nation ! '

Thus far she. Then sudden weeping—
'Son beware sin's awful reaping
   Hell-seed sown, bears ever fruit ! '—
Mocking heard Earl Hugh the maiden,
Drave her forth all woe-beladen.
   But that very night came bruit

Of Llewellyn's force in order,
Of the Welshmen o'er the border,
   Death and horror every side.
'Constable of England, hasten !
Pride of prince and chieftain chasten
   Save the land with carnage dyed !

'Spur and spare not ! Spur and spare not ! '
  So the wailful summons came,
Every hour sees homestead, farm-oot,
  Hamlet frighting heav'n with flame ;
Every hour an age of weeping,
Hell burst loose and England sleeping !

Noise of naker, blare of horn,
  Swift the setting in array,
Wife and maid and child forlorn,
  Husband, lover torn away !
    All the night,
    Warlike might,
Pouring in from hall and hold,
    Serf and yeoman,
    Spearman, bowman,
Gath'ring, while th' alarum tolled,
Clanging, ceaseless overhead,
Direful, dirgeful, till the dead
Stirr'd within their charnel cells.

    Hell rejoices ;
    Demon voices
Swell the tumult. Moloch tells
Hurrying Horror, tales of slaughter,
Butcher'd wife and child and daughter,
Lust triumphant, rage unbridled,
Burning hamlets smoke enstifled,
Devil deeds of death, with blood
Poured like water, hideous flood !

Never resting, ever hasting,
  Soon he reached the world of war,
Swift amid the wreck and wasting,
  Rolled his welcome from afar,
'Essex! Essex!' Shouted loudly
All the March, exulting proudly.

Joining now his royal master,
Never recked he of disaster,
  Hastening Fate and hurrying Doom.
But with morning came the battle,
Ring of lance with buckler rattle,
  Charging squadrons trampling boom.

Arrows death-winged fleetly flying,
Shriek of wounded, groan of dying,
  Shout of conflict, yell of hate.
Hauberk pierced and helmet dinted,
Earth bedewed with blood unstinted,
  Winnowing Death afield with Fate.

England's standard proudly soaring,
  High o'er footman, steed and knight,
Foe and fear alike abhorring
  Who is he, that heads the fight?
Hero strokes incessant raining,
Every stroke a foe attaining,
England's warrior Marshal he,
In whose presence, victory.

Sudden! see the standard falling
  Out his terror-stricken hand!
What is this—this form appalling
  Ghastlier queen of ghastly band?
Dim her eyes and wan, with weeping
  Wound nor priest nor leach can heal;
On his head confusion heaping—
  'Tis the shade of dead Adele!

He—his courser swerving, rearing,
  Checks him not by curb or rein,
But the nearing phantom fearing,
  Reckless flies along the plain;
In his track, disaster, sorrow,
  Scorn, dishonour, foul acclaim—
Heedless, may but terror borrow
  Wings to flee from shade of shame.

Youth beware! God's judgment speeding
  Like to bolt out summer sky,
Kings and princes, all unheeding
  Warning, crushed before Him lie!
In a moment—sentence spoken—
  From His seat, empyreal host,
Flame-winged speed, man's pride is broken,
  Gone his strength, his might, his trost!

Like to bubble sunbeam painted—
  Wondrous rich and fair and gay.
Gorgeous! Till by breath attainted
  Gleam and sheen are gone for aye,

So is man, his God despising,
  Wrapt in robe of rainbow pride,
Till the vengeful flood uprising,
  Doomful whelms him in its tide!

Hugh of Essex! Hugh of Essex!
  Like to Lucifer o'erthrown,
Constable at morn and Marshal
  Yet at noon for nidding known.
How his star is set whose radiance,
  Lustre lent to royal throne.

Brought before the king thereafter—
  Furious he at foul defeat—
'Standard captured, field forsaken,
  Traitor, say what doom is meet?'
Thus he rageful, as when billows,
  Tempest flung, on breakers beat.

Pale the earl as lily blossom,
  Only like to living coal
Blazed his eyes, the while he laboured—
  Breast upheaved by bursting soul—
Words to utter, till escaped him—
  'Right of combat.' This the whole.

'Right of combat!' Bitter smiling
  Gazed the king on lord and knight.
'Say then, gentles, who will venture,
  Who for me maintain the right?
Well ye know the Earl of Essex,
  England's arm and England's might!'

HUGH OF ESSEX

Flushed the Marshal's face with fury,
  Came the words as rush of storm—
'Earl or knight or king I fear not!
  Nothing living!—But the form
That o'ercame me was a spirit!
  Woe is me! Adele Delorme!

All or one I care not! Come ye
  As ye will, no wight of earth
Feared I ever! Lance and broadsword
  Left me, still I'll prove their worth!
Set the lists and heav'n befriend me
  Bann'd and bound in ghostly girth!'

Then the king—'Thou shalt have champion
  And from these thou hast defied.
Set the lists! Let fall of even
  Troth or treason now decide!
But and if thou dost not conquer
  Better far hadst battling died.'

    *   *   *   *

Fierce the day, but cooler evening
  Saw the Marshal in the list.
But the king delaying signal
  Till the sun the river kist,
Blare of trumpet, break the stillness,
  Pealing out the nether mist.

And a horseman, eager riding
  Over hillock, meadow, plain,
Spurred him till the royal presence
  Reaching, halting, drawing rein,

'Justice, justice!' shouted loudly
  Till the dais rang amain.

'King, I claim to meet this traitor!
  See this cambrai kerchief laid
In my helmet, torn and crumpled,
  Bloodied and with blood of maid,
Shamed at night, by England's Marshal
  In his hold afar from aid!

'Knight and kinsman, when the maiden
  Dying, sought me, then I swore
By the blessed rood to venge her,
  By God's Mother, nevermore
Rest to know, till retribution
  Had avenged her suffering sore!

'So I claim of right the conflict!'
  Sternly hearing—'Knight 'tis thine,'
Spake the king—'But thou art weary
  And the battle part is mine,
Yet methinks thou canst but prosper
  Go, and Christ the meed assign!'

Slowly sank the sun, as lothful
  Peaceful earth to leave for sea;
Sinking, lit the lake with crimson,
  Gilding roof and tow'r and tree,
Then at royal sign, the clarion
  Woke the vale with warrior glee.

Now from either course careering,
  Rage and dread together greet,
Lances splint'ring, while their chargers
  Shake the ground with thund'rous feet.
Now to earth they spring, their falchions
  Sweeping, flashing, lightning fleet.

Hugh of Essex! Hugh of Essex!
  Vain thy valour, prowess, skill.
Weak as babe is he that ventures—
  Though his strength a giant's still—
Godless, war against Jehovah,
  Impious, braving holy will!

So his glimmering sword descending,
  Hissing, oft the echoes woke,
Yet in vain the foe attainted
  On his helmet harmless broke.
'Twas as if that bloodied kerchief
  Fas'nous turned each deadly stroke!

Now he weary fails in combat,
  But with fierce ingath'ring might
In his turn the foe remorseless
  Rushing on renews the fight,
While death-silence held the gazers
  Spell-bound they at wondrous sight!

For the stranger onward pressing
  Sudden aims a victor blow;
Full on crest and helm it lightens
  And the earl is stricken low.

Now the dag against his gorget—
　'Yield thee or thy doomstroke know!'

Then he through his visor fiercely—
　'Slay me, curst of God and man!
Yield I will not! Slay me quickly!
　Ah! for death ere shame began!'
Then he softly—'Nay I slay not,
　Bear thou still thy penance ban!'

Then uprising, lift his visor—
　God 'twas face of dead Adele—
Calm and cold as face of angel
　Altar carved in cloistral pale—
'Sent am I of Christ to punish,
　Pray—for prayer may yet avail!'

Loud the triumph-trumpets sounding,
　Squires and heralds drawing nigh,
Springing lightly on his charger
　Rode the ghostly champion by;
Passing made the king obeisance—
　Spoken, ne'er vouchsafed reply.

They astounded, raised the Marshal,
　Sunken he in deathlike swound,
''Twas a champion sent of Mary,
　See! he bears not hurt nor wound!'
Thus said they with prayer and crossing
　As they trembling gather'd round.

Then the king in solemn judgment,
' 'Tis the retribute of God.
Wrong were we, I trow, to venture
  Aught against His royal rod!
Be his doom then, Reading cloister,
  Shaveling henceforth, sandal-shod! '

    *   *   *   *   *

' Youth, in me behold the witness!
  I am he that wrought the deed!
Ruthless, he who snared of Satan
  Bade Adele despairing bleed.
Then adoomed, lost honour, station—
Henceforth shame and lamentation!

' Youth!'—But here he ceased heartbroken;
  Yet the robin joyous sang,
While the convent bell for matins
  Softly out the belfry clang!
Then the youth—' Great Earl, thy sorrow
  Hath my soul with ruth attaint;
Shall for me contrition borrow,
  Purge from sinful aim and taint! '

    *   *   *   *

    Now returning,
    Bosom burning,
But from load of pain released,
Sought the monk again his pallet,
Slept like babe, whom lover callet
Scolds to rest, its plaint appeased.

Slept so long his brethren wond'ring
 Why so late he kept his cell,
Mass and vigil all unheeding,
 Altar-psalm and sacring bell,
Came to find him peaceful sleeping,
 But the sleep of dead Adele!

THEYDON BOIS

THE following is a ballad of Thoydon dans le bois,
to give it its full name. It is still in the wood, as
is a portion of its brother village Thoydon Garnon,
so called after Robert de Gernon who owned it in
'Richard' Conqueror's time. But Thoydon Mont,
with its stately Hill Hall and park, is now quite outside
the forest boundaries.

Of Thoydon Bois itself a rather good story is told
of a Government school inspector, the first I believe
to visit the delightful little woodland village after
the railway to Epping had made it accessible—without
a four-mile walk from Loughton. Over the window
of the village school is a tablet with the inscription
'Theydon Bois School.' Catching sight of this, the
learned newcomer remarked to the venerable vicar
—I had the story from the latter—'Ah! It's high
time we routed you up here, if that's the way you
people spell "boys." '

Which thing, as *Punch* puts it, he 'would much

rather have left unsaid,' after explanation and reflection.

But the ' Bois ' is not what it was. True its fine old green remains, thanks to the Corporation of the City of London, and *no* thanks to the greedy farming folk, who cast such hungry eyes upon it, in the good old days of land-grabbing under its euphemism, enclosure. The green, I say, remains, with its giant elms looking down somewhat superciliously upon the young but noble oak avenue leading up to them —but where are the stocks that stood under the trees at the roadside corner ? Did mine host of the *Bull Inn* remove them stealthily by night ? They stood not a stone's throw from his porchway, ever a patent and pertinent warning to topers in general, and to the ' consumers ' of his old brown October in particular. Or did they decay of sheer old age and lack of use ?—God wot many a leg nowadays could find them plenty of employment as in the days of my boyhood.—Or, to make a shrewder guess, did some sickly sentimentalist upon the village vestry urge their removal as signs of a past and barbarous polity, unduly interfering with the liberty of the (drunken) subject ?

Still, as in these changeful times much must be made of small mercies, let us be glad and rejoice that the *Bull Inn* stands much as it did generations ago. We will forgive, too, the theft of the stocks, in consideration of the glee that must have filled the breast of old Tom Maynard, as cosily smoking and drinking by the huge chimney corner of the ancient hostelry, he chuckled over the fall of the enemy that had given his own unsteady shanks many a sore pinch in days gone by, and, now smitten hip and thigh itself and sawn into sorry logs, filled the capacious chimney with the wrath of its roaring, with noisy spittings and splutterings, and showers of disconsolate sparks ! Long may the old inn stand !

But as in the days of Rip Van—so in all probability in these. Some soulless ' *proprietor* ' will come along—we are all proprietors in this twentieth century—and with the connivance of some equally soulless brewery firm, will turn the rustic ' house of call ' into a modern gin palace, under the high-sounding title of ' The Theydon Hotel,' like to its once ancient and venerable neighbour the *King's Oak* at High Beech.

BALLAD

HUBERT LOVES ONLY BUT ME

SIR OSWALD, 'tis he that rides over the lea,
  Of Thoydon its lord and its knight.
He cometh from warring in far Picardie
  With gallant King Harry his might.

He meeteth a maiden. Oh ! fairer than fay
  Is she in her kirtle of blue.
Her goldilocks brighter than sunbeam in May,
  Her bonny cheeks rosy of hue.

L.L.   G

'And whither thus eager, thou maiden so bright?
　Oh, whither so fleet and so free?'—
'I seek my true lover, ere fall of the night—
　Must hasten, he tarries for me.'

'And who is thy lover? Now tell me aright,
　His calling too—what may it be?'
'Oh, yonder he dwelleth—his father's a knight,
　But Hubert loves only but me.'

'If yonder he dwelleth—then maiden beware,
　Thy lover unfaithful will be!
Hawks mate not with turtles, though gentle and fair,
　Nor lordings beneath their degree.'

'Oh, hedgerows are bonny with roses between,
　And woodbine all golden to see;
And maidens are many, but were she a queen
　Would Hubert love only but me.'

'And where doth he meet thee, thou maiden so fair?
　Thy trysting place fain would I see.'
'Not so, sir, to stranger I may not declare
　The tryst of my lover and me.'

'And what saith the father, thou maiden so mild?
　His mother, what saith she to thee?'
'Oh, she was to heaven by angels beguiled—
　His father is over the sea.'

'And came he to Thoydon, fair maiden, say now
　What manner his greeting would be?'

'Oh, boldly I'd meet him with Hubert, I trow,
　And plead his forgiveness at knee.'

'Oh! I am that father, from Azincourt fight,
　And Hubert may mate not with thee!'—
'Say not so beseech thee, in cruel despight,
　For Hubert loves only but me.'

'Oh! I am his father, thou damozel bold,
　And Hubert far banished shall be.'—
'Though ocean on ocean between us there rolled
　Would Hubert be faithful to me.'

'Oh! absence makes traitors, believe me fair maid,
　Once parted forgotten thou'lt be.'—
'Though evening were morning, and sunshine were
　　shade
　Would Hubert be faithful to me.'

'Oh! I am of Thoydon, its lord and its pride,
　And thou its fair lady shalt be.'—
'And wert thou King Harry, I'd be not thy bride,
　While Hubert loves only but me.'

'Oh! deep is my dungeon, where darkness is light,
　Its horrors thou surely shalt see.'—
'For dungeon or darkness, for fear or for fright
　No bride will I be unto thee.'

Sir Oswald alighted.　'Now by my good roan
　A kiss thou shalt give me for fee.'
'No kiss will I give thee—my kisses alone
　Are his who loves only but me.'

Sir Oswald he marvelled. 'Now by my good troth
　　Right dear art thou maiden to me,
So comely and constant!—I benison both
　　Doth Hubert love only but thee.'

'Oh! then am I lady of Thoydon, sir knight
　　And sire, that full surely wilt be,
And kisses a score will I give thee to-night
　　With Hubert beside me to see.'

COOPERSALE

COOPERSALE, a hamlet of Thoydon Gernon, lies about
a mile from the town of Epping, at the foot of a steep
hill affording a fine prospect over a still well-wooded
district. It is close to the woodland beyond Epping,
which here is locally known as Coopersale Forest.
Beyond it, almost into Greenstead, the wood stretches
under various names, for it has long since passed
into private hands, enriching at small cost, or none
at all, beyond that of enclosure, the owners of sundry
parks and places to right and left.

For as, nowadays, in this twentieth century of
civilization, a woman guilty of cruelty to her children, being a nobody, will be sentenced to 'three
months hard,' as the phrase is, or longer, while another,
convicted of the same crime, but being a lady of
position, will escape with a nominal fine, thanks to

an over complaisant judge; so in earlier times the
stealer of a deer, being a servile person, would ' lose
his skinne,' while the robber of a hundred acres. or
more of public land would contrive to survive and
retain his spoil.

Indeed, as in the New Forest, so half the parks
and places about the Forest of Essex are simple
robberies of common land, connived at or condoned.

Coopersale church, the scene of the legend, is a
quaint old building in a delightful out of the way
district. It stands on a slight eminence and is almost
buried in trees, but its lofty turreted tower is quite
a feature in the landscape. Of late years, unfortunately, a huge red-brick parsonage has sprung up in
the meadow adjoining the churchyard, and con-
siderably spoilt the view from the lime tree avenue
that runs from the side of the old rectory up to the
churchyard gate.

From the churchyard, grassy paths run in several
directions; and it is a goodly sight to see the little
congregation going home after service; lads and lasses
loitering behind the forefathers and foremothers of
the hamlet, telling, doubtless, the old old story that
happily is ever so fresh and new; while the babelings,
ignorant alike of the fire of youth, or the chills of age,
chase each other merrily hither and thither, little
heedful of reproving looks or half hearted admonitions.

The church itself is quaint with dormer windows;
while wood being more plentiful than stone in the
days of its building, there are pillars of oak dividing
the nave from its northern aisle. For those who are

curious in such matters, there is the brass effigy of a fourteenth century rector, in eucharistic vestments; but the screen climbed by high-hearted Margaret Clare and her girl companions is gone, with the rood that she clung to, ere descending again, the sweet brave girl knelt by the side of her spectral betrothed.

Hill Hall, hidden away amid its mighty forest giants on the top of a neighbouring height, is within half an hour's walking; while Abridge, the scene of the catastrophe, lies in the valley beneath, the Roding flowing through it as of yore, and as of yore flooding field and meadow and marsh when the winter rains rushing down from Navestock and Stapleford Tany, or Lambourn and the Mont, turn the quiet pebbly wanderer of the summer into a hurrying stream, wide almost in parts as the broad-bosomed river into which it empties itself,

> Though deep, yet clear; though gentle yet not dull.
> Strong without rage; without o'erflowing full.

But this was over a couple of centuries ago in the days of Denham and before the epoch of sewer outfalls, replete with the exuviæ of a four-millioned metropolis.

ST. MARK'S EVE

A LEGEND OF COOPERSALE

I

'AND who, then, with me in the chancel to-night
  Will watch, while the silver-rayed queen
Slow rides through the night in her vesture of light,
  O'er hilltop and valley between ?
While solemn the tempest sweeps thorough the wood,
  And spectre and goblin and elve
Come forth from the gloom of charnel and tomb
  At boom of the turret at twelve !

'For they that the vigil of blessed St. Mark
  Dare keep at the holy rood-screen,
Strange vision shall see, ere the morrowing be—
  Most wondrous apparence, I ween.
For all they of Thoydon the weary year through
  That perish by land or by sea,
At midnight must pass through the churchyard to
      Mass
  With their priest and his acolytes three.'

Oh, fair beyond telling was Margaret Clare
  Who bade to that vigil unblest ;
Her forehead was bold, while her tresses of gold,
  Wind-frolicked, kissed bosom and breast.
Her eyes they were limpid and blue as the wave
  That, breezeless and laid to repose,
In soft southern bay at the close of the day
  Like amethyst glistens and glows.

High-hearted she came from the coppice, her hands
   Befilled with the spoils of the wood—
With daffodils pale and anemones frail,
   And cuckoo-buds redder than blood.
Queen-crowned with a chaplet of daisies she stood—
   'Twas plaited by Laura Lestrange,
The maid at her feet : so winsome and sweet,
   Child Laura of Coopersale Grange ?

'And I then !—I also ! And, Margaret, I ! '
   Her comrades made answer with glee ;
Save Rosamond, pale as the luce of the vale,
   Who, trembling, knelt down at her knee.
And 'Sister, dear sister,' she earnest replied ;
   'Forbear ! oh, forbear now your quest ! '
So pleaded the maid as her forehead she laid
   In terror on Margaret's breast.

But Margaret, laughing, ' My bonny white Rose,
   Thou ever wert troubled with fear
For me, from the day of our sisterly play—
   Sweet Rose without rival or peer !
But happen what may, in the chancel to-night
   I watch till the dawning of day.
So they now that dare in my vigil may share,
   And they that are fearful may stay.'

But Rosamond, sighing, uplifted her head,
   And sadly her sister she kist ;
Yet scarcely could see, for the fast-falling sea
   Of sorrow, love's soul-springing mist ;

And, clinging, entreated in tremulous tone :
  ' Dear sister, if any must go.
Let me be that one, for no peril I'll shun
  To save thee from danger or woe.'

' Not so. None shall venture for sparing of me,'
  Said Margaret, proud as the day
At morn, that with beam and with fervour and gleam
  Recks not of night's sable array.
' I go, and go fearless ; but, Rosamond, you
  Shall not, lest misfortune befall ;
So stay you and pray till the breaking of day,
  And carol of lark at its call.'

II

Not yet from her couch in the lonely firwood
  The moon had arisen serene,
Though silvery-white was the canopy bright
  That hung o'er the wakening queen.
And soft was the breeze as the murmur of harp,
  Or fountain's Eolian strain,
Or sighing of maid with her cherry lips laid
  To the lips of her passionate swain.

And dark was the chapel enshrouded in trees
  O'erhanging the grave-chequered knoll ;
The clang of its bell, as the midnight befell,
  Like knell for a moribund soul.

But bravely the maid with her tryst-fellows three
  Hid up in the oaken rood-loft,
With fond arms entwined as their heads they inclined
  Full oft to her whispering soft.

Hush! hush! for the hour it is knelling. And see
  Yon light with its corpse-kindled gleam!
The chancel is gray with its shadowless ray;
  It spreads over pillar and beam.
And list, too, the organ beginning to roll!
  But softly! and see, too, the bread
Is set with the cup of which only may sup
  The priest at the Mass of the dead!

They fearfully watching, the prodigy grew,
  And ever the requiem rolled
Its withering strain, as again and again
  The passing-bell drearily tolled.
While noiseless, at bidding of grave-quickened hand,
  The portal wide open was flung,
As slow on the wall, to the requiem's fall,
  The bannerols mournfully swung.

And weirdly the glamour streamed onward, and lit
  The yews and the cypresses low,
Each sorrow-twined wreath, with the gravestone
    beneath,
  Ablaze with the marvellous glow.
And awful! see now in the fascinous light
  That ghostly funereal band,
The pathway upled by their priest at their head,
  Close now to the charnel-house stand!

And babelings were there that as yet were unborn,
  With wives that as yet were unwed !
And schoolmaidens fair that unhappy should share
  The grave with the silver-thatched head.
And all as they halted the sign of the cross
  Made slowly on bosom and brow ;
Then silently came, while the space-filling flame
  Beat wanly on hillock and bough.

Still onward, while, swelling, the weird organ-strain
  Was sad as the wail of the wave
That sweeps o'er the deck of the rock-splintered wreck,
  And beats at the mariner's grave.
Now halting, close gathered, beneath the rood-screen,
  They kneel while their passionless priest,
His antiphons said, incenses the bread
  And wine for the marvellous feast.

Oh, dauntless as eagle was Margaret Clare ;
  What dread in that bosom might hide,
Which never had known a desire that had grown
  To sin against virginal pride ?
And often alone with her staghound at night
  She walked in the forestal glade,
No fear at her heart though her comrade should start
  And bay at the quivering shade.

But now she knew terror, and clung to the rood,
  Her forehead embracing its feet ;
It shook with her clasp and the fire of her grasp,
  And her bosom's impetuous beat.

But bravely she battled the fear in her soul,
  And conquered—her conquest how sore!
Less happy than they, her companions, who lay
  A-swooned at her feet on the floor.

For three of those ghastly life shadows she knew,
  And one was child Laura, that lay
Already as dead, in her horror and dread,
  Her face ashen-pallid, and gray;
The others—ah, God! for the pang in her breast!—
  The last of the phantomic train:
A youth and a lass; 'twas herself that did pass
  With him that was sailing the main.

The gold on his shoulder was fleckered with blood,
  The blue was commingled with red
By broiderer Death, when the laborous breath,
  Fate-bidden, the conqueror fled.
And she: the marshweed on her bosom lay dank;
  The clotted blood hung in her hair;
Her kirtle was wet, and her gaze it was set,
  With the drowning girl's agonized stare.

But either yet turned on the other a look
  Of love all unquenchable still;
For Love liveth aye, though ocean, its prey,
  And earth, claim her children at will!
And peaceful, hands clasping, together they knelt,
  While wondrous the melody rolled
Through chancel and aisle, as slowly the while
  The sanctus-bell solemnly tolled.

Now slowly the celebrant lifted the cup
  And signed the blest sign in the air;
Then worshipped the Host, while Margaret crost
  Her breast at the measureless glare
That burst from the chalice and patine, and fell
  Aflame on her bosom and brow,
As low at the screen, as yet all unseen,
  She knelt with the phantoms below.

Was't hazard or purpose? Her lover looked up;
  He saw her, and bending his head
With unearthly grace, did he show her a place
  Beside him—a place with the dead!
Ah, wondrous life-ruler! Fate monarch! Ah, Love!
  Thou victor and spoiler of Death!
No terror she knew, but undauntedly drew
  To the shade of her lover beneath.

The organ note sank to a murmurous fall;
  The glamour redoubled its light;
As calm in its sheen, all untroubled, serene,
  Like to star in the tiar of night,
She came to the side of her lover; and, lo!
  The shadow departed that dwelt
Beside him erewhile, as with welcoming smile
  He bent, while she silently knelt.

And calmly beside him she knelt, and her soul
  Went up to Jehovah in prayer:
' On earth or in heav'n, my troth-pledge is giv'n
  To him, and his hazard I share.

Forgive, if thus loving I sin, Lord, for love
   Of Thee is begotten alone ;
I do but keep troth, assoil Thou then both ;
   Let Mass for misdoing atone.'

Now drew the priest near ; all untroubled she bore
   His death-gaze, as, crossing her hands,
She shared with the rest, in the Sacrament blest,
   Its Giver and Given, commands.
And sudden her spirit, complacent, beheld,
   In faithful foreshadowing clear,
The doom that should be, upon land and on sea,
   To each ere the death of the year.

Mass ended, the pageant slow faded away ;
   And, people and celebrant gone,
Night's cloud-girdled queen, with her crystalline sheen,
   Looked down on the maiden alone.
And placid its beam through the checkering pane
   Came flooding the chorestal floor,
Like angel of light, with a message of might
   To spirits earth-wearied and sore.

And, lo ! to her fancy the face of the Christ,
   Thorn-crowned, in the traceried frame,
Shone out in the ray in a mystical way,
   With love and compassion aflame.
And tearful she worshipped : ' O Fountain of love !
   Grant now I may service Thee well,
Whate'er may befall, till Thy welcoming call,
   And close of life's wearisome spell ! '

Thereafter uprising, she went to the stair,
  And, climbing its newel-stone steep,
' Wake, Catherine, wake ! or my kisses shall break
  The charm of thy merciful sleep !
And, Laura, dear comrade, unconscious of fate,
  Awake ! for thy lifehood is fleet.
Rise, Emily, rise ! we must home ere the skies
  Morn's embassy lovingly greet.'

And sighing they woke at the call of the voice,
  So passionless, tranquil, and clear ;
Untroubled they woke, but as memory broke,
  They trembled and murmured with fear.
But cheerful she chid them : ' Ah, cowards ! afraid
  Of naught but the silver moonbeam ; '
But nothing they said, as they eagerly fled
  The scene of their terrible dream.

But Margaret held in her embrace a hand—
  'Twas Laura's, full clammy, and cold—
And lifted it oft to her bosom so soft,
  Yet ever so dauntless and bold.
And hastening onward, ere long there shone out
  The lights from the hill-topping hall ;
But bodingly howled in their kennels, and growled,
  The dogs, as they sped by the wall.

And Rosamond springing to Margaret's arms,
  For gladness her pearly tears fell.
' And what did you see ? ' did she ask in her glee ;
  But Margaret nothing would tell ;

But, gently caressing the eager young face,
    Uplifted in love to her own :
' Ask nothing, my sweet ! for I may not repeat
    What to me was in secrecy shown.'

The others but little could proffer, so soon
    Their senses by terror opprest :
The gleaming could tell, with the slow-swinging bell,
    The organ—but naught of the rest.
And morning came filling the landskip with light,
    And evening succeeded to-day ;
But ne'er from each heart did remembrance depart,
    Or sorrow surrender its sway.

III

Oh, Margaret Clare she was wealthy and great,
    Far-stretching her manors and wide,
And if she were proud, e'en detraction allowed
    Her noble, spite glozing of pride.
'Twas pride that, disdaining the grudging of greed
    Ne'er snatched from the few-friended poor,
The way-gotten plot or the shingle-thatched cot
    That crouched at the edge of the moor.

And often, nor waiting for word of distress,
    She went through the welcoming street,
A smile for each door, with a gift for the poor,
    And the children she lingered to meet.

For lonely she dwelt in her hall on the hill—
  All dead were her kith and her kin,
Save Rosamond gay, whose feet the whole day
  Made life with their musical din.

And both were troth-plighted. But Margaret's heart
  Was won by Sir Reginald Hood,
Awatch on the main for the galleons of Spain,
  Curse-laden of carnage and blood.
He homeward returning, the clamorous bells
  Would tell of the wedding and feast—
The wide-opened hall and the fleet-footed ball,
  With largess for greatest and least.

But now there came tidings from over the sea
  Of victory wrought on the main,
Of battle by night and the Spaniards in flight,
  But also—Sir Reginald slain!
And softly, long doubtful, they ventured the tale;
  She heard them as one that hath share
No longer in life—in its joy or its strife,
  Its happiness, misery, care.

But only she went to the chancel at noon,
  And knelt on the knee-furrowed stone,
And gazed on the face of the Christ-God whose grace
  Gives peace to the weary alone,
Oft pleading : ' O Lamb of the aye-living God,
  Who bleeding didst die, and for me,
Ah ! comfort me now, for in sorrow I bow,
  And lift up my soul unto Thee.'
L.L.   H

And summer departing, the mellowing mist
  Came up from the stream-threaded lea;
Its vaporous breath, like funereal wreath,
  Hung ghostly on hedgerow and tree.
And borne on its pinions, death-fretted, it brought,
  Relentless, fate-message for one;
And Margaret sighed, for at Hallowmas-tide
  Was Laura's life-voyaging done.

And kissing the maiden's cold forehead, full low
  She whispered: 'Not long now, and I
Shall sleep by thy side, nor shall foolishly chide
  The days that they sluggishly fly.'   .
And all about marvelled that never a tear
  She shed, nor complaining let fall,
For love-dream at end, or for loss of the friend
  She cherished as dearest of all.   .

'Twas eve of the Mass of the Saviour—blest time
  Of peace upon earth and in air;
The louvre bells rang, and the carollers sang
  Their songs on the terracèd stair.
And Margaret listened beside the yule-fire,
  A smile on her high-thoughted face—
The summons so near, with the death of the year,
  That now was departing apace.

'Oh, worship the King!' so the carollers sang;
  Her spirit went up with the strain
To regions of light, where in measureless might
  The King of all kinglets doth reign.

And ' " Nowell," ' she murmured ; ' Thou all-
   gracious God !—
" Nowell " on this heart-thrilling eve—
Thou Well-spring of love that of mercy didst move
   Man's burden to prove and reprieve ! '

And after she summoned the carollers in,
   And tankard and wassail went round,
While nigh to her knee was the eldest of three
   Whose father in autumn was drowned.
And laying her hand on the chorister's head,
   She blessed him, and bade him beware ;
True son he should show to his mother, nor know
   A thought that she never might share.

They gone with her largess, she sat by the blaze,
   Her thought with the two that were dead ;
Till Rosamond came, and, with pleasure aflame,
   Bent mirthfully over her head.
And suddenly circling her neck with her arms,
   Her face she drew close to her own—
' Oh, far-away queen, with the morrow, I ween,
   Must pleasure for brooding atone.'

And ' Harold is going,' she said with a blush ;
   ' But early to-morrow at morn
Is coming with Kate ; and all's well, we will skate
   On the lake by the three-parted thorn.'
Then Margaret rose ; and her sister for long
   Remembered, with yearning and pain,
The look in her face, with her silent embrace,
   Her kiss, and her lingering strain,

And presently taking the youth by the hand,
  'A word with you, Harold, aside.
Nay, Rosamond, nay! What to Harold I say
  From you I do purposely hide.'
Then told she the tale of that marvellous night—
  He speechless through grief and dismay—
That she on her bier ere the close of the year
  Must lie in sepulchral array.

And straitly she charged him to treasure his bride—
  Be husband and brother in one,
For the sake of the friend, who, her sorrow at end,
  For aye had her rapture begun.
Then sisterly parting she set on his cheek,
  His sorrow so truthfully shown;
'Twas lofty-souled youth, whose honour and truth
  She knew and could trust as her own.

'And when thou art master, and fillest my place,
  Think oft of the poor and the old:
For life is at best but a struggle for rest,
  And gratitude better than gold.
And he who that garners is richer by far
  Than he, the false steward of God,
Of charity bare, whose wealth is a snare,
  And misapplied talent a rod.

'And now fare thee well! for to-night I must ride
  To Lambourne. Nurse Alice would grieve
Full sore did she miss of her foster-child's kiss
  And God-speed ere ending of eve.

Good-bye, then. Come early, for Rosamond's sake.
  Yet see in this oaken bureau
My testament set, with a word for my pet—
  God lighten her burden of woe!'

IV

O lovely the even, as Margaret rode
  To Lambourne by hedgerow and lane;
And lustre streamed down from the Lyre and the
      Crown,
  And the Dogs by the Waggoner's Wain.
Beside her ran Victor, her staghound that now
  Would leap at her steed in his glee;
Then, bounding off, bark, to pursue in the dark
  The hare o'er the snow-whitened lea.

And firm was the seal of the frost on the road,
  On brooklet and millstream and pond;
The ice it gleamed white, in the nebulous light,
  On river and marshes beyond.
And sparkling the snowdrift lay deep in the dell,
  And under the slant of the hedge;
While keen the wind blew, as, the osier-beds through,
  A-sweeping it snarled at the sedge.

The welkin was loud with the musical clang
  Of the bells in their turreted lair;
The song and the din of the broad-gabled inn
  Swept merrily out on the air:

While lightsome the lilt of the viola rose,
  With harp in the many-voiced street;
And cheery each tongue with a welcoming rung,
  Where neighbours and relatives meet.

Now reaching the cottage, she gave up the rein
  To one that ran out to the gate;
Where also the dame in her eagerness came,
  The light on her white-kerchiefed pate.
And clasping her charge to her motherly breast,
  She kissed her in pride and in glee:
'My darling is late, but as steadfast as fate;
  I knew that her face I should see.'

And restful awhile in the snow-covered cot
  She lay in the arms of her friend;
The moments how fast do they speed!—they are
      past!
  'Now hallow me, Christ, to the end.'
A motherly clasp and a lingering kiss,
  But hearken her whinnying horse!
A smile from the dame, and good-bye!—But she came
  In an hour to her bosom a corse.

All heedless she rode, for her heart it was full
  Of peace, and her spirit away
From pulsing of life with its turmoil and strife,
  Its prison and fetters of clay.
Unhindered her palfrey returned by a road,
  A way she was wonted to choose
When summer had drunk at the river, and shrunk
  Its waters to streamlet and ooze.

But ere that the car of the snow-cradled king
　Rolled down on the quivering ground,
All over the mead had the waters outspread,
　Full soon to be fettered and bound.
Ice-fettered and bound at the breath of the king,
　And rigid for many a rood,
The ice-ichor gleamed, where the bulrushes streamed
　Acrest of the meadow-spread flood.

A star now a-sudden flashed out in the night,
　And system and planet grew dim
In blaze of the world, death-bidden and hurled
　To ruin, restoreless and grim!
And, startled, the palfrey sprang forward! In vain
　Awak'ning, she caught at the rein;
Regardless he fled, and the fire from his tread
　Leapt out of the crystalline plain.

And stumbling of terror, he brake the ice through,
　And rolled in the turgidous flood;
She fell from her seat—with his adamant feet
　He struck—she was blinded with blood!
And clutching full wildly at saddle and band,
　She clutched in her anguish in vain;
But fainting could hear, and her covert anear,
　The carollers chaunting again.

'Adeste fideles,' they carolled, the strain
　All solemnly blessing the air;
She echoed the word: 'I come, then, dear Lord!
　Hail, Babe of the manger-cratch bare!'

And sullen the waters closed over her head;
  But joyous her spirit returned
To land of its birth, as the trammels of earth,
  Ecstatic, it evermore spurned.

His foothold regaining, the fallen horse smote
  The ice till he stood on the bank;
But Victor loud bayed, and his mistress essayed
  To reach where she silently sank.
For swiftly he plunged in the black-bosomed pool
  And catching her dress with his teeth,
He drew her to shore, his companion no more
  By hamlet or woodland or heath.

And ever he bayed, till the star-circled night
  Was full of his sorrowful cry,
As, crouched in the sedge, he kept watch at the edge
  Of the river his mistress anigh.
And, wond'ring, the carollers ceased in their song,
  And hearkened again and again;
Then followed the sound, till their lady they found,
  A corpse on the treacherous plain.

And weeping they lifted her out of the weed,
  And bearing her slow to the cot,
Dame Alice drew nigh, with a terrible cry:
  'Ah, God, is Thy mercy forgot?'
Then kissing in frenzy the blood-oozing brow,
  And lips that yet lovingly smiled.
She laid on her breast the maiden to rest,
  As oft when a light-hearted child.

At daybreak full early the ringers came forth,
  And mad was each clangorous bell,
Until the tale spread of their liege lady dead,
  When jubilance ended in knell.
And after was offered, with sighing and tears,
  The Christ-mass ; and service was sung
By lips that with pain but essayed the refrain,
  Their hearts all too bitterly wrung.

But dead she yet lived, and her wishes were law
  Long after in cottage and hall :
For she dwelt in each heart—a presence apart
  From death and the funeral-pall.
And years they drew by, but unceasing her tomb
  Was bright with the flowerets sweet
She loved as a maid, by Rosamond laid
  With tears at her Margaret's feet.

But none ever after dare venture within
  The churchyard at vigil of Mark,
And children still run from its precincts, and shun
  Its causey at falling of dark.
For still it is whispered at midnight the door
  Swings ope, and the anthem again
Is heard as to Mass, in the chorestry pass
  The priest and his moribund train.

MONKSWOOD

MONKSWOOD is, perhaps, the finest piece of woodland in the whole forest. It has its name from the monks of Waltham, who possessed it as an outlying part of their fair estate of Copped Hall. Hence it was exempt from the pollarding that converted so much of the forest into a woody fastness; and its stately groves of oaks and beeches are, as of yore, 'things of beauty and a joy for'—well, let us say, poets and painters, *et hoc genus omne*—with brainwearied toilers after the mammon of unrighteousness, for others, in our lucre-devoted city.

Last, but not least, it is just the place for inspiring 'the lips of lying lovers'—I thank thee Holmes of the Breakfast Table for that line—with many a loverly lie, that, at the time, doubtless, seems as true as the coo of the dove in the overhanging trees.

Monkswood is in Loughton parish, but a mile from the village and Hall. It is on the left of the old coach road to Epping, on high ground, at the commencement of the wooded tableland, if I may so term it, that extends from hereabouts to Wintrywood and the lower forest, some miles on the road to Harlow.

The wood itself is divided by a brook, flowing through a valley of considerable slope in parts, and winding about very picturesquely beneath widespreading beeches, oaks and birches. Great and

Little Monkswood are the names of the divisions,
and both have special features of beauty.

Autumn is a fine time for a ramble hereabouts
by daylight. Then standing beneath the monster
beeches of the lesser wood upon the carpet of soft
brown beech mast—nothing grows here in the eternal
shade—and looking through the boles of the time-
stained giants across the valley to the opposite slope,
the crimson of the leaves is as a glorious sunset, when
all the West is aglow, and the pavilion of the departing
Lord of day is afire with purple and gold.

But winter is a better time still; and chiefly at
night, when Nature for the greater part at rest,
the stormblast whirls out for a frolic. From other
parts of the forest there arises a dull sighing and
soughing, for there the trees are huddled together
and are mostly of a lesser growth and height, and
the gale-fiend sweeps over them and, except in glade
and slade, can achieve but little.

But here there is a fight for mastery—such a fight!
—And the shrieking, raging, and roaring is terrific;
with ever and anon the added crash of a torn-off
bough or limb from some unconquered oak—flung
down in sullen rage and as gage of battle merely—
his other hundred arms maintaining the contest
and filling all the countryside with the noise of
conflict. Then of a truth Monkswood is grand.
Then, if the listener be of the kin of the poets, his
soul expands and exults. He looks up and around—
like the warhorse of the patriarch, he saith Ha! Ha!
to the shoutings and the thunderings—he revels

in the fray ;—the howling charges of the blast, with
the answering roar of the shaken but defiant forest,
filling his breast with rapture! He is in bliss
for the nonce, and perchance patteth his favourite
tree, praising and encouraging till the midnight
chimes surge across from High Beech, when reluctant
and sorrowful he turneth him homeward to prepare
for his own everyday humdrum struggle by a few
hours sleep.

There is a shelvy nook in particular,

> Under an oak whose antique root peeps out
> Upon the brook that brawls along the wood.

that would have served 'the melancholy Jacques'
for his moralizing passing well.

But the 'malisoned tree' of the legend will be
sought for in vain. It stood in that portion of Great
Monkswood overhanging the brook to the south near
to the Green Ride. It is as sequestered a spot as
any in the forest even now, and in the old days must
have been extremely so.

The legend itself is wild—not to say extravagant.
Saxon mythology is blended, curiously enough,
with medieval superstitions, for Hecate is plainly
but another name for Hel, daughter of Loke, and
goddess of the netherworld, with misery for her
dwelling, hunger for her table, and cursings and blas-
phemings for the hangings of her bed.

The hellwain, too, is a feature uncommon, I believe,
in our southern counties, but then, who shall say

what myths and beliefs of our ancestors linger in our coppice hamlets ?

Education, like 'instinct, is a great matter.' But the harmless simple faiths and beliefs of the past die out before it. Soon the touchstone of reason will be applied to everything that is not ' plain as a pike-staff,' and that most scorching of all scorching flames, ridicule, burn up much that is both interesting and instructive.

Are there not amongst us, even now, schoolboys of eighteen or nineteen, whose reasoning powers are such that they cannot accept the faith that Bacon and Shakespeare, Milton and Newton were proud to live and die in ? And, indeed, if happiness be the topstone of national welfare,—and who dares question it ?—then is our much-lauded education but a lament-able failure. For decidedly we are not happier as a people than our fathers or our grandfathers, though some of them never got beyond the three Rs, and we are learned in ' ologies,' ' isms ' and what not without number.

> Each in his narrow cell for ever laid
> The rude forefathers of the hamlet sleep—

and we, their children, ere long, will be laid in hideous, carefully kept, urn-bedecked cemeteries, but unless we do as much for the maintaining of the empire as our ancestors did for its upbuilding, wherein are we the better for all our learning.

And we do not, but are steadily falling behind our neighbours, whereupon the wiseacre rulers of

the land shout out 'educate ! educate ! ' as if the
hungry could be fed with words, or the evils of an
ever-overgrowing population be cured by a shibboleth.
Besides, what real education can you give children
who leave school at thirteen or fourteen, the poverty
of their parents compelling them to turn to, as we
say at sea, thus early ?

While to make matters worse 'the curriculum
of study' as medical student Barnes of Bartholo-
mew's has it, instead of consisting of two or three
subjects properly taught, upon which any lad or lass
of ordirary ability can afterward build if he or she
will, is a medley of a dozen that simply muddle the
brain of poor Hodgkin and give him, not unnaturally,
a hatred of booklearning for the rest of his days.

May a not unthoughtful nobody suggest a far better
thing for the work of the new century than this
played-out education fad.

Restore the land to the people. Put the labourer
back to the soil his forefathers tilled generation
after generation to the benefit of the whole kingdom.
Split up your overgrown farms,—curtail your spacious
parks,—break up your dukeries and deer forests,—
get back the peasantry, if it be not already too late,
and the words of Goldsmith are not all too true,
unhappily,

> But a bold peasantry, their country's pride,
> When once destroyed, can never be supplied.

At any rate, try ! Half the money squandered on
so-called education, which, in ninety-nine cases out

of a hundred is all thrown away, would enable thousands of hard-handed, brave-hearted, honest-minded English countrymen to get a fair living out of croft and field. Forbid, too, altogether, or if that cannot be, restrain into decent limits, the ever-increasing plague of foreign pauper immigrants! Keep out the wretched outcasts of Russia, Germany and Austria that come to us by thousands every year, and come to stay, driving out our own poor people from their homes, and turning the East of London in parts into huge ghetti, of unparalleled poverty and misery.

Again. Don't, when you send men to prison, leave their wives and children to starve, for that is but to make crime hereditary, by training up a newer race of criminals. Take the little ones by the hand—teach them that evil as necessarily begets evil, and good, good, as sown seed of corn begets corn, and of barley, barley. Then give them some handicraft that will make useful men and women of them and their children after them.

And, above all, organize a national system of emigration. Land in abundance has the Giver of all good gifts bestowed upon us. Truly 'He hath not dealt so with any nation,' nor, humanly foreseeing, will He ever again. Also, He has given us much people wherewith the wilderness and the solitary place may be made glad, and the desert rejoice and blossom as the rose.

For the land at home is become much too strait for us, while Canada, Australia, New Zealand, and our colonies generally cry out for citizens.

Will you send them, ye that rule, or will you stick to your shibboleth ?

I can answer for you. You will not! For that would mean higher wages for those that remain, with smaller profits for yourselves, with smaller houses and smaller estates. It would mean also less money for luxury, less to be flung away year after year at Epsom and Newmarket, and less for the many selfish pleasures you have come to consider necessaries of life and position.

Worship of Mammon and his golden calf, the worst of all religions, is, I fear, much too firmly established among us now.

' Each for himself and Allah for all ' is the motto carved over our modern Moloch's temple gate, and he that has it most by heart is his most cherished and successful devotee. For myself, I think I prefer the English equivalent, as altogether devoid of cant, though blunt even to cynicism, ' Each for himself and the devil take the hindermost.' This as yet is not written up, but soon will be, the ' hard-as-nails ' sect daily increasing and coming rapidly to the front.

But what boots preaching in the face of the old, old question, ' Who is my neighbour ? ' repeated with a smug complacency that is quite delightful by all our so-called statesmen and politicians.

ADA OF ENEVER

A LEGEND OF MONKSWOOD

'Twas eve of Saint John, and the hillside upon,
  The village was gathered in glee ;
'Mid merriment wild, the faggots were piled
  That kindled would redden the lea,
When first the lone star should herald the car
  Of Night, o'er the malisoned tree.

Adown the broad glade went singing a maid,
  None surely more lovely than she !
Her heart it was light, and her eyes they were bright,
  And her face was as sunshine to see !
' Oh, Love, he is lord—of each maiden adored—
  And a right gentle sovran is he ! '

With close-shaven crown, and with visage cast down,
  With cross and with rosary,
A monk came her by, with sob and with sigh,
  While evermore murmurèd he
' Accursèd for aye till maiden shall pray
  For me at the malisoned tree ! '

' Now Jesu thee save ! thou friar so grave,
  Good sir, benedicite !
And why dost thou creep beside me and weep
  And sigh like to sighing of sea ?
'Tis sprite-haunted ground about and round
  The shade of the malisoned tree ! '

L.L.   I

He lift up his head—'twas the face of the dead
  His garish eyes ghastly to see—
No life-living priest but a spirit surceast,
  Hell-tost and tormented was he.
His lank hands he wrung, where the death beetle clung
  To the bole of the malisoned tree.

From his presence she shrank, while the terror drops
     dank
  Were thick on her forehead to see.—
'Thou fear-filling priest of Gehenna releast
  Say now why accostest thou me !
Canst work me no harm—for thrice blessed charm
  I wear of our Lady so free ! '

In hollow tones low—while she hallowed her brow
  And called her on holy Marie—
He told her his tale, while the summering gale
  Grew soft as in sympathy ;
'I wander for aye 'less maiden shall pray
  For me at the malisoned tree ! '

'Pure maiden am I as angel in sky,
  And gladly I'll benison thee—
But tell to me first—thou beadsman accurst
  And doomed to such terrible dree—
Why maiden must pray for thee, or for aye
  Thou hauntest the malisoned tree ? '

'Then if thou wilt hear, nor shun me of fear,
  My tale I will tell unto thee—

I murdered a maid, and her bones they are laid
  In the shade of the malisoned tree !
Wo's me ! well away ! 'less maiden will pray
  I must mourn through eternity.

' Ah, me ! for the wrong !   But I loved her for long—
  Oh ! fairer than fairest was she !—
But dedicate priest, again to my breast
  No maiden appressed might be.
Yet tempted I fell, and my love I dared tell
  At eve 'neath the malisoned tree.

' With madness I burned—my pleading she spurned—
  Oh, chaste as Cecilia was she !
Then hell-gotten thought, of Beelzebub brought,
  I thought in my misery.
Accursed the day, and accursed for aye,
  My sin 'neath the malisoned tree !

' And if never mine,—of her beauty divine
  None other possessor should be.
Oh, God, that frail breath should be doomsman of
    death
  For pride or for misery !
Oh, fiendish my heart, and fiendish the part
  I played 'neath the malisoned tree !

' And thus I begun—" Oh, chaste as the sun
  That kisses the dew-spangled lea.
Not passion to move, but thy virtue to prove
  I said what I said unto thee.
Now kneel at my feet and an ave repeat
  And I shrive thee as clean as the sea."

' So knelt she, fair queen, and I shrivèd her clean,
  In the shade of the shuddering tree,
Then cruel death-blow did I smite on her brow—
  Oh, Christ, that the horror could be !
I loved her for all, Hell's new-gotten thrall,
  I slew 'neath the malisoned tree.

'With camelet bands I bound her white hands—
  So small and so pretty to see !
I shed not her blood, but by Calvary's rood
  I hangèd her there on the tree ;
Nor ever I fled till her spirit was sped,
  And she livingless swung on the tree.

' But her tender eyes sweet, for cherubim meet,
  So blue and so trustful and free,
They froze my soul there, with their terrible stare,
  I see them, and ever must see
For aye and for aye, 'less maiden will pray
  For me at the malisoned tree !

' And her death-parted mouth with its horrible drouth,
  It turnèd and turnèd on me.
She spake never word, yet as thunder I heard
  Within me God's awful decree—
" Accursed for aye, until maiden shall pray
  For thee, at the malisoned tree ! "

' And her tresses of gold from their snood-loosened fold
  Downfalling from forehead to knee,—
Each tress was a snake that hissing bespake
  God's wrath on my cruelty—

" Accursed for aye until maiden shall pray
   For thee, at the malisoned tree !"

' Then I fled ! But at night, by the yellow moonlight
   I came in all secrecy ;
And her cold lips I kist, as Judas I wist
   His Lord in Gethsemane—
Then I buried her deep, where the cankerworms creep
   Through the roots of the malisoned tree.

' No masses I said.—For her that was dead
   What prayer might be prayèd by me ?
But I grovelled all night, in the ghastly moonlight,
   My soul like to storm-tossèd sea—
While demon fires glanced, and ouphen they danced
   In the shade of the malisoned tree.

' At midnight's lone hour, from out the old tow'r
   That shadows the slope of the lea,
The passing bell rang, with its pitiful clang—
   'Twas tolled of diablerie !
Dear Christ ! how each stroke anathema spoke
   " Accurst for eternity ! "

' Till, pure as the day, a maiden shall pray
   That the ban may be lifted from me,
While demon fires glance, and ouphen they dance
   With hags in their wizardry,
My spirit must stay upon earth and for aye
   Beharrow the malisoned tree ! '

*   *   *   *   *

The monk now was gone, and the maiden alone
  Stood now by the malisoned tree—
' 'Twas devilish deed, and right justly decreed
  His penance for ever should be !
And shall I then pray, 'mid goblin and fay,
  At night, for such traitor as he ? '

Thus she in her pride—Yet often she sighed
  As slow to her manor went she,
While demon fires glanced, and ouphen they danced
  That night by the malisoned tree.—
Ha ! Ha !—shouted they—for aye and for aye,
  Sir Wilfred our comrade shall be !

II

Oh, Luketon its manor is pleasant to see,
  Its walks and its alleys so green—
There are chambers a score, with towerets three,
And a hall that's as broad as a royal causey
  And a parlour that's fit for a queen !

And Ada of all she is mistress of right—
  What mistress more gentle than she ?
Her locks are of gold, and her eyes they are bright
As the sheen of the drops that are shed by the night
  When morn bids her waken and flee.

Her hands they are white, O, so white ! and her feet
  So shapely and dainty to see !
Her mouth it is small, and her teeth they are meet

As pearls to be set in an earl's coronet!—
  Her laughter like rippling of sea!

And Ada is gone to her boweret bright
  With its arras of damascene,
For day it is gone, and the short summer night
Right welcome is come with its cool wannish light,
  The crescent moon smiling serene.

Oh, fair, and oh, fair, with her goldilocks gay,
  And her kirtle looped up to her knee,
The gleam of her neck in the silvery ray,
And the snow of her breast, as she kneeleth to pray
  To Mary the star of the sea!

Like angel aslumber'd was Ada at rest,
  Or cherub in cloisteral fane,
Her lily hands crost on her virginal breast,
Her fair face by beamlet and raylet carest
  That lovingly flooded the pane.

And peaceful she slept till the toweret bell
  Spake midnight with tremulous stroke,
When wondrous occurrence the maiden befell,
Weird light filled her chamber, and, sudden, the spell
  Of her slumber dissolving, she woke.

All startled she woke, with a cry and a thrill—
  'Is it phantasy, vision or dream?
Is it mortal or spirit, that standeth so still—
So clear, and so near I could touch it at will—
  Begirt with mysterious beam?'

Sweet maiden, she came of a masterful line,
  No maiden was braver than she,
But her bosom beat fast, as she fashioned the sign
Of the cross on her forehead, while ' Jesu divine,'
  She whispered—' now benison me ! '

The blood it came back to her bosom so cold,
  At the pray'r and the lifegiving name !—
' Those sad eyes, so blue, and those tresses of gold
They are mine, and mine also that forehead so bold,
  That mien all unconscious of blame.

' And is it then shape of hereafter,'—she said—
  ' That I see in the ghostly moonshine ? '
' Not so,' said the phantom, ' I am of the dead !
Fear not, we are kindred, begot of the bed
  Of Enever's warrior line !

' And since thou hast spoken may hope then begin.
  Ah, precious those accents of thine !
I loved—yet for lover nor passion would sin,
But died, and would gladly thrice over to win
  The peace for him that became mine.

' Ah, long has his spirit repented the deed,
  To save him pertains not to me ;
For He that all judgeth, by Him 'twas decreed
From penance his spirit should never be freed
  Till maiden should plead at the tree.

' Sweet sister, earth trammell'd, unless thou wilt pray
  One night for his spirit's repose,
Beneath that fell gibbet,—he wanders for aye,

Unhousel'd, unpardoned, tormented, the prey
  Of fiends, till eternity's close.

'And if thou wilt venture, then look not behind
  But ever regard thou the tree !
For threat or for murmur, for whisper unkind,
For wail or for laughter for storm or for wind,
  Stir not but remain on thy knee !

'And oft as thou prayest, weave into thy pray'r
  The name that no fiend may abide.
And oft to thy succour bid him that could dare
With Satan to conflict, and him that doth share
  The strength of Jehovah His pride ! '

*   *   *   *   *

Bright Phosphor, thereafter, afflaming the crest
  And gemming the brow of the morn,
The maiden uprose with resolve in her breast
And long time she knelt 'neath the effigy blest,
  Aglow in the gleam of the dawn.

'Now haste thee, now haste thee, child Edward my
      page,
  Go featly and bring unto me
Dan John the chirurgeon, whom men call the sage ;
Go quickly and bring him—there's gold for his wage,
  And, pageling, a guerdon for thee ! '

*   *   *   *   *

'Dan John, thou art wise and but little I ween
  Outrunneth or letteth thy skill !
The planets thy loresmen, with Luna their queen,

Reveal thee their secrets—earth's sullen unseen
  Its treasures unfold at thy will.

'And no man may tell thee the tale of the years
  That have furrowed thy face and thy brow;
But gentlest of sages, life's hopings and fears,
Its calms and its tempests, its joys and its tears,
  None share them more bravely than thou.

'And well, too, the secrets of Enever's race,
  True leech, dost thou hide in thy breast.
So tell me the tale of yon maiden whose face
Looks down from the wall with such innocent grace
  Like babeling by seraph carest.'

'Nay, lady, first tell me what thing thou would'st do,'
  Full gravely the master replied;
'Beware lest that malison light upon you,
Last daughter of Enever, lovely and true,
  Beware thee Eve's folly and pride!

'And seek not at midnight for spirit or shade
  The tree that is cursèd for aye.
Untold are the toils, and the snares that are laid
By demons and devils to harrow the maid
  That dareth thereunder to pray.'

'Dan John and Dan John, what I do, that I do!
  No danger my purpose shall stay.
Thou readest my project—'tis plain, to thy view
My heart then is open,—why then must I rue
  For long troubled spirit to pray!'

'Oh, twice then, dear lady, that spirit has met
   A daughter of Enever's line;
And twice have I guarded.—Beware, then, nor set,
For sorrow or pity, for ruth or regret,
   Thy will 'gainst a greater than thine!

'Of her then whose semblance yet hangs on the wall,
   Of her I will readily tell—
Thou, lady, art lovely—thy charms yet are small
Compared with that maiden's, for fairest of all
   Earth maidens was lady Iselle!

'Yet loved she unwisely below her estate
   A youth of but yeoman degree;
Her father was wroth :—Can the eyriebird mate
With chough or with gannet ?   'Twas ordered of fate
   Their happiness never should be !

And long time secluded in convent and cell
   That lady lamented the day.
Young Wilfred, too, cloister'd, so hoping to quell
Youth's passion unruly, that fiercer doth swell
   With obstacle, loss or delay.

'Sad, sad, was the ending !—The maiden must wed—
   No choice in her spousals had she—
Despairing and tempted, 'tis said that she fled
By night with her lover—— ' ' 'Tis false, she is dead,
   She died at the malison'd tree ! '

Low laughed the chirurgeon.   ' Dear lady full well
   I see all is known unto thee
Of Wilfred the monk, and of lady Iselle,

Her fate, and his penance, what boots then to tell
  The tale of the malisoned tree ?

Yet knowing, art purposed their weal to essay,
  True daughter of Enever's line !
I fain then would help thee.—Heed then what I say,
The night thou dost venture, first kneel thee and pray
  For aid at Saint Nicholas' shrine !

' Next bind on thy forehead the triple leaf blest,
  The sign of the sweet Trinitie.
With wort of Saint John on thy hair and thy breast ;
And gathered at eve, in thy girdle comprest,
  The gold of our lady Marie.

' Barefooted must venture !—Ah ! lady, the way
  Is ragged with bramble and thorn !
Barekneed too must kneel thee, unfriended till day,
Flesh torn and besullied—bethink thee and say,
  Dear lady, canst thus await morn ? '

' Dan John and Dan John, what I do, that I do !
  No danger my purpose shall stay ;
That maiden so helpless, forgiving and true,
Her lover's dread penance no longer shall rue,
  Christ aiding, I free him for aye ! '

' And canst thou endure, all is well !—But beware
  Lest, wearied, thou fallest asleep !
That moment the spirits of earth and of air,
Malefic, have power to assail and ensnare
  To revelry hellish and deep ! '

III.

'Tis night ! But undaunted, the maiden behold
Slow stealing by coppice and meadow and fold.

Oh, fairer than lily, in vesture of white,
Or vestal gold-girdled, or angel of light
On earth-flight of mercy, she goeth. The moon
Bedazzled beholds, but of charity soon,
Her splendour withdrawing, bids cloud unto cloud
From Night's murky garner, the maiden to shroud
From mortal espial, or gloating of fay,
Or spirit of ill as she goes on her way.

The thicket she reacheth. The wind, that was still,
Now waking and wailing, the fir-crested hill
Makes answer, low sighing. Gloom-canopied, dark,
The forest moans fretful, while hearken ! oh, hark !
The fiend-frolic laughter that frighteth the wood,
That thrilleth her bosom and chilleth her blood.
Ah, lady, high-purposed, brave maiden and queen !
How deadly thy devoir, the dangers unseen,
And seen that thou darest ! Alas ! that the morn
Afar yet doth linger. Befriend her, forlorn,
Ye spirits angelic, joy-pinioned, that speed
To succour and solace earth's children at need !

The brook now she crosseth. Awhile in the wave
Her wounded feet linger their bleeding to lave.
What whispers the streamlet caressing her feet ?
' Back lady, while yet there is hope of retreat !

Who cross me at midnight to yonder fell tree
The gleam of my wavelets shall never more see!'
Full sadly she heareth. 'Alas! is there naught,
Above or beneath but with warning is fraught?'
Yet falters she never but enters the glade
That dirgeful enfolds her with glooming and shade.

All fearful she enters, but resolute still,
Represseth rebellion of dolour, and thrill
Of maidhood fear-falter'd, with low-voicèd prayer—
'Oh, Jesu! sweet Jesu! the thing that I dare
Is direful and grievous; befriend me, I pray,
And guard from the dangers that darken my way;
Nor suffer to perish the spirit for whom
Thou payed'st the ransom of death and the tomb;
But save thine own image, pure Son of pure Maid,
And keep from betrayal—Thou sometime betrayed!'

The moon now is hidden—cloud warreth with cloud—
The troubled wind labours—in grave-gotten shroud
Glide pale shapes beside her, while fen fires reveal
The flaming-eyed vipers crest arching that steal
The forest path over, with lizards that show
Abhorrent and loathsome in luridous glow.
Now waketh the tempest, and shrieks through the
    chace—
Storm-smitten, rack-driven the clouds flee apace.
Asudden the lightning with far-reaching glare
Illumines the woodland—the tree, it is there!

Who standeth beside it ? And ah ! what doth hang
Dread fruit from its branches ?—With cling and with
   clang
Of hell-stithered fetters, around the foul tree
A death dance is circling ! Their horrible glee
The phantoms forsaking, about her chill form
Loud mocking begather ! Yet fiercer the storm
Shocks onward terrific—A thunderbolt falls !—
Oaks crash down heart-shatter'd ! In terror she
   calls
Again and for succour—' Blest Jesu, be near !
My soul is sore troubled, I fear, oh, I fear ! '

Wild shrieking the demons give place at the name
That boweth creation to praise and acclaim.
While yet these are stricken she hastens and kneels
Beneath the tree-gibbet, and kneeling appeals
From powers of darkness and princes of night,
To Mary queen-mother of God, and His might—
' Hail Mary ! blest Virgin and Mother, befriend
Earth maiden on mission of mercy ; defend
From demon and devil, from goblin and ghost,
And comrade pure maiden, 'mid satanist host ! '

Now slow from the belfry the solemn notes roll
Like passing-bell mourning for moribund soul.
'Tis midnight ! Now dead men their sepulchres quit ;
And spirits self-perished, unhouseled, the pit
Behaunt them, where scornful with torch and with bell
Men flung them, disdainful. Now life-blighting spell

Foul sorcerers fashion ; while corpeelings at rest
Hags quicken and waken with bidding unblest.
Now devils to virginal pillowings creep
And whisper ill fancies unfitting sweet sleep.
While warlocks malefic, to revelries ride,
Satanic, with Baal their master beside.

Chill, chill, was the sod ! Ah me ! but the chill
Of soul and of spirit environed with ill !
Yet bravely she battles with ever restraint
Of murmur, or thought of return or complaint.
Nor ever for whisper of evil, or jeer
Of spirit unbodied, gives homage to fear ;
But vigilant kneels, while the moments slow run
Till grace be to Mary, an hour it is done.

Now Hecate came raging encircled with storm,
Fell-headed, snake-girdled ; malefic her form
Uncouth and large-looming in vaporous wreath
Partparted and torn by the fire of her breath.
The whirl of her coming fills welkin and air
Bestartling the stag in his fern-hidden lair.
Her haggard hand lifting, she points to the tree,
And mocking, the maiden bids up from her knee.
' The moments are fleeting—his sabbath's begun,
Why then dost thou linger ? let homage be done !
Up sister ! up sister ! and follow with speed
Where Satan doth summon, and Hecate doth lead ! '

' Oh, Gabriel, puissant envoy of peace,
Thou strength of Jehovah, from terror release

The cords of my tongue that I answer aright
The summons of hell and the spirits of night !'
So prayed she low-bending, and sudden her tongue
Was loosed and she spake while the far forest rung
With tones of defiance, so lofty and clear
From mortal lips scarcely they seemed to appear—
'No sister of evil, thou hell-hag, am I !
Thy mandate I scorn, and thy summons defy !
By God and His Jesu I bid thee away
Nor dare to molest me, that innocent pray !'

Low-crouched the foul queen, at the sound of the
    name
Rejoicing the faithful, o'erwhelming with shame
Imp, infidel, devil, with aught that shall dare
Of ill to be nigh when it blesseth the air—
Then fled, idly raging, with turbulent crew ;
While Ada, unharassed, gave honour anew.

Now cometh upon her allurement of sleep,
Life-balm when its moments too wearily creep ;
When summer-joys ended, but shadows are left,
With mournful remembrance of pleasure, bereft
Of all but the flush of recall, or the goad
Of ill past retrieval, immitigate load !
But sleep now were fatal ! 'tis fascinous snare !
'Tis evil conceived of the princelings of air.

Full heedful of warning, she wars with the spell
That is death ; and the better its tempting to quell
With self-imposed rigour, her wounded feet press
The cold ground ungrateful, nor shun the caress

L.L.   K

Of blood-blossomed bramble that nigh to her knee
Its spine-girdled trailings spread under the tree.
Thus fights she, nor falters at misery, oft
More loyal companion than pleasuring soft ;
And helpfuller far to the soul that would rise
From earth joy to joy with the meine of the skies.

Thereafter is going about and around—
The woodland is stirred to its coverts profound.
With creaking of axle and clanking of chain,
The hellwain comes laden with spirits in pain !
With flame-breathing nostrils, its chargers obey
Apollyon their master, and fiendishly neigh ;
While chauntings funereal dolefully rise,
With pleadings and wailings and cursings and cries.
The dread cortège halting the maiden anigh,
O'er weeping and wailing and cursing and cry
The fiend spake her gleeful—'Thou earthling, that knee
At midnight hast bent at the corpse-fruited tree,
My wain is well freighted, but yet there is room,
Thou Ada of En'ver, arise to thy doom !
Hast worshipt at gibbet, at hell garnished shrine,
Hast homaged red Moloch, thy soul it is mine ! '

'Michael !   Archangel, majestic of might,
Who warring with Satan didst force him to flight ;
Great Sabaoth captain, that workest God's will,
Now save from the fiend that my spirit would spill ! '
So prayed she, yet scarce 'twas a prayer but a moan
Of misery nigh to despondency grown.

Yet scarce was it uttered, or birthed in the soul
Than thought-fleet it sped to its haven and goal.

Now lo! from the welkin came wondrous reply
In accents majestic—'Thou, Satan, dost lie!
Speed on thy foul garner, no prey hast thou here,
Perceive it proud demon, in sign thou must fear.'
Now leaped forth the lightning, and lo! in its glare
Like cross shone the wildings entwined in her hair!
With outcry terrific and awful, the wain
Shot off like to star that is hurled from the main;
While see o'er the thicket, glad herald of day,
Fair Phosphor aflame with beneficent ray

Who is it now glides from the covert and kneels
Beside her in silence! His presence she feels
Instinctive, yet turns not her head to behold.
'Tis he! 'Tis the friar, Sir Wilfred!—Oh, cold
As ice-ichor now is the blood in her veins!
But hark! all about her rise jubilant strains
Unearthly but lovely and soft as a gale
Of Auster begotten in valley and dale.

Now Morn in her mantle of purple and gold
Day's azure gates open—with glory untold
The Orient kindles. There's joy as at birth
Of spirit escaped from the thraldom of earth.
Night flies at her challenge. The sun now uprist,
Hell's myrmidons vanish with murk and with mist.
There's music, there's incense on earth and in air,
Ne'er morrowing yet was more lovely and fair!

The skylark, forsaking his turf-hidden bed,
Bears part in the pæan—the gladsome notes spread,
The cushat soft plaining awakens the wood,
The merle bravely pipes to her yellow-billed brood ;
His bracken couch spurning, the stag sniffs the breeze
And tosses his antlers, disdainful of ease ;
Nought is, but is joyous, so perfect the morn,
So peaceful and comely, field, forest, and lawn !

But she worn of watching and conflict, to ground
Prone-fallen lies heedless in slumber profound ;
So lies while the morrow enlarges to day
And freed from Night's clutches exults in the sway
Of Phœbus reseated on ambergris throne
With canope of crimson, low-hanging, and grown
To purple o'erhead, where unwilling of flight
Yet lingers, slow yielding, the rearguard of Night.

In haste now there cometh Dan John to the tree.
All night long, sore troubled, his vigil kept he ;
But distant, perforce, both from conflict and cry,
Since none that essaying dare ever espy.
All night long he wandered, and worshipt, and prayed,
Till morn, when emboldened he entered the glade
And made for the hillock. Now swift to the tree
He hastens, good leecher, and kneeling on knee
With skilful hand labours to succour the maid,
Who thanks to the mercy of Mary, and aid
Of leechcraft awakens !—She trembles—a cry—
' Dan John is it thou ! ' Then, twixt moaning and
        sigh,

An ave she murmurs. Now loudly he blows
His bugle for bearers ; then tenderly throws
His gaberdine o'er her, within its warm fold
Her rigid form wrapping, so gelid and cold.

At midnight calm sleeping her chamber within
Like chrisomed babe houseled from soilure of sin,
As slow from the turret the warning notes sweep
Again that weird splendour dispelleth her sleep.
And 'mid its effulgence, like vestal arrayed
For temple and altar, that virginal shade.
Nor Isabel only, for see ! by her side
Sir Wilfred assoiled from his madness and pride !
Forgiven, henceforth where she goeth, goes he
Where love ever dwelleth unpassioned and free.

And bending they blessed her with uplifted hand
And accents as soft as the sea on the sand
When winds are aslumbered, and waves do but kiss
And waken the duneing to loverly bliss.
They blessed her brave daughter of Enever's race
As bravest and purest and fullest of grace.
Thereafter sweet comrade of God-fearing spouse
And love-filling mistress of heart-serviced house ;
Chaste mother of children, as fair as the day ;
Of daughters unblemished, sons braver than they
That humbled the crescent on Ascalon's plain,
And trampled the lilies by Somme and by Seine
In life ever blissful, and blest at the last,
With haven in heaven, earth's voyaging past.

CHINGFORD

A HOUSEHOLD word is Chingford, with all the citizens of that portion of 'the wen' lately discovered, as some say, by that indefatigable and delightful explorer, Sir Walter Besant.

Easy of access, and less wooded than some other parts of the forest—a large tract of the woodland having been 'hainaulted,' in the good old days of lord of the manor spoliation—the plain behind the old hunting lodge, and the new hotel, is a sight to be seen on any feast-day of that most popular of all modern saints, St. Lubbock.

For then thousands of our humblest cits disport themselves upon the grass, or in swing or booth. Then for the time being is Aunt Sally the most beloved and belaboured of relatives by the strong-armed coster. Then, too, the merry but shrill voices of be-feathered damsels, eager for asinine racings, rise up on every hand to the accompaniment of roundabout steam-organs pouring out by the hour together the choice and enlivening strains of the latest music-hall ditty that has 'caught on.' Then, to misquote Shelley, 'all the earth and air is loud' with the din of a myriad voices, amongst them, easily to be distinguished, the cry of a hundred peripatetic ice-cream sellers, who make a small fortune for themselves to-day, and another for the East-end medicine-men on the morrow; while the popping of innumerable corks—a sound in itself provocative of thirst—

goes up incessant from gingerbeer bottles and eke of lemonade—the glucose compound ycleped beer for the most part being unobtainable.

Which gathering of cits the villa people of Chingford call a pandemonium, and retire from it in high dudgeon to their back parlours; but the East-enders, caring nothing for them, account it bliss and enjoy it accordingly.

Quot homines tot sententiae! But for my own part I would much rather see the poor of London enjoying themselves on a week-day holiday on the broad plains, than the said villa folks in their red coats and buskins playing golf on Sunday to the annoyance of all the more reverent portion of the community, and the danger of the little ones walking across the grass.

By the way, was it not a Chingford man—of course not a golfer himself—who described the game thus—

'Golf—a game of stick and ball, much in vogue with members of both sexes strong of arm, but weak in brain. It is greatly recommended by proprietors of private lunatic asylums, as a valuable outdoor exercise imposing no strain upon the intellect, however small. It is itself a mania, and like another well-known affliction, had its origin in Scotland. Unfortunately, up to the present, no good duke has done anything to mitigate the misery it occasions the rest of the community.'

But putting aside red-coated Sunday golfers, and shabby-coated week-day excursionists, the great charm of Chingford is its ancient and ruined church.

Till lately the picturesque old ruin stood almost by itself a mile away from the village proper. But now there is a horrid cemetery right opposite to it; houses have been built hard by; and misery of miseries a cruel gas lamp, mainly for the benefit of backbowed ' scorchers,' casts its ghastly glare upon the ivied church and the mouldering headstones of its once sequestered churchyard. By day, too, ' the sound of the ' corpse-greeting ' bell, goes on with demoniacal clangour, persistent as the temptation it engenders, to execrate cemetery and chaplain, sexton and bell, shareholders and directors to the bitter end.

In the wintertime especially, with just enough snow about to whiten the churchyard, and always by moonlight, Chingford old church in the sixties was worth journeying a hundred miles to see. So many a time have I seen it from the stile by ' the ivy-mantled tower ' that overlooks the river and the mill, when there was not a sound to break the night-stillness but the occasional rattle of a nightjar, the shrill cry of a circling bat, or the stir of a bird in the leaves of the matted ivy whose stems were as thick as the age-bowed pillars of the church itself. Presently the barking of a dog, softened by distance, would come up the hill; or the bleating of sheep from ' woolly fold,' but both were musical and added to the charm of time and scene. But now—Well! Edmonton's merry devil would himself be scared could he revisit the scene of his exploits; and, forgetful of pranks and deviltries, would hurry him back to the netherworld symposium of choice but departed spirits.

A hamlet school stands by a bit of green at the break of the hill that leads to Sewardstone and Waltham. Here, it is said, a rather amusing incident took place a year or two ago. It was Sunday afternoon, early in the new year, and monsieur le Curé was catechising after the latest and most approved style, i.e., walking up and down the schoolroom and questioning certain of his younger flock by name.

'Now, Jane Maynard, what was the name of the mother of our Lord ?'

'Mary Free, sir.'

'What !'

'Mary Free, sir !'

'I don't understand you, child ! What do you mean ?'

'Please, sir, we sang it at Christmas. It's in one of the carols.'

'Nonsense ! Sit down ! I shall give you half a dozen bad marks.'

'But it is, sir.' And here Jane Maynard, getting angry in turn, piped out in a piercing treble—

> When Christ was born of *Mary free*,
> In Bethlehem that fair citie,
> Angels sang there in mirth and glee
> In excelsis gloria !

which quite settled the matter, at any rate so far as the rest of the little ones was concerned.

AGNES LEIGH

A LEGEND OF CHINGFORD

'Twas pride of morn, and all the waking wood
Was wrapt in mist, and cloud of dewy rain,
A moment falling, softly weeping, then
Withheld, like tears of coquet fair, intent
To be consoled with lover kiss and smile,
Maids longed-for sunshine !
                  So the morning mist,
Disparting slowly at caress of day,
Rolled off in aëry fragments, sportive borne
Now here, now there at will of wayward breeze,
By ferny holm, or dell and babblet brook !

Full-throated, jubilant, as pris'ner freed
From dungeon gloom and fetters, whom the light,
The stir, the breeze, the very face of earth
Awakes to untold ecstasy of joy—
The nightingale, scarce hidden, sat and filled
The wood with music.
                Yet more lofty strain
The skylark poured, as nearer heav'n than she
That loves the night, or screen of darkling bough ;
While loud o'er all rang out the cuckoo's note,
Spring's vagrant minstrel, Ishmael of the woods.

Within the grove upon a fallen bough—
Almost itself a tree, so great its girth—
Flung down by vengeful tempest, two men sat,

And watched the play of light amid the leaves;
The lifting mist; and whirl of beechen sheaves,
Broadcast by frolic winds.

                    'How like a prayer
The forest shows, friend Geoffrey, at the morn,
All things to joy address! Methinks I'd give
My gentle life, with all the gauds of Court,
To change with thee, and keep her highness' deer.
What church so fair as yonder shadowy aisle
With floor of sunbeams, where the flickering light
Steals in to pray and kiss the chequered ground?
What sheen of altar tapers mates the gleam
Of yonder beechen leaves, newborn, their pale
And silken heads bent down to mother earth,
As frighted at the flush and glare of day?
See! too, that birch slow waving o'er the pool,
Its tasseled sprays—the pool that is no pool
But snow wreath laid within the shelving bank
So thick and white the crowfoots matted bloom.
I would thou wert Sir Henry More, and I
Good Geoffrey Joyce of Chingford!'

                    'Aye 'tis gay,
Sir Henry now, but comfortless enow,
Frosts locking yonder pool. Then drifted snow
Bars path and glade; while cutting breezes sweep
Athwart the naked woodland. Then's the morn
Most like a dirge, for wail of angry wind,
And groan of breaking bough, and slide of sleet,
With bite of sharptoothed frost on hand and cheek.
Nay! Nay! An could'st thou change, full soon I trow
Sir Henry More would tell another tale.

So best as 'tis. The forest staff for me,
For you the ruff and rapier. Yet I mind
The time we roamed the woodland, careless boys
And lightsome as yon squirrel leaping free
From bole to bough. To think a few short years
Should make such change ! '
                    ' But not in love, dear lad !
I oft bethink me, Geoffrey, of the morn
You pulled me out the pit, beside the haye,
My long hair dripping like a Nereid's tress
Braided with duckweed.'
                    ' Aye ! 'twas happy chance
I learned betimes to swim. Your father else
Had gone a-mourning for his only son,
And Lady Mary lost a gallant knight.
But tell me now—no currish knave is nigh
To play eavesdropper. Is it true the queen
Is moved to put in force bluff Harry's laws
'Gainst heretics and Lollard out-of-faiths ?
I know not but the penalty outcrimes
The crime ; for ever in a monarch's crown
The fairest gem is mercy ! '
                    ' Hush ! no word,
Good lad, against my mistress ! She, forsooth,
Is but a woman swayed by love, and faith,
And just resentment of her mother's wrongs.
True friend—true child of holy mother church,
Herself is gentle as the morrowing breeze.
This cross of gold she gave me but of late
For trifling service, and with sad grave face,
Said as she gave—" As friend to friend, and not

As queen to subject!"   Then with pleading look—
"Sir Henry More, I trust, will not forsake
The one true faith, his father's and his queen's!"
"And if I do, may Christ forsake me too!"
I answered warmly, meaning every word.
"The good Christ ne'er forsakes the souls He loves
Although in blindness they may traitor him,"
She gave me back and with her own rare smile.
Oh, she's a queen for whom each loyal knight
Would battle e'en to death, and cry well won!'

'And yet she sent to scaffold Janet Grey,
And eke the poor lad Dudley,' said the reeve.
'But puppets both, at pull of crafty hand.'
'Puppet or not, she wore her sov'reign's crown.
And 'tis a saw with every Colin Clout,
"Treason's akin to murder!"   Think you now
Northumberland had spared his lady's life,
She in his pow'r?   Did Richard Crookback spare
His nephews laid to sleep in harmless cratch?
Or Yorkist Edward turn aside the dag
That spilt the blood of Anjou's princely heir?
Yet did the queen spare lady Jane; and still
Forsooth had spared her with her younker spouse,
Had not ungrateful Suffolk taken arms
To set her once again upon the throne
By toppling down his rightful queen, who gave
Him life, of grace, when cold and prudent wit
Loud clamoured at the council for his head.'

'Well! well! may be!   But see! the glozing sun
Gath'ring his strength, the more to welkin seat

He sturdy climbs, has sped the night-bred mist
Like ghost at cockcrow.   We'll to Barns and crave
A bowl of milk, and cakelet for a sop.
This way, Sir Henry, 'neath yon hanging thorn,
That crowns the slope, and drips regretful tears,
His brave array of Mayborn blossoms, pranked
With pink, at fing'ring of still-tongued decay.'

'So, Hector, so !   Good hound dost sniff the deer ?
And faith ! there goes a lusty roe.   Good lack !
The queen to-day should have fair sport.   There's
        truth
I' the old saw, we Essex woodmen quote—
   " A misty morn and a roving roe
   Up ! for the chase will featly go."
And since her grace but seldom visits now
Our homely shaws, so have she goodly sport.'

So said the woodman, as with lissom tread,
He led the way beneath the waving trees ;
And down the slope along the dewy sward
Of Fairmead, where was set a modest cot,
With porch o'erclung of woodbine, while a rose
Garnished the wall and peeped the casements in.
On either hand grew cullumbines and rue,
With gilliflowers and pinks along the path ;
And marygolds, a wealth of glory set
About a rustic arbour.   Simples all
And costless ; yet had never pleasaunce gay,
In castle court, a fairer mistress, nor
A gentler or a truer.   In the midst
She stood, most lovely ! like to pictured sylph—

Her light blue eyes ablaze with God's own light;
The light of love for all things, whatsoe'er,
Or tree, or flow'r, or bird—since all are His
And fashioned of His care for careless. man.
Uncoiffed she stood amid the walks, her hair
Close cut about her broad and sunny brow;
But, as rebellious still at spoiler hand,
All into ringlets sunny bright as gold
Thick-clustering grew.
        Her rounded cheek was flushed
With kissing of the sun, too favoured swain!
Her cherry lips full ripe for lover kiss,
Half-parted, showed the pearly teeth within,
What time she smiled upon the eglantine,
Whose dainty rose, fresh pluckt, lay in her hand.

So fair the maid the courtier's heart leapt up,
And eager hand he laid on Geoffrey's arm,
Low whispering—'Nay, friend Joyce, what nymph
    is this
You secret keep in yonder forest cot?
Full many a damsel, mansion born and bred,
And beautiful as Dian have I seen,
Here and abroad, yet never like to this.
But hark she sings! Leash Hector for awhile,
The hound will tell our presence else. Keep close
Behind this friendly oak, and tangling hedge!'

   'Passions which thou didst endure,
    Sweete Saviour for my sake;

My soule's salvation did procure
   Though earthe my bodie take—
My bodie fraile that oft for sin
   Must penance do and feel—'

Thus far the maiden, when the restive hound,
Bayed loudly and disturbed her guileless song.
A muttered curse the knight bestowed ; then moved
Full into view and doffed his feathered cap.—
'Fair morrow to you, maiden !—if the wish
To one so fair be not vain courtesy.
Where beauty smiles, must nature aye be gay.'—
She blushed, unused to courtly speech and phrase,
And blushing heightened all her loveliness.
Now soft as siren tone came meet reply—
'And eke to you, Sir Knight, and neighbour Joyce!'
And then more slowly—'Everything is fair
To them that see aright ; sith He that made
All things at first, did call them very good.'—

So said the maiden calmly passing by
The knight's soft flatt'ry.—All surprised he stood
And thoughtful, then—'By Barnaby, well said,
And wisely too ! Whence got you such address
In foiling laud or courtier compliment ?
Yet of a truth, 'tis truth. Had I but met
Yourself within the wood an hour agone,
In sylvan dress and garnished for the chase,
I had methought you Dian, come again
To faint our English hearts with gladsome sight
Of beauty all too rare for mortal eyes.'

She heard him gravely, as of duty, then,
Her watchet eyes with half reproachful look
Uplift to his—' Sir Knight I am but that
My Maker shaped me in His wiser will.
No better than the worst—if there be aught
Of better or of worse 'mongst men—if not
The best in worth for gift of greater gift!
All tell me I am fair. And once I saw
At Copped Hall a picture of a dame
Accompted fair, and after in a glass
Myself, and truly thought I saw again
That lady, save for humbler garb and mien.
But what of that? They too were very fair—
The deathless host, that foolish warred of old
Against th' Archangel and were cast for pride.'

Abashed, the knight was silent. Geoffrey laughed—
' Thus Agnes answers flatt'rers. Not the first
Are you, Sir Hal, to entertain reproof
For fautor speech un-welcome. Hector now
Pays wiser homage. See! he licks her hand,
That deals him in return such kind caress
A score of Chingford swains would die to win.—
But time bids hasten!—Agnes we are come
To beg a bowl of milk, and crust of bread
The sweeter much for kneading of soft hands.—
Plague o' my tongue! I too must needs offend.—
Well, let it be!—Yet know Sir Henry More,
Whilom a gallant of Queen Mary's court,
And now a penitent in quest of peace
In forest holt and covert.'

L.L.   L

                  'Milk I have,'
The maid returned with curtsey to the knight,
'In plenty, and I'll gladly bring you bread.
Sir Henry More is welcome. Neighbour Joyce
Needs never telling of the same. Pray sit
Awhile within the arbour, freshly sweet
With new-blown woodbine, of itself, indeed,
A feast for them that love the dear God's gifts.'

She gone, they sat them down. Unclosed, as used
Of late, there lay a book upon a shelf,
And seeing this the knight bent o'er the page,
And read aloud a verse of Aquinas.
'Marry! good Geoff, what bookish priest doth turn
Green arbour into cloister? 'Ware the maid!
Sir monk, that walks these garden paths among,
Or else 'twill be Saint Anthony again.'

''Tis Agnes' self, the girl is very wise,'
The forester returned. 'Our good old priest
'Twas he that taught her.—Hush! here comes
       herself,
I'll tell you more anon.'
                     With smile and bow
Sir Henry rose to meet the maid. From out
Her hands he took the porringer of milk,
And set the loaf upon the settle board.
''Tis unbecoming task for learnèd hands,'
He said with meaning pointing to the page.
She smiled, then answered gravely from the book—
'Not so, "there's never harm in serving; all

The harm's accounting service, harm to self " '—
Then curtseying low,—' Pray you excuse me now
But my sweet slugabed was waking, when
I left the house, and calling sister Ness.'—

She turned, the hound slow following as she trod
With easy gait the flowery garden path.
Silent Sir Henry stood, until again
The cot received its mistress, then he laughed—
' Mine eyes have drunk so deep of beauty, Geoff,
Your milky meal for me has lost its charm.
Love's thirst alone is quenched with draught of
 love.'
The woodman smiled—' Yet taste the milk, Sir Hal.
Remember how 'twas drawn by comely hands.'
Then, more in earnest,—' And remember too
Though poor, the maid is honest. Do not bring
Your courtly arts to sorrow Agnes Leigh.
No moth to flutter round unwonted light,
And singe, and die, in unrelentful flame
Is she, but one that loving, loves till death
Or disappointed dies to willing tomb.'

With stern proud look and flashing eye the knight
Replied full hotly, ' Friend ! Sir Henry More
Needs ne'er reminding of his duty, nor
Recall of knightly faith at cotter mouth.'
So said, then all repentant of his heat
Stretched out his hand,—' Forgive me !   I am like
A smould'ring coal, that fanned o' sudden flames
And burns th' unwary chafer.—Do not fear

Unholy tempting of the maid by me.
Fair as an angel, she should be as pure!
God's wrath upon the traitor that would soil
Her chrisom soul with thought unworthy heav'n!'

'Forgive me too!' the reeve replied and grasped
Sir Henry's hand. 'Forgive me if I deemed
A courtier's life, perchance, had dulled the soul
Of him I loved as brother, and so do.
Command me what you will Sir Hal, nor doubt
I'll e'er forget the nuzzling of your arm
About my ruder neck, when childish grief
Made life a penance. We were brothers then,
Geoff Joyce the ranger's son and Henry More,
Kinsman of England's Chancellor, true knight,
And martyr for the faith, what time the king
Demanded of his subjects more than they
Could give, as subjects still of mightier King.
But yet beware! The girl is strangely wise.
I'll swear her good as blessed Agnes' self
Her namesake! But '—and here the sturdy reeve
Lift up his hand, and made in haste the sign,
Christ's holy sign upon his suntanned brow—
'She reads strange books.—Yet never word of this
To other! I'd the rather lose my tongue
Than harm her by an hair!—Sir William May,
Our parson heretofore—God rest his soul!—
Of love for learning, taught her all she knows.
His niece some say, but some indeed have doubt;
No likeness she to mistress Margery Leigh
His callet sister, hatchetfaced and grim,

Who came to keep his house these fifteen years.
But after, spouseld goodman Will o' Barns.
With her the child, she called, forsooth, her own
But mother'd harshly. So the good priest took
The little maid and kept her till his death.

Shrew Margery then, bed-ridden, bade her here
To prove hale dame to her own puling brats.
So Agnes came, and, sweet as sunbeam, filled
A dolesome house with music.—Many a lad
Would free her, an she would, by honest love.'
'Yourself among them, Geoffrey ? ' laughed the
          knight,
Yet anxious still to catch the reeve's reply.
'Nay! Nay! The maid is never wife for me.
Not but I'd love her dearly ; only this,
There's never joy where minds unmateful mate !
I should not understand her.   When she tired—
As tire she would of only homely joys—
And sought relief in books and learned lore,
I should be left a-dry.—No pleasure that !
Yet more, the girl's a lollard !   There's the rub.
That's why I said I hoped the fame was false
The queen's restoring bluff king Harry's laws,
King Edward's counting naught.   Hard times are
          these
When kings, uncertain of their faith, atone
For doubt at home by penalty abroad.
But hark ! The horn ! There's gath'ring at the
          lodge.

'Tis early! Yet old Bertram knows his work.
Wilt end the milk ?—Ah well ! we woodmen eat
Against our often fasting.—We must on,
You to the queen and devoirs at her side,
And I to join the meiny for the hunt.
There goes the hound !   Full well he knows the call.
Good dog no need of voicing, we'll anon ! '

II

Without the forest lodge, a space removed
From royal ear, within the sylvan shade,
The rangers stood and careless wiled away
The time with song, till coming of the Queen.
'Twas Joyce who now full blithely woke the wood
At call of brother reeve, whose noisy note
Still shook the birchen bough 'neath which he lay.

Song

A staggard there was, that leaped out of the shaw ;
  Tra la la la, in the greenwood-a !
And after him hurtled his goodly felawe ;
  Tra la la la, in the greenwood-a !

A call then I wound me full loud in my horn ;
  Tra la la la, in the greenwood-a !
The five-year he fled him by thicket and thorn ;
  Tra la la la, in the greenwood-a !

In haste then Sir Richard bestraddled his bay ;
  Tra la la la, in the greenwood-a !

His lady she called for her palefroy gray,
   Tra la la la, in the greenwood-a!

The quarry he stayed him to drink at the brook;
   Tra la la la, in the greenwood-a!
Then turned him again for his dene hidden nook;
   Tra la la la, in the greenwood-a!

A shaft then I drew me right up to the head;
   Tra la la la, in the greenwood-a!
The staggard he shook him then tumbled down
      dead;
   Tra la la la, in the greenwood-a!

The lady too stumbled, 'twas under a thorn;
   Tra la la la, in the greenwood-a!
Sir Richard thereafter he weareth the horn,
   At court and in's hall and the greenwood-a!

———

'Well sung, Geoff Joyce! Well sung, good lad, I say!
"At court and in's hall and the greenwood-a!"
Shalt sing again! Give's now "When shaws ben
      green."'
So said an aged forester, the while
He laid approving hand upon the reeve
Who answered cheer'ly—'Faith! the call is mine.
And see Will Luffman's busy tuning throat.
'Twere shame to spoil his ditty—let him sing!'
Thus bidden, in his turn with right good will
The reeve trolled out his song with merry mien.

Song

O, I am a forester good, boys,
My walk it is Luoton its wood, boys,
  And often I see—
  Well! it's nothing to me
What I see when I'm watching the deer, boys!

There's a dip down at Debden you know, boys,
Where the lads and the lasses they go, boys,
  For the bracken grows high
  So that none can espy
Should Jack—Well! it's nothing to me, boys!

There's a cot in the slade by the brook, boys,
With rosary, bell, and with book, boys,
  There dwelleth a friar
  Who says his desire
Is but to cheat Satan of souls, boys!

His cot is but small, but its snug, boys,
There's a porringer, platter and mug, boys,
  A table and chair
  With a settle to spare—
But that's for some other, you see, boys!

There's a casement high up in the wall, boys,
So you cannot see through if you're small, boys,
  But should you be tall
  It might then befall
You'd see—Well! you'd see what you'd see, boys!

O, I am a forester good, boys,
And I'm watching o' nights in the wood, boys,
  And sometimes I see—
  Well! it's nothing to me,
What I see when I peep through the pane, boys!

Applause and laughter scarcely at an end,
Rebuke unlooked-for came from strident voice—
' I warrant me you see the saint at prayer
For prying knaves ! '   It came from wandering frere,
Whom chance had brought to Chingford overnight,
And now stood scowling by the jovial reeves.
At this fresh laughter filled the glade, and one
Made scoffing answer—' Yea, before the shrine
Of beauty, holy sir ! Ourselves at times
That selfsame way are woundily devout ! '

The weazened frere at this was doubly wroth,
Yet had not time to speed an answering shot,
For now came trumpet blast.—The gates wide thrown
The Queen appears with all her courtier throng.
Now caps are doffed ! A cheer from lusty throats
Goes up, each loyal heart aglad to greet
Their careworn mistress. She, from sceptred toil,
To-day short respite takes within the wood ;
That then as now, sequestered realm of peace,
Calmed troubled hearts and soothed unrestful grief
With sympathy of brook, and swaying bough,
And silence broken only by a sigh
Low-breathed from out the bosom of the shaw.

A royal buck in Blackbush plain is known
To have his haunt. The cortège thither wends
And passing Agnes' cot, the maiden stands
To make obeisance. Joyous at the sight
Of gay-dressed cavalcade, her youngling charge
Make childish clamour, clapping hands and so
Drew all eyes on the girl, who, courtesy given,
Turned half aside to hide the virgin glow
That flushed her cheek at gaze of hundred eyes ;
Yet turning caught a look from him, whose face
Dwelled strangely in remembrance since the morn.

The Queen went on, and soon, the buck aroused,
The hunt began, and all the woodland rang
With horn and halloo. Now the mort is blown.
And now fresh quarry speeds the brakes along,
And climbs the slope, and threads the tangled thick,
Or seeks the devious watercourse, o'erhung
With beechen bough and bramble tenebrous.
Erelong in turn he falls. Thus until noon,
When one outran the weary hounds and made
Escape by way of Chingford. Sport at end,
And fallen quarry borne a space away,
They made the Queen an alcove. 'Neath its shade
Awhile she rested, then again her way
Betook to Copt Hall, there to lie the night.

Meanwhile Sir Henry More, his horse fall'n lame,
Forsook the royal suite and turned him back
To Chingford. There, remounted, but a mile
Or two had gone, when panting, trembling, spent,

A lordly stag ran past him. Drawing rein,
He wound a call, and turning, chased the beast
That followed still the grassy forest lane
To where Allhallows ancient chapel set
Upon a grassy knoll without the wood,
Looks down upon the softly winding Lea.
Full lonely was the place, and here the stag
With bursting heart sought refuge from his foes;
With last brave effort, leaped the oaken pale,
And ent'ring in the peaceful chapelry,
Anigh the altar groaning laid him down.

Now came the knight, and making fast his horse
To mounting-block, sped up the causey green.
But sudden stopt, at sound of tearful voice,
Within the ivied fane—'Poor hunted beast
To seek the shelter thus of holy place,
And at God's altar plain the pride of man!'
The knight was thrilled.—Full well he knew the
        voice—
Once heard, who e'er forgat its angel tone—
And looking through the open casement saw
A sight the like he ne'er had dreamed to see.
Before the screen the forest maiden stood
And suppliant at her feet, the weary stag!

Vast pity filled his breast—his hunting knife
He hid in haste. The couchant prey was safe.
Protected thus, had Dian's self appeared
And claimed the fere, he had gainsaid her will,
For sake of her, as lovely and as chaste,

Who stood before Christ's altar weeping tears
Of purest charity for tortured beast.
Abashed, he doffed his hat and entered in
With rev'rent tread and soft. She quickly heard,
And turned in haste, with outstretched hands to
    shield,
Whate'er she might, the sufferer at her feet.

'God's house!' she cried, 'God's house! Forbear
    pursuit!'
Then blushed and smiled. Like April sun through
    tears
Of glistering rain, her glowing face appeared.
Her bosom lifting with suppressed delight
At sight of friend, she eagerly came down
The chancel step to meet him. 'You will spare,
Sir Henry, will you not for Christ his sake,
The harmless brute that seeks his hallowing house,
To scape His creatures wrath!'

                      'The stag is safe,'
The knight made answer quickly, 'and for sake
Of her who pleads so sweetly for his life.
I only am pursuant!'—here he stayed
Afraid that frown might gather on her face;
Yet had she none for him—'and that by chance.
My horse fell lame, so I returned and met
This fleeing stag, who shall be safe henceforth
From chase and chaser. In my park at Bourne
I'll set him. There till envious age shall let
His running, he shall range wide-antlered lord!

Now aid me to secure him, till my folk
Can come and bear him off unharmed at eve!'

Beneath the tower the stag was pent, yet still
The knight and maiden lingered in the aisle.
The tide of gen'rous impulse past, she stood
With downcast eyes and gave him faltering thanks
He drinking in each look and tone, until
Her image filled each cranny of his heart.
Who heretofore had laughed at love as sport
For idle men and moment, deeming naught
Of worth, save statecraft, embassies and war;
Now felt within his falsely armoured breast
The Lovegod's rankling shaft, and yielded up
The fortress of his soul, contented well
To lie enchained, so sweet, the gilded gyves
Of Love, and duresse lit by beauty's smile!

Yet had he never speech somewhile, the spell
That thralled his heart enchaining still his tongue.
Although but village lass, the flippant phrase
Or careless converse, other, loftier maids
Had not refused, but rather welcomed, such
Full well he knew she would disdain, had not
The place itself forbidden idle speech.
At length recovering heart,—' 'Twas lucky chance,'
He said, 'that led me hither; I am glad
To be your servant, charge me as you will '—
Then stayed in some confusion, as too much
Or all too little said. But calmly she
Made answer gravely—' Was it chance? Ah, no!
I'll ne'er believe a good deed done of hap.

Is it not writ that never sparrow falls
From cloudy welkin, but our Father knows
Its agony of falling and the why?
Who maketh all, doth surely overrule
All things and that for good.   Both you and I,
Though diverse in our station and estate,
Are natheless His, to work His royal will.—
And also I have read '—Abruptly here
She stopped, and gave the knight a questioning look
That said full well—"The times are fateful, dare
I speak thus freely, though my heart be full,
To one so late a stranger.'—Thus indeed
He read her sudden silence and her look
And made her answer,—' Nay, have never fear
But tell me all your thought.   On faith of knight
No word shall pass my lips.'

                          Encouraged thus
She turned and showed him by the chancel pier
A staple and a chain.   ' Here lay till late
Fast chained and kept—so precious was the gift—
God's word of life to all that walk thereby.
While yet 'twas there, each day I gladly came
To read therein, and once when sorely grieved
And sick at heart, I found the cheerful words
" To them that love Him all things work for good ; "
And comfort found, and find it still what time
My wayward soul grows weary of restraint.
And thus to me, Life journeys not with Chance
For doubtful comrade, trustless in its need ;
But rather companied by One, whose faith
And prowess none may question or control ¦ '

' A noble faith ! ' the knight replied.   ' Yet few
I trow are they that grasp it.   Angels may,
And they that most are like them, in this world
That groaneth ever under curse of sin,
As said good father Petre, when he preached
Before her grace at Greenwich.   But for me.
Too abstract far.   I must have aught to hold,
Some nearer presence, mortal like myself,
Or sometime mortal.   Thus the blessed saints
To me are helpful.'—
       Here she interposed
With wistful earnestness, that double charm
Lent to her features, mobile as the stream
When laughing sunbeams lurk in crystal waves
That woodland whisperings wake to life and play.
' And have you not,' she urged, with kindling look—
' Such helpful presence ever nigh, the God—
The Christ that took on flesh, and manlike died ?
What need of saint for intercessor, or
The championship of angel ! '
        ' Prithee, hush !
Sweet girl !   I would not for a kingdom harm
A curl upon thy brow ; but other ears
May hear, and evil come of hearing, so
If that you value liberty or life,
Imprison up that wizard tongue, that speaks
Such liquid heresy, mine ears could drink
Incessant, and ne'er weary of the draught !—
Or speak but low, so none beside may hear.
Till now I thought this lollardy but held
By state upheavers, Lutherites, and they

Who giving rein to flesh, and fleshly greed,
Forswear the faith that damns their evil way.
Sweet Mary shield us, now pure-hearted maids
Take up the parable !—Saint Anthony
Naught yielded till the tempter came in guise
Of girlhood, lovely as Susannah's self ! '

A pallor overspread the maiden's face,
She trembled and was silent. Seeing this
He cheered her gently. ' I am loath to pale
Those damask cheeks an instant, or convey
Your soul a thought of fear, or causeless wake
The pulsings of your heart to fleeter course ;
But 'tis no secret, there are troublous times
In store for them that hold not with her grace
In forms of faith. So give no room for doubt
To any by your 'haviour or your speech !

Now we'll to fairer subject.—Think you not
These lonely walls ; this dreamy shadowy light
Flung darksome from these painted casements down ;
With thought of all the close invaulted dead
That sleep beneath these dusty aisles, will press
Too hardly on your spirit for your weal ?
To me the woodland yields a fresher joy,
That knows no taint of charnel hostelry,
Nor oft pollution of lip-service prayer.
Here men betimes must kneel, and crimes confess
Whose very utterance falls but short of sin.
The very air is thick with sighs and groans,
With plaint of frailty, and repentant tears

That dew perchance the hollow foot-worn slab
Of Maudlin long since houseled and forgot!
Youth should be gay, and beauty ever set
About with beauty. Whispering trees, and streams,
That sing her softly as she passes by,
With flowers to shrine her feet, and bid her know
Herself their mate, however lovely they,
These should attend her ever!'—

Agnes here

Made mild remonstrance. 'So the poets feigned
Erewhile of Flora! I too love the wood,
Its arching glades and ferny solitudes,
The parley of its leaves with kissing winds,
But most of all its nightly dirges, sung
Amid its dim recesses. Yet I love
This chapel more, that ever ope invites
The passer-by to stay awhile and pray
For help in pilgrimage. And if in truth
Its antic aisles are eloquent with sighs,
And fall of tears, do I not sigh as oft,
For that I am, and that I fain would be?
And weep withal when none is nigh to see?
And are not sinners' sighs and groans of all
Most grateful sacrifice to Him, great Lord,
Who also wept, but all for us, and sighed
Not seldom for our sin, His godly strength
And beauty gone with often misery?
And is it wrong to dream, good spirits here
May concourse, all their earthly penance done!
And that of love, may often comrade us
Who pray, where they once prayed, celestial souls

L.L.   M

No longer needing prayer, but bearing ours
On willing wings to Him, the God, that hears
And when He hears forgives ?
　　　　　　　　More nigh to Him
I feel beside yon altar and more safe
Than in His wider world, of care and strife.'

The knight was silent.—' I am overbold,'
She said, ' to speak you thus, but that you bade,
And so tell all my thought ! But see ! the sun
Is flaming Judah's sword ! In summer time,
'Tis sign of noon, and I have stayed too long
For some whose love will chide my late return.—
Your patience yet an instant.'
　　　　　　　　Here she knelt
Before the shrine, her lovely head downbent
Awhile in prayer, then rising, graceful moved
Adown the aisle, and past the wallset stoup,
Regardless, though Sir Henry dipped therein
And set the blessed sign upon his brow.

They parted at the gate. A nearer way
She took by field. He watched her from the stile
Till lost beyond the maple and the thorn
That girt the pasture. Then he hastened back
To bid his people seek the prisoned stag ;
And after máde for Copt Hall and the Queen.

III

Embower'd in woods—a portion of the waste
Of Waltham parked and palisaded—stood
Upon a sunny slope an ancient hall
With gabled roof and turrets. Firm it stood,
Secured with moat and wall and barbican
Against the lawless outcasts of the wood.

For ages held by church of Holy Cross,
A goodly seat it was, wherein the prior
Whene'er he wearied of his cloistral rule
Would make retreat ; to plan amid the copse
That lay within its precinct, fresh essay
Of beauty for the chapel by the gate—
Rich gem of art that each succeeding prior
Made richer by whate'er the centuries
Attained of greater skill in sculptor art !

A lovely place it was with pendant roof,
So dight with fretwork chisellings, and poised
So delicate, it seemed to hang in air,
A floating canopy for aëry wall ;
That seemed not wall but wreath of fruited vine,
With garland grapes that pendulous swung, amid
Broad hawthorn leaves, or oakspray bearing up
Their autumn chalices !
                                   It was a thing
Beheld in dreams, but seldom waking—such,
As slowly moulded age by age, could lift
The gazer heav'nward and compel to pray'r.

A pleasaunce lay anear the outer wall
With grassy alleys, overarched with yew
So greenly thick, that neither nipping breeze,
Nor overfervid beam could incommode.
A plat adjoined with dial, and a green
For bowls, with fishpond where was set in midst
Dan Neptune with his tritons and his steeds.

'Twas eve and freshly fair.   The sinking sun
Shone full upon the windows of the hall;
Which kindling, flashed afar the bloody gleam—
A beacon 'midst the landskip !
                              East and west
Put on eve's rosy vesture. Hanging clouds,
Slow sailing, fringed with gold, made gorgeous pall
For dying day. The rooks, a noisy cloud,
Wore slowly homeward flapping weary wings ;
A breeze awakening, stealthy touched the trees,
But here and there, as timid of advance
To dalliance, till the standard of the Night
Should flaunt the darkening west.
                              The curfew bell
Rolled distant o'er the woods from Epping town,
And pleasing echoes woke from crest and hill.

The Queen was in the pleasaunce.   Nigh a grot
She sat and wistful gazed upon the scene.
A space removed, her maidens athered where,
Made storm-like by the play of gentle hands,
The water lapped the breasts of Neptune's steeds.
Some fed the carp, that flashed their scaly gold

Amid the mimic sea ;—some loftier sport
Made with their courtier mates—arch looks and
    smiles
Bestowing freely, with soft words, most sweet
As born of lips as fair as her's who kist
Adonis coy.
           Aweary sighed the Queen
Beholding these, ' So came to me love's dream,
While yet the shadow of the crown fell not
Upon my girlish brow ! Ah, weary life !
Athirst, and from the cratch, for love, yet aye
The cup withheld ! Not e'en a parting kiss
When death redressed my mother of her wrongs.
And welcome, bore her willing soul to plead
Her cause at just tribunal !
               He, I love,
And so soon wed, I fear me, loves me not,
Or second only to the realm his sire
Would join unto his own—which ne'er shall be !
Ah, me ! Ah, me ! Too sad the thought.—I'll call
These giglot girls about me.
              She whose glance
Too often seeks yon alley's shade to hide
The thoughts that thrall her, may she never know
Such hunger at her heart as pinches me !—
The lad too were becoming mate—her wealth
Would match his worth. Brave stock ! how
    could my sire
Unhead his kinsman chancellor ?—Would I
Had such another now to counsel me ! '

A page stood near, and now at royal call
Made low obeisance. ' Bid my maidens here
And mistress Cath'rine tune her idle lute '—
They coming stood expectant.—' Sing me, Kate !
Your song, perchance, shall still unruly thought
In me, and draw for you Sir Henry More
Out yonder alley.—Tush ! child, never blush !
He is a proper youth, and Kate de Vere
Might further go to fare the worse for mate !—
Now sing and charm yon noisy bird to peace !—
I care not what, so 'tis not over gay
To jar with grief, nor over sad to press
The joyless heart to tears with added woe ' '

Song.

The dew is on the lea,
    The lark is in the sky,
And swift, Morn's splendours fly at dawning of the day.
    On land and lake and sea,
    Is laughter, mirth, and glee,
For all things care defy, at dawning of the day !

The sheep are in the cote,
    The ruddock's on the thorn,
He in his song doth mourn, for dying of the day,
    Within the lazy moat,
    The drowsy moonbeams float,
The world is all forlorn, at dying of the day !

The chough is on the wing,
The seamew wakes her mate,
The rooks hold wild debate, at dawning of the day,
The newborn breezes bring
Fresh perfumes, ploughboys sing,
All things new pleasure take, at dawning of the day !

The night wind whistles shrill,
The owl alarms the wood,
Fear chills the trav'lers blood, at dying of the day,
The robber roams at will,
Death candles burn—there's ill
And terror all abroad, at dying of the day !

But ah ! to me the night
And day are ever one,
While, he, my light, my sun, doth bid old Time delay,
He smiles, and at the sight
Night flies—I bask in light,
And nothing know of dawn, or dying of the day !

———

So sang the maiden bending o'er her lute.
Nor ill bestowed her royal mistress praise.
Her voice was sweet, and as she sang, her soul
Woke at the words, and birthed them into life.
Thereafter sat she silent till the Queen
From reverie awoke and praised the strain,
When all about gave plaudits.—One, a youth,
And over forward, whispered aught that brought
An angry light a moment in her eyes.
And once she beat the ground with dainty foot

As weary of applause, or waiting yet
Impatient, other, dearer voice, whose need
Of praise outweighed all else a hundred fold.

This now the Queen beheld, and, all unused
Herself to hide the workings of her soul ;
Took pity on the maid, and looking round
Bade one go fetch Sir Henry from the gloom
Of yew and holly laboured into shape
Fantastic.   Then with royal gesture called
The singer to her side and spake her low—
' 'Tis hard, good wench, to pipe to careless ears,
Or absent swain—in sooth 'tis sorry work !
And who should know as I, how oft the flower
Of love is hedged about with guard of thorns ?
Here comes our pensive knight !—I bade him here,
Be yours, sweet wench, to keep him.   Idle task
Were that for me.   Young love defies restraint,
And ever frowns on neutral offices,
Or come they from a peasant or a queen.'

Thus far the Queen aside, then louder spake—
' Now, Cath'rine, take again your lute and sing
" Love's Triumph," while Sir Henry More shall hold
Your ballat-book and turn the page at need.'

What could the knight but bow, and take his place
Beside the maid ?   She gave him one swift look,
Part proud, part pleased, and then with skilful hand
Stirred into life the vibrant strings, whose throb

Harmonious and low was like the fall
Of forest water, over fallen tree,
Which erewhile hung above the coquet brook,
Love sick of gleam and music, slowly falls,
Till prone, it checks the wave, that hence must stay
And kiss its sometime suitor, ere it pass
In foamy flight along the shadowy dell,
Complaining loudly at enforced embrace.

Song.

Dan Cupid leapt up from his couching at day,
   And chose him out arrowlets three ;
Sir Rupert shall one—and the Chancellor gray—
   And the novice in cloistery !

Sir Rupert he mocks at my frolicksome shaft,
   While glory is ever his theme ;
The Chancellor busied in cunning and craft,
   Bans love as a pestilent dream !

The shaveling to be, in his cell on the hill
   With psalmery, penance and prayer ;
Doth hide him away, but resolve as he will,
   Love's arrow shall follow him there !

The knight he rode by on his destrier strong,
   With squire and with meiny so gay ;
Hurrah, for the shout and the shock, and the song
   With the feasting, at close of the fray !

But a lady looked out of her jessamine bower
  As the knight and his meiny went by;
Oh, winsome her face as the fragile wind-flower!
  And brighter than dewdrop her eye!

And waving her kerchief, she greeted the knight;
  What could he but smile in reply,
And lift his plumed bonnet—Love smiled at the
    sight
  And swiftly an arrow let fly!

' And whither, Sir Rupert, now whither dost ride,
  So gallant, so youthful and free !
My father is absent—he's wooing!' she sighed;
  ' Were some one but wooing of me!'

Then kisses she cast him, one, two, three—and twain
  She set on a sprig of the tree;
It fell on his saddle—Sir Rupert drew rein—
  ' Dear maiden, I'll wear it for thee!'

I've won and I've won, quoth the god as he fled—
  They may shout and may shock as they may,
Sir Rupert will tarry.—By maiden bested
  Too late will he ride to the fray !

The Chancellor gray in his garden so fair
  Was walking 'twixt briar and bent,
His forehead, thought-furrowed, was knitted with
    care,
  His mind upon grandeur intent.

A laugh, like the rippling of wave on the sand
  At turning of ocean and tide,
Disturbed him in scheming—he lifted his hand—
  A rosebud fell full at his side.

His ward in the pleasaunce, at play with her maid—
  Unseen he had crost their retreat—
Her lap full of roses—her frock disarrayed—
  With glimpsings of bosom and feet!

He gazed in his folly—Dan Cupid, forsooth,
  Need hardly have been at the pains;
Yet shafting an arrow—the fireblood of youth
  Leapt up in the Chancellor's veins.

Oh, ho! and oh, ho! but the state now must wait;
  Yet plead as the Chancellor may—
Laughed Cupid—his lordship must bow to his fate.
  The maiden will ever say, nay!

The novice in chauntry bent over his book,
  His 'gesta sanctorum' at knee,
But ever his thought was of forest and brook,
  Of hamlet, and cottage, and lea.

Again in his fancy he saw the grey mill;
  The millboat with sedge-holden keel;
Again, too, the fall of the light-flashing rill
  He heard, with the whirl of the wheel.

The face of the miller's fair daughter—ah, me
  His playmate and sweetheart of yore ;—
He saw it.—She smiled in her innocent glee—
  His book fell unheeded to floor !

Unquenchable longing sprang up in his heart,
  Love's barb smiting deeply and keen,
He let the book lie, as he rose to depart—
  'His sweetheart to comfort I ween.'

'She wept when he left her to seek the cold cell,
  What now when he lies at her feet ?
Or monkling or miller, I prithee now tell ? '
  Laughed Love, as he made his retreat.

———

Far strayed Queen Mary's thoughts, the while her
    maid
Thus struck her lute.   For aye her lonely heart
Pined after love, and fated ne'er to know
Congenial mate, was famished.   Broodful now
Her soul pursued her promised spouse across
The far-dividing sea.   Her people's hate
She knew him, and she dearly loved her land !
Thus passion strove with passion.   Could she vow
For dream of wedded love, repugnant vows
To all her nation ?   Should a strain arise
'Twixt spouse and people, whether most would reign
Within her heart, and whether final sway ?

Now stood the pearldrops in her mournful eyes,
Downcast to hide the tempest in her soul,

A moment thus, and all her native pride
Rose up impatient! On her pallid lips
Was swift command for silence, but she checked
The haughty words, and spake the maiden fair—
Communing with herself 'Nay, now, the fault
Was mine to bid her sing such skittish song '—
Then out aloud—' Enough, good girl, enough!
It is a fair conceit, this power of love,
If somewhat overtold!—

      Sir Henry More
I have a matter for your private ear;
But first go one and bid my people light
The altar tapers. God be praised for gift
Of prayer and devout heart!—I am not sad
Nor weighted down with loneliness, what time
I have commerce with saints at shrine or tomb!'

So said the Queen withdrawing little space,
Sir Henry in attendance. Then to him,—
'A loving heart, good youth, is pearl of price;
And one is here, your mate in birth, and more
Than mate in wealth, who fain would win a smile
From one who shall be nameless. Is't enough?
The girl has chosen well!—Command may not
Be given in Court of Love, but when the bells
Ring out for me, I would my ward were wed
To him she favours, and her Queen approves.
See yonder where she walks—the yew less dark
And sombre than her thought! You gave no heed,
Nor word of praise, all others loud, although
She mainly sang to you. So glide you in

Yon bosky alley where she downcast walks,
And whisper comfort. 'Twere but kindly task
To lift the gloom that clouds her comely face.'
Thus Mary softly, kindly, then withdrew,
Her maidens following, all but Cath'rine Vere.

Sir Henry made obeisance, but the Queen
Retired, he frowned and coldly turned aside
From maid and alley, 'Yonder haughty girl—
Whose snowwreath face veils scorching vulcan fires—
Is fair enow, yet never fair to me.
Her raven looks remind me of the night;
And aye her piercing eyes, the orbed light
That nightly looks unmoved on right and wrong,
Cold, careless, callous. Nay! Give me the locks
That fall like rippling sunbeams o'er a brow
That's sunny also.—Eyes like violets,
Wide ope and truthful—telltale cheeks that glow
With Phoebus' kissing—teeth of Parian pearl
That gleaming peep from cherry lips that seem
To cry, " Come! love, a kiss, we'll kiss again ! "
And over all a look that's ever kind,
Though often far away, as if she saw
Lost Eden, or the golden portals set
Ajar that she, fair spirit, might behold
Her sometime home !—
                              So! So! With tyro brush
I paint a face that would bemock the skill
Of Master Tintoretto.—Mistress Vere
May mate with whom she will so not with me !—

The woods are cool to-night, I'll walk awhile
By old Bonduca's camp!'
                                        Unheeding all
The curious looks of courtier and of maid,
The knight forsook the pleasaunce. Entering now
The woods that lay without the crenelled gate,
He thoughtful wandered on. The dusk of eve
Soon deepened, while the first faint star appeared
In gloom of eastern glade. The wind uprose
To welcome night; while all the forest woke
To harmony of leaf, soft sighing; stir
Of lightly waving bough; descant of brook;
With drowsy coo of dove, or lazy caw
Of rook belated, sailing slowly home!

Within the camp a tussock of wild thyme
Inviting rest, the knight sat down.—'How sweet
The hush of eve, how calmly still the woods!
And yet 'tis said this spot did sometime ring
With crash of conflict; madd'ning roar of men,
In berserk phrensy frighting Death himself,
With untold uproar; hurricane turmoil;
Curse of despair, or jubilation wild
Of victor over corse of fallen foe!—
How much we mortals in our folly miss
The good, the good God gives us! How we rage
For wealth and fame, and but to rival them
That still outshine us; they the while at pains
To o'ertop others. Happy were I now
To quit this crowd of many-minded knaves,

Gilt weathercocks, that veer with every wind
And court each royal breeze !—

How sick am I
At heart, whene'er these Mammon worshippers
Prate of the state, the church, the people, while
Their thoughts are only, how to wrap themselves
In pride and pomp ; or how convert their theft
Of church and land and wayside commonage,
With woodland field, to lawful appanage.
Who moves his neighbour's landmark, curst is he !—
But then who owns for *neighbour*, poverty
In russet gabardine, or carter smock,
With noisy shoon oft-pieced, and broad-palmed hands
Brown with the blustering of a hundred storms ?
What share has Colin Clout in land or state ?
And yet, God wot ! did he not toil a-field
Our courtly locusts soon were ill bestid,
First bartered all their tinsel state for food !

So !   Something stirs beside the wind, that speaks
The beech-tops waking dirge and monody,
For them that sleep hereunder.   Friend or foe
Come forth nor make a sorry fort of fern !—
Ha !—Footpads !   Well ! who walks the woods o'
     nights
Must look for ill companions.   Folly's mine
To roam thus unattended.'   Thus the knight
In scornful undertone, then—' Keep you back ! '
He called and loudly, while his rapier gleamed
This way and that.   Hardby a friendly tree
Affording vantage, springing thither he

Now stood at bay, close followed by the men
Who clam'rous bade him render up or die!

He careless smiled. ' My purse ?   Alack ! my friends
There's little in't, but what there is I'll keep
As honest got.—Give back again I say !
I am the poor man's friend, make me not foe ! '—
The outlaws laughed—'A gentle and a friend !
Tush !   Yield your purse, or rather, give us back
Our rightful own !   Wilt not ?   Then here's for
      proof ! '

They closing in, he thrust with fearless hand,
And one fell groaning.   Then in turn he knew
The sting of steel, and felt the warm blood gush
Adown his poniard arm.   Some thrustings more
And all were over, had not blare of horn
Spoke help, and scared afar the robber crew.
'Twas Joyce who brought his foster brother aid
With Hector baying loud in fierce pursuit
Of flying foe.
              ' Art hurt, Sir Hal ?   Art hurt ? '
The ranger eager cried.—' Not much ?   That's well !
Rude leechcraft must suffice and woodman skill
In place of court chirurgeon.'—Cheerly thus,
The while with practised hand he bound the wound
And staunched its bleeding.   Then the groaning thief
He bent him over.   ' Yea, a sorry knave,
With weazen face as sharp as misery.
In sooth, Sir Hal, a right good meal of steel
He's had at last—I doubt me he will live !

L.L.   N

He's stuck in's ribs!—Dost hear me out-throat dog!
Art spent, or thinkest room for surgery?
And yet what use, the halter ready noosed?
Shalt swing, i' faith, and soon for this night's work!'

The robber stirred.   Sir Henry interposed
With kindly chiding.—'Geoffrey, let him be!
And, he be sped, vex not the parting soul
With illtimed quip, for often, stroke of Death
Doth quicken hearing.—Not!   Then let us do
For him as for another.   Better work
To make a rogue an honest man, than hang
An hundred knaves to win a little ease!
Speak, friend, can aught be done? I bear thee naught
Of malice, but would render good for ill.'

'I know not, only I am sorely hurt,'
The thief replied.   ''Twere best to let me die!
I was no robbersman till robber king
Despoiled my monkish masters, left myself
And them to starve!   Christ!   Might I but repeat
A pater or an ave ere I speed!'—
So groaned the thief.   Then pitiful the knight—
'Nay tend his wound, good Geoffrey, an you can!
He is your pris'ner—I will ransom him
Restored, if mis'ry drave him to the crime
As well may be.—No aid can I bestow
Thus pinked and bandaged, so I'll back to Hall
And send you present help.'
                              'Nay, never stir,
Sir Hal, the wood is lonesome!   When you left
The gates I followed, fearing ill.   'Twas known

The court would lie the night within the hall.
The fame has garnered rogues, as crows forsooth
Foregather thick at prospect of a feast!
My mot has waked the wood—I'll wind again
And help will be forthcoming.'
                    This he did
And answer came from out the nearer thicks.
First Hector, panting; then a stalwart reeve,
And then another, while a distant mot
Made further question.—'Prithee, Wat, reply
Or all will here anon!' So one gave back
Calm answer while they bore the wounded man
To charcoal hut, anear the shelvy camp,
And laid him down on bed of russet brake.

IV

The Court again at Sheen, Sir Henry More,
Pleading his hurt and business of import,
Returned to London; thence, spurred on by love,
To Chingford and the cottage by Fairmead.
A peerless day it was of peerless June!
The sun shone bright, but yet his steadfast beam,
By woodland breezes tempered, rather fired
The blood to joyous pulsing, than disposed
To idle languor or unrestful rest.
Rich was the breath of eglantine, its few
Pale blossoms set amid its thorny crest.
The furze yet bloomed, a saffron fringe about
The scarcer broom, whose golden drops made faint

With oversweetness.   Here and there the ling
Rang out a sylvan peal from late blown bells,
But mostly sere, spread out a tempting couch
Beside the scarce-trod pathway of the wood.

The knight went slowly on, his soul attuned
To harmony with nature, and the more
His thoughts were gentle, hon'rable and true
To all things and all creatures. He could look
The whole Court in the face, man, maid, and priest,
And fearless say ' None here can lay to me
Wrong done, by word or deed, but otherwise
Have holpen others oft.' Full goodly he,
And stately of his presence. In his face
Was written truth, and in his steadfast gaze
Could friendship read devotion, but a foe
Intensity of purpose, fearless will,
With challenge e'en to death for proven right !

His patrimony small, he owed no man.
But like his royal Queen, his outgoes made
Subserve his purse, yet never niggard, moved
The cynosure of grateful hearts whose need
Or lesser fortunes, craved some welcome aid.

Now urged by love—true love that hourly grew
The more he pictured, ardent, in his soul
The darling of his dreams—and fired by hope,
Sad life's most blest companion, came he now
Along the lane to where the woodside cot
Sent up its twisted wreath of azure smoke.
And favour'd of Dame Fortune, scarce had come,

Before the cottage door was oped and she
Came down the path, equipt for morning walk.
With her a child who joyous ran before
Adown the mead to fill her little hands
With kingcup posy, simple spoil, but yet
Fairer by far to childhood innocence
Than all the flaunting trophies of the plat.

Himself unseen, he stood and watched them pass.
And gazing, breathed a blessing on the maid.
Oh! fair was she in kirtle russet brown
With bodice white as snow, and maiden coif
That fondly clipt her soft and clust'ring curls.
Her movements all were graceful as a fawn's,
And as a fawn unconscious of their grace.
Light was her step as Dryad nymph's what time
They beat the dewy ground in moonlit dance.
Her lovely head she firmly held erect,
As all the world might scan her countenance
To read therein, but virgin purity,
Grave gentleness, and pensiveness begot
Of often converse with the peaceful dead.

So passed she queenly by. A sigh escaped
Her lover's lips, as breaking from his trance
He followed after, keeping still in screen.
Ere long the wood fell back. He crossing now
The open sward, she turning with a smile
To speak her laggard charge, perceived him there,
And startling, blushed like cloud at summer eve
That glowing floats above the couch of day.

Now courteous doffing hat :
                   —' Tis happy chance
Fair maid our meeting.' Then ashamed of craft
Made quick correction. ' Nay, I'll say not so !
I came indeed of purpose, hoping thus
We might encounter. Prithee let me stay !
Since last we met, I've pondered many things,
And chief of those we parleyed. I have set
The stag at large within my park, and round
His neck have hung a circlet, with the saw
" For Agnes' sake." Nay ! look not so disturbed.
Are we not friends by compact, am I not
Your pledged consort in time of adversage ? '

Her head was modest bent, but swift uplift
She gave him grateful look. Now gath'ring hope
From out her aspect, ' Let me share your walk,'
He said, yet diffident as one that courts
Perforce a favour most beyond belief.
' To me as you the woods are more than woods.
They live, they speak, they tell me many things,
While every grove has lore of sprite and fay
And shapes that scorn and mock our feeble ken.'

Here Agnes smiled. ' And is not such a faith
More fit for Trixie here, and foolish folk
Than learned knights and gentles ? See ! she
    laughs
And runs to look for fay in yonder bush.
Yet come you an you will. The woods are free
To all that do no harm to vert or deer
But foin o' season. We were on our way

To view old London, with the spire of Paul's,
From off the mound that hangs o'er Kitty's cave.

Now went they through the woods, the little maid
Oft glancing at the knight with widespread eyes
And grasping Agnes' kirtle. She now moved
More thoughtful, while her bosom rose and fell
As pleasing thoughts were chequer'd still with
    doubt,
And wish and fear were set in counterpoise.
So some short time in silence. Afterward
Attaining where the waving bracken grew
More freely on the hilltop, and the trees
Stood more apart and gave a broader view
Of shelving hill and bosky dell, with here
And there a cot or grange amid the green,
The knight again brake silence. 'Sweetly fair
It is, but yet how lonely! Fear you not
To range these woody wastes all unattent?'

'Not so,' she made him answer. 'Where is fear
Where love abideth? I am not alone
Although I roam these spreading woods among.
Are not good spirits ever in the air
To minister to them that love their Lord?
I know I love Him!—Would indeed 'twere more!—
But yet I love Him, and betimes I deem
To hear Him speak me in the passing breeze
That laps my cheek or plays amid my hair.
Not seldom too, when all is very still,
As if the wood and e'en the busy world
Were given o'er to Death, and he were full,

I feel Him in the depth of silence. So
Am never lonesome.

　　　　　　　　　I am known beside
To all; and who would harm a neighbour maid !
" 'Tis Mistress Agnes ! "   " Good day " or " Good
　　e'en "
From all I counter.—Once indeed a churl
Beset me, so I called aloud and then
Came help incontinent ; while, hapless, he
Fled faster for the bolt, that followed on
For all my pleading !

　　　　　　　　　See, now there is Paul's ! '
She said soon after when the hilly crest
They reached and gazed adown the wooded vale.
' There, where its spire o'ertops yon fleecy cloud,
As if 'twould pierce the very dome of heaven,
And grateful of the skill that lift it up
Would Godward bear the praise of prayerful men !
I fain would see it close. But all agree
The way's too long, and all the road beset
With beggar robbers. Tell me ! is the place
So beautiful, with pillars tall as trees,
And massy roof, stone-ribbed that aches the neck,
And windows vast, and aisles that might enfold
A hundred hamlet churches ? '

　　　　　　　　　' Vast indeed ! '—
The knight made answer, marv'ling at the light
That lit the maiden's eyes the while she spake.—
' Is London's pride, and grand and beautiful

Its organs pompous roll,—but still to me
Dearer by far the chapelry, where late
I met a maid more beautiful than all
Paul's chisel'd saints and painted effigies.'

A shade swept o'er her face.—' Come, Trixie, come,'
She said and hastened on. But yet her breast
Heaved strangely too ; and did she stoop to hide
The blush that sudden crimson'd cheek and neck ?
Perhaps, but yet her look was calm as e'er
When next she spake and showed him in her hand
A forest flower, and smiling gave the saw,
' Poor ragged Robin blooms amid the hay
When tapers burn for bright Saint Barnaby,'
Is't not a pretty wilding ? Do you love
Our woodland bents, as well as trees and groves ?
What were life's pathway, rugged at the best,
If unadeckt with flowers ?   Sweet summer friends !
I never tread them down with careless foot,
Nor pass them by unheedful. Gems they are
Escaped from Eden, ere th' archangel shut
Its golden gate for ever ! Sometimes I
Behastening home at eve, have harmed a bud
That seemed of love to greet me. Then I've stooped
And kist the broken darling.—Ah you smile !
Was't then so foolish ? '

                        ' Nay, sweet mistress, nay !
I had been bruised and doubly for such kiss ! '
So said the knight, then paled, a sudden throb
His wound bestowing. Faint with pain he blanched,
Then grasped a bough and breathless stood awhile.

The damask fading out her sunny cheek,
She startling looked him o'er with anxious look.
' What is it then, Sir Henry ? Do you ail ?
Can I do aught ? '

                He laughed, ' Nay shame is mine
To show such schoolboy blanching. It is naught
But part-healed scratch that gave me sudden
     twinge.'

' There is no war afoot, you should be hurt.'
She gravely said. ' Yet natheless I am sad
To know you suffer. Count me so your friend
To give what aid I may.'

                 ' Indeed 'tis naught
Fair leech,' the knight replied. ' Far deeper wound
Dan Love befetched me, not so long ago.
But this same scratch, by Peter ! never brawl
Bestowed, as you misdeem, but honest fight
For life and purse, a week agone, within
The wood by Copt Hall warren.'

                    In her eyes
He read distress.—' Indeed 'tis truly naught !
King Henry's cloistral laws have left the land
Rich legacy of begg'ry ! Hangmen now
Are ropers best consumers. Death, forsooth,
Has never pinch like hunger. Men must live,
While sorry laws make ever knaves ! So now
An honest man has much ado to keep
His purse from playing changeling at a call,
And guard his head from clubbing ! '

'Tell me more,'
She said, he silent.—'Joyce proclaims you brave
And gentle '—Here she stayed, as discomposed
The knight should know her thoughts had been of
    him.
Then blushing added—' Woodward Joyce is friend
To me, as more to you, so 'tis not strange
That he should talk of you but yesternight.
But here's the camp! And see! the bracken
  grows
More grossly broad and tall, luxuriate
In dust of buried men.—Your cheek is pale
As pain still held you. Pray you rest awhile!
Here where yon beech, twin-boled, o'erhangs the
    mound
And wide disparted yields sequester'd seat,
I often sit and feign me many things.'

Thus urged he spread his cloke, o'erjoyed to win
Such all unlooked for mateship. Side by side
Now sat they—Trixie playing at their feet—
Sometime in silence, silence eloquent
As orat'ry, when hearts in unison
Leap at a look, and sigh responses sigh.
Ah! day of days when first a maiden knows
Herself beloved. When first her timid eyes,
Of virgin love illumed, are lifted up—
Part veiled part wondrous—lifted but to fall
Confused, abashed at deeper fiercer gaze.
And Agnes knew herself beloved and knew
Her lover brave and virtuous. Knew him true

In thought and purpose.   One, too, that his Queen
High-honoured and designed for lofty place.

But knowing this, her heart was sorely tried.
She, simple village maid—though beautiful
And learned more than many a courtly dame,—
How could he stoop to mate with her, and not
Forego his fortunes, Queen and courtly friends ?
Such penalty for love were all too great !
She could not love, who thus could disarray
Her lover of his garnish. Least of all
Could Agnes Leigh thus spoil her noble fere.

Thus thinking, in her soul grew stern resolve.
Quick rising up—' Come, Trixie, we must home ! '
She said, enfolding to her breast the child.
' The sun is kissing High Beech shaw, 'tis hint
We were at Fairmead, and Sir Henry More
Again on's way to London and the Queen.'

He fain had stayed.   But reading in her look
Resolve he could not conquer, howe'er fought,
Stilled on his lips the wistful words that love
Had wellnigh shafted, and complaisant bowed.
' Your pleasure is my duty.' Only this
He said, but with a meaning. Now they turned
Again and passing through the hollow, roused
A fallow deer, asleep beside the stream.

He flying, scatter'd scent of mint and thyme,
And shook the woodbine twirl, till all the path

Was odorous with floating sweets, most meet
For maiden fair, and noble swain, and thoughts
Born of the lovegod mild!

                        Against the gate
They parted. She with half-averted face,
Bidding adieu full coldly, though her cheek
Burned damask, and her eyes with wistful light
Were all afire, what time he lifted up
The child, and kissed the baby lips, that smiled
Contented welcoming to soft caress
Of gay-deckt gallant.

                    Agnes' hand he took
And lifted to his lips. Unwonted thrill
Enkindling at the touch—'Farewell! Farewell!'
She hasty said, and hurried in to hide
Her bosom's tumult. Trixie coming in
A moment after, full of babbling glee,
Quick, Agnes caught her up, and blushing hushed
The prattling lips with—'Playmate, tell no tales!'
Then to herself—'That kiss was meant for me.
It lingers still—I do but take my own.'
So kissed her o'er and o'er, then sat her down
To quell in household task distressful thought.

V

The Queen was wed.   From spire to spire the tale
Rang out and all the realm was full of noise.
But not of joy ; too full the folk of dread
And hatred of the Spaniard.   Evil days
Bethreat'ning, some, took flight incontinent
For Lucerne or Geneve.   Of nobler mould,
The most remained to dare what might befall,
Death at the stake, or dungeon, worse than death.

But this apart, the Chingford bells were rung
While holiday was made upon the green.
The pipe gave forth its strident call to dance ;
The tabor drummed and jingled ; garlands wreathed
The shaft ; while circling lads and lasses filled
The air with mirth and laughter.   Booths were set
A mighty elm beneath, whose goodly boughs
Stretched every way, more lordly than the oak
Its older comrade.

         Here the grand-dams sat
And gossiped, while their goodmen willing quaffed,
In honour of the Queen, if not her spouse,
Full draughts of old October.   Ancient quip,
And oft-told jest, or merry tale, with these
Held sway ; the lightsome pleasure of the dance,
Or frolic catch and kiss, forbad of age.

A little way removed, as shunned of all,
A beldam sat, her wrinkled hands and chin

Upon a stick strange carved and intertwined.
As ebon still, her scraggy elfin locks ;
And bright her sunken eyes, that restless turned
From lad to lass, goodman and wife, and all
That came within the ken of malice look.
It happening now that Joyce passed careless by,
She called him—harsh her voice as shriek of jay—
' Ho ! Geoffrey Joyce !   Good Geoffrey, hark awhile !
Where's she, I say, your sweeting, Mistress Leigh ?
Can she not foot a measure for her Queen ?
Ho ! Ho !   These lollard maids !   'Tis heathenhood
To trip about a garland-shaft, with lads,
Who hustling kirtles, snatch a willing kiss.'
So said she weirdly laughing,—but a frown
Of deep resentment spread o'er Geoffrey's face.

' And what,' he sternly asked, ' is Agnes Leigh
To you, good mistress Savill, you should reck
Whether she sport or other ?—She is not
Your fere for devil-dance, or blackman feast
O' nights in Monkwood hollow ! '

                              Bitter laughed
The beldam.   ' Nay, friend Joyce, keep civil tongue,
Hadst better ; while for Mistress Agnes Leigh
There's storm a-brewing.   Best, my lad, be friends !
The rack's worse work than dancing late o' night
With fire-tongued pipers ; and the faggot-flame
More scorching morsel far for maids, than feast
With wild stormriders.'

'Out upon you hag!'
The reeve replied in fury. 'Devil dam,
Go seek your wizard crew! Your sabbath court
Will end ere long. I would there were a law,
To burn each hell-cat sorceress ; or else
Your demon prenticeship were at an end,
And your foul master claimed you. Witch away!
I'll have thee ducked for railing. Hector here
Has better sense than Christian men. He'd tear
Thee limb from limb, and gladly.'

Thus the reeve,
His anger conq'ring fear, though thrice he crost
His brow and breast, and flung his doublet ope.
She cruel sneered and shook her skinny hand—
'Good youth I'll mind thy threat. When next there's
    court,
I'll have thee registered in Satan's book.
And Mistress Leigh, so, ho! the Lollard jade!
The ducking stool, brave lad! In sooth the pool
Thou'lt want ere long for other need, yet not
Put out the flame that laps her dainty limbs.
Wilt look in's glass ?—I'll show thee wondrous sport.'

She hobbling off, Joyce crost himself again,
And sore disturbed in mind went other way.
Alone within the wood he spake his thought.
'This piping irks me! Evil days forsooth
All men foretell—this match begot of hell.
God wot! there's ill enough, we want no more
At Spanish hand. For Mistress Agnes now,

Sir Henry loves her; best to speed his suit.
He may protect her.   All I can I'll urge
Herself to favour loyal lover, such
A royal dame might count his wooing gain.
So! Here's the letter! Doubtless in the church
Or graveyard I may find her.   Happy day!
That sees her wed and safe in husband's arm.
For me I'll never wed.   Too good is she—
None other good enough.   But he's the choice
I would persuade her.   Grant them happy days!'

The churchyard gained, Joyce looked him all about,
A stile there was that overhung a mead
With grassy path that lead to Edmonton.
Midway the river, like to glittering snake,
Wound here and there through low and rushy banks.
The broad-stepped stile o'ershadowed by an oak
Made pleasant seat, and here the maiden sat
To list the bells' glad music. Sweetly sweet
It was, the welkin full of harmony,
That floating, now, was soft as virgin dream
Of love, and now, was loud as tempest shout
Through mighty trees.   As sound of surf on shore
Borne inland on the breeze, betimes it was
Then loud-voiced like the storming of sea caves
Whose mermaid denizens pursued, bemoaned
The fierce assault and wooing of the waves.

With upturned face she sat, her parted lips
Soft smiling, all her soul within her look.
'She is a spirit, come awhile to earth'

L.L.   O

The woodman said. 'Just such an angel face
Looks down at Waltham out the abbey roof.'
Still unperceived, his staff against a stone
He struck and so recalled the maid to earth.
Disturbed she turned, then smiling, shut the book
That lay upon her lap and gave her hand.
'Good neighbour, you are welcome, though you mar
My musing and disperse a troop of friends
Invisible to all but only me.'

'Good spirits tend you ever, Mistress Leigh ! '
He said, then took from out his breast a scroll.
'These from Sir Henry More. His serving man
Came with them yestereve. Himself must keep
At Winchester awhile.'

                              Her lovely face
Looked doubly lovely now. A moment fell
Her eyes before the woodman's earnest gaze,
Then met his frankly. Very soft and low
Her tones and clear—

                         'Sir Henry More is kind
To think of lowly me. Yet am I glad
To have such constant friend ; and Joyce, the more
You ever speak him hon'rable and true.'

She took the note, that fluttered in her hand,
The while her quick gaze travelled down the page.
Joyce all observant, what time now she bent
Her head yet deeper, made resolved reply—
'Aye, good and true ! None like ! His word is sure.

Courts have not changed him. Mistress Leigh, the
    maid
He chooses, is most honoured in his choice!
He's pow'rful with the Queen ; and there are days
When power at court, and that alone, may make
The turn twixt life and death. So should he choose
Him out a wife, from high or low estate,
If she be wise, she'll gladly say him yea,
And that right quickly.'

                 Here the woodman paused
To mark how speeded home his friendship shaft.
Then bolden'd of her blushes, spake again
In earnest pleading—

            ' Agnes ! Mistress Leigh !
I am true friend in saying, scorn you not
The noblest heart in England. Were I you,
As you, indeed, are she Sir Henry loves,
With love as true as star to pole, I'd leap
To meet his love as fast as fawn to doe
When direful danger threatens—Danger ! There !
The word is out. Forgive me when I say,
Would God I now might greet you Mistress More.
There's harm abrooding, be you sure. Ere long
This Spanish match will work all England ill.
For nowadays three men are hardly met,
But, such the folly ! two will disagree
And daggers draw, for singing of a mass
Or lighting of a taper.—I'll ne'er join
In such mad trifling. Let them burn who will !

For me enough to guard the royal deer
Each day, and say a pater at its close.
But now what says the letter ?—Word of love ?
If so take friendly reed. Bethink you well
And give not prudish answer. I would bear—
Did not Sir Henry's body-servant wait
My cot within to take your answer back—
Your greeting to him, an I trudged afoot
From Chingford Green to Winchester, if but
Your word be yea, as Mary grant it be ! '

Thus Joyce in gen'rous love. She heard him out
Then grateful laid her hand again in his.
' Kind friend I thank you !   Gladly would I say
The word you wish, if but at single stroke
To gain a brother such as Geoffrey Joyce.
But I am sore perplext, and for his sake.
He honours me too much.—I'll not deny
I love him, if indeed 'tis love, to love
When loving harms what one the most would bless.—
I would I could resolve ! Yet wait you here,
The bells awhile a-resting from their mirth,
The church is still as grave. I'll in and pray
For Godly guidance.'

                    Kneeling now before
The chancel screen, she laid the letter down
Upon the step, and prayed with childlike faith
For guidance in decision. Coming back
With grave and earnest face—

'Good friend, I go
To write Sir Henry answer.—For yourself—
Sith you so love your foster-brother—this.
I'll wed him, an he promise certain things!
Content you thus! But, Geoffrey, never word
Of this to other. Be you circumspect!
You are my brother now, if all be well!'

A light lit up the woodman's comely face,
As drawing nigh he kissed her lifted hand.
'Sweet Sister Agnes,—if I may be bold
To name you so—your honour is mine own,
From this time forth,—your welfare mine,—your ill
My hurt, yet truly none shall hap that love
Can ward or minish. Be you very sure,
No word of mine shall blush your maiden cheek.
But write you now your letter. Marry! now
There's meaning in the bells and music too,
For all some losel tugs a trifle late.
Dost walk toward the village? 'Void the green.
There's skipping round the pole, and for to-day
Free kissing of the maids; so prithee keep
From view those tempting lips, that none may taste
Without a broken head, Geoff Joyce anigh.'

A little way they went across the fields,
By maple hedge that sweetened all the path.
Then parted; he, to duteous forest walk,
She, home to write her letter. Arduous task
To coquet jade or prude, but not to her
Whose soul was crystal white, and all her thoughts

Pure as the light that threads the firmament
For cheer of wayward earth.

                      The day gone by,
Her task at end ; her charges laid to sleep ;
Her letter writ, and given into hand
Of trusty messenger, she went again
Along the lane to Lippets hill, to view
The Chingford hill-top all ablaze with flame.
'Twas answer'd soon by Lucton ; then the crests
Of Enfield flamed till all the sky was red,
And all the air with wind-borne shoutings loud.

Upon a bank, close cropt, she sat her down
And watched the blaze that bloodied Waltham's tower.
' God grant ! '—she sighed,—' it be not omen ill
For those that love Him after simple wise ;
Nor lean on plausive doctrine ; ornaments
That gaud the eye, but dull the ghostly sense.
But if't should come, and come to me, in love
Lay never more on me, dear Lord, than I
Can bear, thine handmaid, willing unto death,
Yet weak with all a woman's feebleness.'

Thus Agnes prayerful. Sudden in the sky,
Amid the ruddy gleaming of the clouds,
She saw—her spirit for a space released
From bond of flesh and chain of earthly cloy—
Fire upon fire, with stakes and them that hung
Tortured,—to sense of fearstruck crowd, and them
That minister'd to cruel state and law—

But not to her whose inner sight was cleansed.
For, scatheless through the torment fire and smoke,
She saw a royal form glide to and fro,
With uplift hand that shrank the greedy flame
Like churl at foot of lord. Thereafter laid
Compassionate, on heart and brain of them
That hung supine, they kindling at the touch
Celestial, knew no longer pang of pain,
But sang amid the flame and singing died !

Others, again she saw in dungeon drear
Close manacled, and wrung with anguish throe.
Pallid with cold, yet scorched with hunger fang.
Void of all earthly cheer, but earnest hope
Of God-sent death to bid their dolour cease.
Some yet again were laid on iron bed ;
Nor men alone, but matrons, tender maids,
Unrobed at bidding of lascivious men,
And stretched and torn by fearful engine framed
By devil-craft in man.—All this she saw,
And seeing, in herself felt all the pain,
And shuddering cried—' Lord, can it be Thy will ! '

Now out a neighbouring tree, there burst a song
Loud-voiced and clear, from blackcap full of glee.
All resonant the air, the hymn of joy
Woke in her heart responsive thrill. The tears
Shone in her eyes—her heart was glad—her soul
Commixt with Him, whose breathing gave it birth.
And rising up to tread her homeward way,

The vision gone, she sang with bated voice
Her lollard song, and knew no more distress.

Passions which Thou didst endure,
　Sweete Saviour, for my sake;
My soule's salvation did procure,
　Though earth my bodie take.

My bodie fraile, that oft for sinne
　Must penance do, and feel
Itselfe undone, nor pardon win
　Didst Thou not piteous heal.

Though ache and anguish be my lot,
　And dethe be dethe of paine;
Of Thee, sweete Saviour, ne'er forgot
　I shall newe life attaine.

VI.

An oak there was, that riven, yet was green
And crowned the breezy orest of High-beach hill.
'Twas said the bolt that rived it, fell the day
Bluff Harry shelt'ring in its shade from storm
Was met and curst of frenzied Francis Lane.
This all believed, yet careless made a seat
Of knotty boughs, beneath, by tempests torn
From off the dying tree, and dashed to ground.

Here Agnes sat, one August morn, when sheen
Of sun and radiant sky uplit the land

Refreshed by showers that fell, the overeve,
From clouds that doubtful swept this way and that;
Withholding now—now yielding up their store
Of garnered fruitfulness and foison sweet.

A smile was on her lips. Her eyes were full
Of dreamy thought. And though the landskip lay
Far stretching from her seat, diversified
With sloping meads, and winding roads and paths
Just seen, light threads within a verdant maze;
With hilltop woods, that lay against the sky
Like curly-headed bantlings on the breast
Of some sweet mother, mighty of her love;
She nothing saw, but only in her mind
Perceived and pictured him who came to-day
Her promised lord.

           For now the twain had met
And vows exchanged. Again upon her lips
She felt his trothal kiss—what kiss so sweet!
Again she felt the clasping of his arms
As closely laid against his throbbing breast
She whispered—' Yes, I love thee,' while he swore
To keep her ever in his heart, and guard
As prize more fair than Eden paradise.

But now her thoughts recalled, she looked about,
And lovely in herself, drank double joy
From loveliness in Nature.—' Wondrous fair
Those crystal drops that stud this bramble spray,
Small worlds in truth, but yet how beautiful!

Though kissed to death by all too ardent ray,
Lo! how they gleam and glitter, hundred-hued!
So Semele in ancient story died
Absorbed in hot embrace of Jupiter.
Deep mystery there!—Sir William, rest his soul!
Was ever wont to say, these heathen myths
Had meaning for ourselves.—Would he had lived
To know his childmate happy in the love
Of worthy suitor!—Let me read again
The pretty song he sent me yestereve,
With promise of his coming—better still.

Morning Song.

Wake Agnes! Wake! Night's spectral shades have
    fled
Aurora's steeds before, and seek their bed
Deep, deep i' the mirky sea. See! Morn bestrews
Out her full lap replenteous, thousand hues
O'er all the orient sky! Awake! Arise!
Mark yonder star dissolved in kindling skies!
'Tis Lucifer! that ling'ring pales his ray
Amid the flush of crimson-pinioned day.
See! too, how Cynthia, stainless queen, awhile
Her night-worn car arrests, so she may smile
Upon thee, ere beneath the forest verge
She sink to claim the rest her vigils urge.

Lo! now the sun, 'neath cloud-wrought canopy
Of glittering gold, resumes his sovranty.

Kissing the morn, that trembling, panting, weeps
Joyous at his embrace, and weeping, steeps
In sheeny dew each bud, and bell, and flower,
Whose glistening cup perfumes fair Flora's bower !
Up ! Up ! The lark seeks yonder roseate cloud
On flashing pinion borne. Ecstatic, proud,—
Where blazoning gold o'erlays his purple wings—
He hails the new-throned sun, and welcome sings ;
Flooding the sky with such melodious sweets
That cloud to cloud, th' impassioned strain repeats ;
Till earthward borne, refreshful Nature wakes
From drowse and sleep, and swift her couch forsakes
To lave her emerald locks, and fresh her brow
In love-lit Morn's impulsive overflow.

Agnes ! see Aurora here,
Beckoning at thy casement clear !
Flora with her smiling stands
Garlands streaming from her hands.
Haste thee ! Quit thy maiden bed !
She will tress thy virgin head,
Tint thy cheek with vermeil dye,
Stol'n from out th' enkindling sky,
Arm thy glance with housling fire
Born of love and pure desire ;
Crown thee morrowings fairest queen
High in soul as in demean.
Thou canst ne'er such gifts despise,
Agnes wake !   Arise ! Arise !

The Tyrian tints of the morn must fade,
        And fading die.   .

The 'broidery pearls on leaf and blade
    Must heav'nward fly.
These in the wave of advancing day,
These in the morn's affervid ray.
Flora ere long to her bower must hie,
Lest Phoebus too fiercely inflaming the sky,
The glare of the noon, with its sweltering heat
Too full on her dearlings should lighten and beat.
Then Agnes arise, and forsake .thy bed
Ere Flora, Aurora, and the Morn be sped!

    Wide! Wide! your crystal gates
Unfold, ye nymphs of golden-sandalled day!
    Behold! my lady waits,
Impatient all to tread morn's lightsome way.
    Let forth the flood of light,
    That all the murmurous night,
Ye have confined within your stargirt walls!
    For her exalted gaze,
    Nor heaven's supernal blaze,
Nor blinding beam of dazzling day appals.
For she hath shared of Aurora's cup
And tost the Elysian goblet up.
    Now shall she ride
    On the roseate tide,
And list how wave to wave melodious calls.

    Agnes know,
    The day must go,
Back to the womb of devouring Night!

Agnes think!
We near the brink
Of the deep, whose billows incessant arise
Tost from its bosom to challenge the skies.
Evermore chaunting funereal strain,
With ever for burden wave-wakened refrain—
Life is naught but the foam o' the sea
Of Time, firstborn of Eternity!

Dull thought begone! Away!
Back to your sunless cells,
Where black Discomfort dwells,
Your mother—she of black-browed chaos born.
Back to your caves forlorn!
Nor longer dare intrude
With envious mien and rude
Your sullen shapes where Agnes decks the way.

But oh! ye thoughts serene,
Of winsome shape and mien,
Ye sportive nymphs of Love in aëry dress,
Come in your daintiness,
And Agnes greet with virgin mirth and song.
For ye to her belong,
Your gentle queen, and ye shall drive afar
Each envious shade that nears her triumph car.
Now lovely by her side,—
Your mistress and your pride,—
Ye joyous sit, and guide her proud-stept steeds.
She all your music heeds,
While blissful ye, from out her lustrous eyes
Fresh rapture take, to fire your symphonies!

So, Agnes, mayst thou ride, secure from harm,
With gentle fancies girt, and music's charm,
Adown the stream of life ; while Love shall lend
His crimson wing to fan thee, and shall blend
All hours in one sweet morn, till morns shall end.

The paper read with often pause and smile
She hid it in her bosom, sighing low—
' How much he loves me ! Everywhere my name
Inwoven in his song.'   Then looking round
Beheld him standing by, and springing up
Was clasped in eager arms.   None there to see
How oft her lips he worshipped with his own,
Drinking rich draught of happiness ; while she
Clung timid, Helen-like for loveliness,
And blushing like Aurore at Phoebus' kiss.
' My queen ! My queen ! '—twixt every kiss he said—
' I love you, sweeting ! Agnes, love you me ? '
She answering aye, with tender look and sigh
And pressure of the hand that locked her own.

Now moving slow they sought the deeper woods,
She sometime gazing up with modest glance ;
But yet more oft, her soft eyes cast adown
When drawn of guardian arm her curly head
Drooped on his shoulder, while her sunny brow
He mated with his lips.
                        The ring-dove cooed
His spouse and frequent, as he bade her see
True lover mortals, souls impulsed as one.

The deer went trooping by, all unafeared.
The woodlark, jocund, poured his blithest strain
Above them, as he welcomed worthy mates
To his green solitude, and waited oft
Whene'er they loiter'd to renew his lay.
The very trees seemed glad of their approach,
And yet more softly sang their breeze-born song
' Earth children, come ! within our leafy shade
Repose ye, rest ye, dream love's opiate dream ! '

At last she spake, unclosed a little way
His clasping arm, so she might deeper gaze
Within his truthful eyes, ' I cannot deem
It aught but phantasy—a wizard dream
Awaiting waking.—I who never thought
To have such gift, such priceless gift of love,
As all unworthy ! ' Here her trembling lips
He closed with kiss and protest. ' You are she
I'd choose from out ten thousand ! None so sweet
So lovely and so worthy ! '—
                                Sank her head
Again upon his shoulder. Afterward—
'There is a glamour on you, Henry, so,
You may not see aright. A village maid
Am I, a little learnèd, an' you will,
In godly books, all out the love of one,
Who, lonely as the golden star of Eve,
Took pity on me, lonely as himself,
And, taught me, how the God-giv'n soul should mate
With all good things in Nature, thus to be
Companion of Himself that made them all.

But woman still, I hunger'd oft—he gone—
For sister or for brother; some fair face
To mirror mine with equal beam of love:
Or goodly mind—beyond my youngling charge—
To link with mine, in spirit sympathy,
And chain of pure affection.—Then you came!'
No more she said, but closer laid her head
Against his breast, while he with lover thrill
Her soft hair kissed again and yet again.

Proceeding now they reached a wattled cot
Beside the path, where dwelled an outcast monk.
From Waltham here—its convent rule suppressed—
Aged and worn he came, 'mid cloistral boughs
And sighing winds less mournful than his soul,
To end in peace his nigh-spent pilgrimage.
Of pity, to his need the forest folk
Administered, while he their care repaid
With orison and blessing, all he had,
Yet much, as gift from lips of godly man.

The cot seemed empty. But the knight at sight
Of cross and wooden platter set outside,
Bestowed an alms. So Agnes too, but sighed
And timid glanced within.
                              'What is't to fear!'
Her lover questioned. 'Nay, he loves me not,'
She said regretful. 'Yet I would be friends,
While long time Joyce has giv'n him alms of me.
But that he knows not, nor how oft o' nights,
When warmly laid within my pallet bed,

I think of him, so harshly pillowing here
On rushen couch, 'mid ague-mist, and strife
Of struggling boughs rude-grappled of the wind,
And pray his soul may have the cheer he scorns
To use his body.—Surely something stirs
Within the hut ! There ! didst not hear a groan ?
And now again ! Perchance the frere is sick.—
I'll look within.'

      'Nay, nay ! the task is mine,'
The knight replied, and quickly entered in.
Behind an osier screen, the old man lay
And moribund, his mis'ry nigh to end.
Beside him lay an empty cup, and eke
A morsel of black bread. Upon his breast
A crucifix he clutched, in vain essay
To lift it to his lips. Of ruth the knight
This did, while Agnes kneeling, piteous wept,
Her gentle heart sore smitten at the sight
Of homeless grey-head priest, within the grasp
Of grisly Death, and, friendless, left to die.

But sudden as they gazed, his eyes unclosed.
He looked around and saw the weeping maid.
He trembled ; then half rose from off his bed
And cried in feeble tone through parching lips—
' Accursèd daughter of accursèd sire,
Seed of unhousel'd bed, what dost thou here ? '
More had he said, but that speech-sealing Death
His hand set on his lips, that vainly moved,
As falling back, he gasped and peaceful died.

L.L.   P

Amazed the knight looked now upon the dead,
And now on Agnes. She with equal doubt
On him, then knelt and prayed through rain of tears
A bidding prayer. Meanwhile a hundred thoughts
Disturbed the knight. Who then and what the maid
So fiercely challenged ? Who and what her sire,
So curst by dying lips of holy man ?
Or was it but illusion—phantasy—
Mindnumbing phrensy of anearing Death ?
But, be she what she might, he loved her still
Void of all thought of change ; and, happy day !
Her love was his, whate'er her hidden state.
So thought he, then o'erbent the kneeling girl,
And loverly upraised her when he deemed
Her prayer at end.

         'Come, sweeting, I will send
Some cotter hither. Tapers shall be his,
And all that fits a good man's funeral,
With obits after for his soul's repose.
But 'tis no place for tender-hearted maid.
Nor sight for gentle eyes, whose piteous pearls
Are ever prone to falling at distress.'

So Henry said and drew the weeping girl
Without the hut ; then turned and closed the door.
In silence now they homeward trod the glade,
The golden sunbeams stealing through the trees
To dance and chequer all the russet floor ;
The light wind whispering ; birds on every side
Athirst with joy that only song could slake ;

All nature joyous, careless, knowing not
Of death, or knowing, fearing naught at hand
Of him earth's shadowy visitant who bids
To other, loftier lot.
                    Sir Henry first
Brake silence.—'Sweetheart, why so dull and sad ?
Set never store on witless babbling. Oft
At death, men's tongues are loosed to little worth,
Restraint of mind forgone. Belike yon priest
Mistook you in his folly for some maid,
Acquaint of better days.'
                        Here Agnes raised
Her face to his with wistful pensive look.
'So thought I at the first, but strangely now
Comes recollection of a place and scene
All unremembered since a mindless child :
I trod a lofty hall with doubtful feet,
Afeared for very vastness of the place,
And stumbling 'mid rush strewings. Something more
But indistinct—a tall grave man in dress
As yours, with sword and poniard in his belt.—
A face or two of women.—Then a flame,
A mighty flame ! and after Chingford cot.'

Sir Henry mused. Then, 'Be you what you may
Or simple village maid, or damosel
Begot of knightly loins—to me for aye
You are my queen, my Agnes, only joy !
Good birth is accident, but loveliness
Dame Nature's own bestowal.—Sweet ! alone
Is good accomptable in good men's eyes.

But beauty wed to goodness ? Happy swain
Is he whose 'tis to compass such rare prize !
Then who so blest as I ? Come, smile again,
Ere long I'll thrid this labyrinth, if so
You will it. Now and presently dispel
These mists of doubt by anodyne of love.'

His proud arm circling now her virgin waist,
Again her eyes lit up with bashful fire.
Her lips half parting, showed the pearly spoil
They hid, the while her bosom rose and fell.
He smiling waited answer, bending low,
Proud of his power to stir such noble soul.
When out the thicket rose a sturdy voice
In cheerful song scarce half a shot away.
' 'Tis Joyce,' Sir Henry whispered, ' well I know
That voice and ditty. Full is he of mirth
And lay and carol as a lark of song.
Still ! love, and hear him ! Here's a heather seat.
My cloke shall do you service, sit you down.'

SONG

WHETHER she praise me, or whether she blame,
　Or pout she or laugh she or sorrow,
For ever to me is my darling the same,
　Good-morrow then, sweeting, good-morrow.
　　　　My queen, I would not have you
　　　　Dull as December day !
　　　　But mistress, pray you, crave you,
　　　　Give love and fancy play !

Spring-time is merrie in coppice and lea,
　When cowslips are nodding and blowing;
Vi'lets are lovely, but never to me
　Such sweets as my sweeting bestowing.
　　　　My queen, I would not have you
　　　　All as the soft Spring-day.
　　　　But mistress, pray you, crave you,
　　　　Give love and fancy play!

Summer is sultry; but laid in the shade,
　On thyme or on tussock of heather,
'Mid murmur of bee, and the sough of the glade
　We kiss and we mock at the weather.
　　　　My queen, I would not have you
　　　　All as the Summer day,
　　　　But mistress, pray you, crave you,
　　　　Give love and fancy play!

Autumn is mellow; the fruit on the tree
　Is ruddy and ready for eating;
Peach, apple or plum, what dainty dost see
　So ripe as the lips of my sweeting?
　　　　My queen, I would not have you
　　　　All as the Autumn day,
　　　　But mistress, pray you, crave you,
　　　　Give love and fancy play!

Winter is restful; there's snow in the street,
　And icicles hang from the gable;
Come kindle the ingle to welcome my sweet,
　So winsome in tippet and sable.

My queen, I would not have you
All as the Winter day,
But mistress, pray you, crave you,
Give love and fancy play !

Here Geoffrey ceased. The knight with laughing face
Rose up, with Agnes blushing at his side—
'My queen, I would not have you
Dull as December day,
But Agnes, pray you, crave you,
Give love and fancy play ! '
Repeated he. Then—'Geoffrey, Geoffrey Joyce,'
Called loudly out, till all the woodland rang.
Halloo ! came back, and soon adown the glade
The reeve came striding, Hector at his heel.
' Good morrow, Mistress Agnes, and again
To you, Sir Hal ! ' he said with merry voice,
While Hector fawning licked the maiden's hand.
' Meseems I sang o' purpose, so to judge
By look of pretty face ! Anon you called,
Sir Hal, so need must be afoot, since third
Makes never company when lovers meet.'

Thus Geoffrey mirthful, till Sir Henry told
Of Waltham's monk, when changed his face to grave.
His brow he crost in haste, and murmured aught
Part prayer part valediction, then replied,
' It shall be done ! Leave all, Sir Hal, to me !
Will Bourne, now somewhat past his hurt, for sake
Of past employ, will cheerly do what needs.
I'll give your message. Twenty years agone,
Or had not royal law broke convent garth,

Brave obsequies were his with pompous dirge.
Well! Well! what matters howso laid to rest,
So grateful hearts speak blessings o'er one's grave,
Or tearful eyes bedew the funeral pall?
What recks the maiden, snatcht her morrowing breath
Of virgin crants and chaplet? Death is death!
Whene'er he comes, unwelcome, and howe'er.—
Now holy Mary grant her beadsman rest!

VII

Limpid mirror of the sky,
Twixt thy shelvy banks of green,
Silent gliding, glistening by,
Cygnet ait and isle between.
    Wavelets murmur soft your song,
    Maidens sweet ye bear along!

Happy thou! Within thy flood
Virgin faces softly gleam;
While escaped from gaoler snood,
Silken tresses kiss thy stream.
    Wavelets murmur soft your song,
    Maidens sweet ye bear along!

Cheeks of damask, red as rose
Waked at morn by virgin kiss;
Teeth of pearl your mirror shows
Naught your love-lit waters miss.
    Wavelets murmur soft your song,
    Maidens sweet ye bear along!

Bodiced bosoms, snowy white,
Where the love-god cagèd lies,
Willing captive, waiting night
Ere his wily craft he tries.
    Wavelets murmur soft your song,
    Maidens sweet ye bear along!

Happy stream, whose waters flow,
Beauty laden, clear and deep;
Beauty such as lovers know,
Visioned only in their sleep.
    Wavelets murmur soft your song,
    Maidens sweet ye bear along!

Thus sung a page, as down Thames' lordly stream
A royal barge swept slowly to its bourne.
'Twas Autumn! But as yet the breeze was soft
The sun still hot as summer still kept court.
While, flamed of golden ray, the silvery flood
Flung back the beam that aëry quivering
Danced rainbow-hued about the barge's side.
The margent woods still fringed the banks with green,
Though golden-patched in places, where some elm
Displayed a burnished bough, or, chestnut donned
Its russet robe—fore-ensign of decay—
Loose-hung and ragged.
                        Overhead there lay
Scarce moving—as within the lucid stream
It loved its own resemblance—one white cloud;
While graceful, here and there, the cygnets swept—
Down-cloudlets they—with wake of crystal sheen.

His song at end, and guerdon rich bestowed
In smile and sparkling eye, the pageling laid
Himself again at feet of her who seemed
The chief amid the maidens. Men were none
To-day among them ; only they that rowed,
And they apart, and out of hearing, ev'n
Of sight betimes, the crimson canopy
Let fall between them. Courtly maidens all,
That waited on the Queen, their converse turned
On statecraft, aye with underlying thought
Of them that ruled. What matters to a maid
Who sways the state, so she, fair despot, sway
One heart, her Eldorado, haply found !

Aweary of the theme, spake one at length
The common thought.—' And tell me, Vere,' she said
With archful look and smile of covert mirth,
' Where goes so oft our knightly paladin ?
Since Chingford hunt he shows an altered face :
Is oft afield and early, late o' nights
Returning. One can scarcely win a smile,
Still less attain to speech.—Our sometime monk
Methinks is snared.—I fear Sir Hal's in love ! '

Vere frowned, and marking laughing mocking eyes,
Made answer hotly—' Prithee ask himself,
Good Mistress Clifford. I—I nothing know.—
Nor care ! What's then to me Sir Henry More ? '—
' Much,' whispered one, whose soft and dimpled arm
Lay round her comrade's neck. ' But she to him
Is naught, and well she knows it.—Were she not
So cruel proud, I'd feel for her despight.

But hurt, she's tigress, and anon she'll spring.
He'll scape, but woe to her that whets her claws!'

Annoyed at smile and whisper, Vere again
Brake forth impetuous—'Sing boy! sing, again!
Coy Gertrude here shall follow. Sing, I say!'
Thus she with angry look. The lad obeyed
With timid glance at one whose kindly eyes
Smiled in reply and chid his mistress' rage.

Song

Under the bushes I lie and I sing,
  La, tra la la! tra la la la!
Mavis he's jealous and preeneth his wing,
  La, tra la la! tra la la la!
He preeneth his wing and he shaketh his poll,
The song that I sing from his mother I stole,
  La, tra la la! tra la la la!

How now, Sir Robin, art blither than I?
  La, tra la la! tra la la la!
Out in the woodland beneath the blue sky,
  La, tra la la! tra la la la!
Chaffinch and cushat a fig for your notes,
Blackbird and throstle come swell out your throats,
  La, tra la la! tra la la la!

Hither, good Jenny, thou pert little thing,
  La, tra la la! tra la la la!
Come and I'll teach thee a carol to sing,
  La, tra la la! tra la la la!

Cuckoo, thou bastard, come hie thee away,
Mate an' thou wilt with the jar and the jay,
   La, tra la la ! tra la la la !

Listen the ditty I learned of the thrush,
   La, tra la la ! tra la la la.
See, there be lovers, laid under a bush,
   La, tra la la ! tra la la la !
Maiden so pretty, come tell me the why
Thy comrade so often should kiss thee and sigh ?
   La, tra la la ! tra la la la !

Now laughter filled the barge. ' A pretty song !
Here's kiss for 't child. Where learned you such a
      lay ? '
Thus she that cheered the lad with kindly look.
' It has a rustic savour. Woodland born
Was he that made it, couched beneath a tree.'—
' In sooth,' the boy replied, ' but yestereve
I had it of Ralph Grey, Sir Henry More
His page as wot you all, and he from one
At Chingford, where he went on matter close,
But not so close I gathered it anon.'

Now lovely heads were laid about the boy,
And eager voices gently urged him on.
Alone of all Vere showed disdainful look,
Though inward, every sense was strained to hear.
' Ralph there goes oft. 'Tis given out to see

One Joyce, Sir Henry's friend and foster-frere.
But more's behind. A maid, he says, as fair
As day, or Mistress Gertrude. That is much
To say I trow.'—Hereat a maiden laughed
Thus open praised. ' A kiss shalt have, good lad,
For such fair speech, but, sweetheart, tell us more
Who is she, Hab ? '
                              'I know not ! I had known
But at the moment came Sir Henry in
And bade Ralph hasten.'
                              Gentle faces now
Wore looks ungentle.   Vere with scornful laugh
Made answer through her pale and quivering lips.
' Some alehouse wench, forsooth, whose pretty face
Has caught Sir Henry's fancy ! '
                              ' Yet 'tis strange ,'
Said one more thoughtful.—' Cosset ! art thou sure ?
'Tis little like Sir Henry More to urge
Some village chit to folly.'—Here again
Vere interposed.—' Run not still waters deep ?
There's wisdom in the proverb. But enough
Of knights and base-born wenches ! Have you heard
The council at its sitting made resolve
By way of parliament to bring to end
The strife twixt truth and Lollard heresy.
So now our out-o'-faiths must turn or burn.
That's news an' if you will ! Now, Kate, beware,
Your goldilocks and pretty face will naught
Against the bishop's sentence.'
                              All aghast
The maiden trembled, white as aspen spray

Bestirred by zephyr.—'Mistress Vere, forbear
Your venom taunts, I am good Catholic.
Yet Holy Jesu keep me safe from craft
Of false-tongued foe!'
                    Vere laughed—'Good Kate, I spake
But japingly. To die for faith needs soul,
And that you lack. Flush hair and ruddy cheeks,
Your mother dow'r. Tell you full oft your beads,
Be seen at mass, make shrift, and flame will ne'er
Assail a tress.'
                    Now anger conq'ring fear,
The girl rose up. Her late so pallid cheeks
Aflame, she stood, with words of fierce retort
And hot remonstrance. Yet was never need,
For springing from his seat, the pageling stood,
Brave scion of brave line, before the maid
And took her hand, and kist it twice or thrice.
'Nay, never heed unkindly look and speech.
My uncle shall protect you. Mistress Vere
Speaks that she knows not. If must be, I'll fight—
Nay, burn—for thee and never flinch a hair!'

Now anger dying out, the maiden's eyes
Shone limpid, as her pretty hand she laid
Upon her champion's head. 'Fair cousin, I
Do thank thee, and will treasure up thy words.
Wilt be my knight? Here's gage of loyalty.'
A golden circlet off her panting breast
She took and wound it round the supple neck

Downbent before her. All about them smiled,
But all were pleased and murmured pleasant words.

Vere bit her lips, but secret in her soul
Was angry with herself and not with him.
' Would God,' she thought, ' I might attain such joy
Of love from him, whose Ethiop slave I'd be,
And guerdon love with love a thousandfold.'

Withal she coldly spake,—' Come hither, sir !
Too forward you,—I'll send you back to Gore.
Remember this, for future, page of mine
Must be less lavish of his tongue.   'Tis writ,
Man cannot serve two masters, less a page
Two mistresses.   Come ! hold me here my book.'
He lothful rising, with resentful look,
To do her bidding—' Tush,' she whispered low,
' I am not vext with you, but wounded sore.
Sit now, I'll sing and give these chits the dor.'

SONG

Glints the river, glides the stream
    Softly, calmly, flowing ;
Willows wave where maidens dream,
    Cheeks and eyen glowing.
Me ! Ah me ! my heart is broken,
Churlish Joy has ne'er a token.

Lilies white as new-fall'n snow,
    O'er the landskip lying ;
Cold as ye my heart I trow,
    Faint and worn with sighing.
Me ! Ah me ! my heart is broken,
Churlish Joy has ne'er a token.

Sunbeam, God-sent imp of light,
  Gladd'ning, glist'ning, glowing,
Thou to me art dull as night.
  Hope nor cheer bestowing.
Me! Ah me! my heart is broken,
Churlish Joy has ne'er a token.

Willow, waving calm and slow,
  O'er the laughing river,
Canst no joy my heart bestow,
  Ne'er from care deliver.
Me! Ah me! my heart is broken,
Churlish Joy has ne'er a token.

Swallow, skimming low and light,
  Lend thy pens I prithee.
Happy! might I wing my flight,
  Ocean over with thee.
Me! Ah me! my heart is broken,
Churlish Joy has ne'er a token.

I'll away where osiers wave
  Dirgeful by the river.
Gladly there I'll make my grave!
  Death from woe deliver.
Me! Ah me! my heart is broken,
Churlish Joy has ne'er a token.

There's for you, mistresses, a doleful song
To suit distressful maiden.' Thus with scorn
Said Vere, her face stern set, her liquid eyes
Aglow with mixt emotions. Then her gaze

She turned upon the river and was still.
They too awhile were silent. Then restraint,
Grown irksome, whispering grew again to speech,
And erelong speech to mirth, another theme
Unlocking tongues. Meanwhile, the page disturbed
By sight of Vere's dejection, laid his hand
Upon her arm, but doubtful of her mood,
With half beseechful look. She, looking round,
Beheld the boyish comforter and gave
Him gracious smile for guerdon. Sudden then
His hand took in her own, and set an arm
About his neck, but uttered never word.

But now proud Wolsey's stately pile attained
The pennoned barge was moored beside the pier.
Attendants hast'ning, brought the maids to land.
Who gleeful made for court and palace hall.
But Vere remained apart, with gesture proud
And look forbidding question. With her stayed
The page of duty. 'Cosset, I would walk,'
She said, the rest withdrawn their several ways,
'Enough of idle gossip for a morn.'
By terraced walk and devious path she went,
Slow moving, till within the wilderness
She sat her down beneath a thorn, long time
In silence brooding. Rising up at length,
With haughty lift of hand—"The maze is nigh,
Come thither, boy!' Now in and out she wound,
The way well known, till, in its secret heart.
Again she rested. Sighing now she bade
Her wondering pageling seat him at her side.

Again her arm caressed his boyish neck,
As bending down she kissed him on his cheek.
And after, searched his eyes with quest'ning look—
Brave honest eyes of hazel, flinching not
For all her fiery gaze. As satisfied
The lad was true, and she might safely bend—
' And am I then so hard a mistress, Hab,
Thou hast no love for Catherine de Vere ? '
He halting in his speech with doubtful words,
She bitter laughed. ' Nay, boy, but now thy tongue
Was fluent as the sea for Kate Lestrange.
But then you twain are children still, some day
You'll wake to find her woman—fair one too !—
She, proper man in Herbert Pole.—What now !
Art so far gone ? Dear lad, that blushing face
Betrays thee. So ! that glistering chain, forsooth,
Tells double tale. But yet thou hast not asked
My leave to wear it. Still no tongue ? Poor boy !
Must mine then service both ? '

                              Ceasing now
From badinage, she spake in kinder tone—
' When late I took you out your father's hall,
I gave my troth to service you in all.
De Vere keeps ever faith. Wear then the chain,
And may it presage lifelong happiness,
God and all-hallows willing ! '

                              Now the lad
Brake forth impetuous.—' I would love you well
Did you but let me ! But betimes you show
So cold I think you never friend to me,
And sorely wish myself again at home.'

L.L.   Q

Vere smiled—' 'Tis said by some that range afar
There are vast mountains in the further deeps,
Snow-clad, ice-capped, that yet within their womb
Breed flame eternal, sometime bursting forth
To plume their crests with wavy pens of fire,
And paint their nether plains with horrid glow.
If, cosset, then, betimes I show so cold,
'Tis but a seeming frostiness; beneath
Is fire enough to lift you into heav'n,
If so I did but will it.   Trust me then.
And I am cold, with summer-soft caress,
Then thaw me, Hab! Like snow in May I'll melt
At threat of southern gale.—Is't now a pact?'

Abruptly now she changed the theme, the boy
Won over wholly.—'Tell me now—this jade!—
This Chingford slut!—and is she then so fair?'
'So Ralpho says, and courteous as a dame.
Of goodly presence, yet not over tall;
With watchet eyes like wells for depth of blue:
And step as light as tread of upland fay.
And when she smiles, Ralph says——'
                            'Enough, enough!
Goodlack! if thus you younglings prate of maids,
Forsooth, there'll be but few when you are men!
Yet, cosset, tell me, can you better keep
Your mistress' secrets, than this braggart boy
His master's?—Well, I ween Sir Henry More
Would trounce him, known the wagging of his tongue.'

He promising with eager speech, and oath,
Checked on his lips by touch of jewelled hand—

'Nay, sweetheart! nay! Ne'er soil these pretty lips
With uncouth speech! Leave oaths to bearded men.—
This then I wish. Learn all you can from Ralph,
Of message and pursuit.—Where dwells the maid?
Her station and—aye, that indeed may prove
Brave weapon to my hand—her faith. In full,
Find out whate'er you can, but all by craft,
With never word of me in all the quest.
Show careless oft, as 'twere but idle mood;
And sometimes contradict, to urge the more
Your comrade to assertion. Naught in this
I purpose but for good, yet secret be
As miser over store.—And now, awhile
We'll join the rest. Childlike, the revelry
You'd doubtless share. Ah me! would I were child!'

VIII

Now Autumn waning, Winter 'gan to spread
His frosty breath o'er mead and hill, and whirl
Amid the woods, and toss the ruddy leaves
About the rimy way. Yet still the year,
As loth to farewell Autumn's fruitful reign,
Betimes was mild and gracious, genial days
O'ertaking gelid nights, and summer breaths
Succeeding blustrous gales. The air was rich
With scent of fallen leaf, and fresh-turned field;
And loud with caw of idle rook, and cry
Of gate-perched urchin twirling clapper toy.

The day was clear withal, and calmly still
When Henry More resought the Chingford wood.
The blue smoke, out the cottage chimney-top
That crowned the leaf-strewn hill, rose thinly up
Amid the elm-tree's yellowing branches tall.
The beeches all were bare, but these as yet
Refused to doff their golden-fringèd robe
So late put on ; while, still about the meads
The monarch oaks stretched out their umbrous arms,
In careless grace of strength ; no leaf surrent
To bidding of the blast, that followed on
The footsteps of the frost, like plunderers
In rear of warfare, stripping fallen foe.

Beyond rose up the woods, rich-purpled, where
The noonbeam lit them—blacker on the slope
And sombre as the pall of hearse-borne dead.
Save where some holly, glassy green, stood out,
Disdainful, 'mid the pollard borde, and laughed
Defiance at white winter's wuthering call.
All overhead the rooks with rugged throats
Made answer to the breeze, or pattering fall
Of chaliced acorns careless cast adown ;
Rich Danae shower, swift sought of noisy swine,
That now were free to roam the thinning glade
Till fall of eve and wind of keeper horn.

Unmoved the knight beheld the scene—his thoughts
Fast fixed on her, his gentle cynosure
So menaced and so dangered. What could she
So mild and helpless, did malignant tongue,

Or conscience-twisting zealot, name her now;
' Out of belief ?—Or what, if ta'en to task
By cold stern men, relentless ?—Men who deemed
They did their God good service, by restraint
Of all their God-giv'n instincts.—Mercy, grace,
And charity dethroned at bid of faith,
And dungeoned-deep of duty, falsely called.
And brooding thus—' Fools ! fools ! wit-starving
    fools ! '
The knight exclaimed, as o'er a fresh-sown field
He gazed, but idly, resting at a gate.
' For never evil done,—but only thought
Adverse to thought,—to prison,—torture,—burn !
And think to serve their life-bestowing King
By slaying of His image ! "

                  Now arose
Nor far removed the scarecrow's strident note.
Which heard, Sir Henry muttered—' Yonder clown
Has ears to hear, and tongue withal to prate.
Here's court'sy for your warning, honest lout !—
' Tis folly now to voice conceit.   God wot !
His pleasant world were hell, could man read man
Without the aid of speech !

                My queen ! those lips
That trill so softly in my ears, must learn
To prison language, and be wisely still.
Dear God forbid that jealous swain should set
The bishop's bloodhounds on the harmless track
Of my fair doe ! "

             So sighed he as he turned
Thoughtful away.   Erelong, her humble home

The view disclosing—' Agnes, every straw
That roofs thy cot is precious, and for thee
The very bird that perches on the sill
Far comelier than his mates, and aye his song
More rich and tuneful, since he sings to thee ! '

Thus he anigh, while she,—Ah ! spell of Love !—
As she had heard her lover's voice, drew nigh
Her casement and beheld him where he stood
Amid the whirling leaves and bracken sere.
Now, fired of love, the rich blood flushed her face
To deeper beauty. Then her little hand
She waved in greeting and came quickly down.
Now blushing—' Henry !—And to-day ! But yet
It is no portent. All the morn my thoughts
Would run on you, and so you come. See now
How magnet love can draw us at its will.'
So said she laughing, all her peerless face
Aglow with guileless pleasure. Quickly now
He took her hand and kissed it. ' Dearest, come
Awhile with me away from field and cote.
I have a matter I must forthwith tell,
Of utter moment, none may hear't beside
Our very selves. Put on your snood and cloke,
And come away from ken of eave-drop knave.'

The graveness of his face now robbed her own
Of blush and smile, ' Dear love, I'll come and soon,'
She said with trembling accents. ' Go you on.
Await me by the thorn. A little while
And I will follow. Go you then before.'

In haste she left him. Slowly he withdrew
And sought the thorn, the trysting thorn, blood-red
With ripened haw, and sat upon the log
That lay beside, and list the robin's song,
Who perched on upper spray, his liquid notes
Trilled soberly for psalm at eventide.

Soon Agnes came. Her willing, yielding hands
He took in his, and set her by his side.
Then ardent gazed deep down into the lake
The soft cerulean lake of her pure eyes.—
'My queen, I love you! Never harm shall light
Upon this golden head while life is mine,
And strength is left to guard it. This my queen
Doth surely know. But, Agnes, yestereve
The parliament—God vex it for the deed!—
Did re-enact the laws King Edward purged
From out the book 'gainst Lollardy. Nay, worse,
Enacted others, such, a careless word
Or even look may peril liberty,
Perchance lose life. This drew me here to-day,
In haste, to warn my darling, lest by speech
Or 'haviour she should jeopardize her weal
And break her lover's heart.—So hide away
Your harmful books. Forget your Lollard lore,
And next when mass is sung, conceal your soul,
And worship with the rest. All else I'll take
Upon myself, but this must Agnes do
For love of me.'
                    With sad and troubled face
She heard him to the end, then deeply sighed—

'I love you, Henry! Yea, I love you true,—
I cannot say how much, and for your sake
I'll hide my books and keep a careful tongue.
But more I may not—dare not!—Can I bow
The knee to Baal, shaped in shape of bread?
All holy things forfend!—My own, my lord,
The rather bid me worship thee, for thou
At least art man, and represent of God,
So 'twere the smaller sin. Christ aid me now
In this my strait, for I am but a maid,
And weak, while pain and misery are strong!'
But here a light illumed her pallid face
As angel wing had touched her cheek and filled
Her soul with blessing out supernal height.
And sudden rising up with claspéd hands,
And eyes uplift to heaven, life's only hold,
She cried in tones that thrilled him through and
    through—
'Yet are we more than conquerors through Him—
The mighty Lord of all—that loveth us!'

Too beautiful, too lofty in her look
She seemed for earth. Sir Henry, awestruck, gazed
Through film of tears that blurred his ardent sight.
Full noble-minded he, he could not speak
A word to shake her purpose, only gazed
With pleading eyes that urged the more, for tears
Unwonted, not unwelcome. Now she came
Again, and tearful also, kissed his brow—
'My love! my love! and if the Master will,
My sometime lord—think not my heart is cold

Because I dare not do this evil thing.
Ah no! Ah no! Bethink you yet again:
I love you well, but must I then deny
My God and Lord? Indeed I love you well!
And ne'er as now you do not urge to ill,
Nor tempt me of my weakness, nor of love
Make devil-engine to assault my soul.
Full well I know you would not change your faith
For aught but force of faith-compelling truth.
What good man could? And so unworthy mate,
Of worthy lord, were I to show less true.
Say yes to that, my darling. Give the heart—
That beats for you and only next to God—
The comfort of your blessing, thus distressed.

Her pleading hands he set against his lips
That trembled as he made her meet reply—
'Yea, God forbid, that I should urge my queen
For life or death to wrong her noble soul!
But only if you suffer, I must bear
Your dolour thousandfold.—And should you die,
Ah me! that e'er such fiendish thing could be!—
I also die, a death of life-long woe,
Too slow destroying while it keeps from thee.'

Her head she laid upon his lifting breast,
Her grateful ears drank in the loving words,
But only sighs made answer.
                              'Is there not,'
He urged her now,—'My Agnes, other way?
Say, yes—say. yes and I will wed thee straight

And fly the Court for Zurich.' Proudly now
She lift her head.—'I love thee, Henry, well,
But sith I do, I will not drag thee down
To level of an alien. You are high
In favour of the Queen. To mate with me
Against her will were but to blast your hopes
Of honour and advancement—hopeless make
Your efforts to befriend God's faithful folk,
As pledged to me when first I pledged my love.
Nay, never so, but let us wait the will
Of Him that placed us each in several state.
You, noble, of your greatness to solace
Whate'er you may, His people in distress ;
Me, humble, to confess, perchance to win
Life's proudest guerdon, crown of martyrdom.'

With hasty clasp, he drew her to his breast.
' Nay, speak not thus ! Forbid the very thought !
'Tis like invoking Satan to his worst,
And tempting of the doom we most do dread.
Is there indeed none other way ?—At Bourne,
Wilt hide thee, love, away ? My people there
Are staunch, and, if the fame be not untrue,
My steward Benson, Lollard in his heart.
But 'tis an honest swain of wit and worth,
Who now would serve our purpose. Say then, love,
Wilt hide with him till better may appear ? '

' So would I do and gladly, dearest heart,'
She made reply with sad and wistful smile—
' But cannot. 'Twas but yestereve I spake
True word to mistress Marg'ry not to leave

Her pallet, she all surely failing now.
Yet more at Bourne, should treachery hap, on you
Might evil fall for harbourage of me.
It may not be! Abide we still and wait
God's purpose, sure no harm can happen each,
Unwilling He.—Hark! love, how yonder bird
Full-throated trills his simple song unmoved
At threat of nearing winter. Yet the blast
Fills all the glade with fluttering leaves, that sere
And shrivelled, tell the tale of frosty fang,
Their late affliction. See his bloodied breast!
God's gracious recognition of the deed
He did what time, distrest, he plucked the thorn
From out the Christ-god brow, so he might give
Him all he could of solace.'
                                        Thus the maid,
What time the bird with swelling breast poured forth
An ampler song as conscious of her praise,
Then plumed his wing and flew a little off,
Her mild gaze following, while she pensive blessed
Him in his covert. Deeply moved, the knight
Her hand lift to his lips and so recalled
Her thoughts to earth and him.

                              ' Enough! Enough!
It shall be as you will. I'll urge no more.
E'en as you will, so be it! All my soul
Suffused in thine as rivers in the flood
Of earth-engirdling sea, or matin star
In golden blaze of day. But yet I'll guard
Thee what I may from danger. All about

Thy cot I'll set my lackeys; these to watch
Most presently for threat of ill, and these
To ward the blow should danger grow to proof.'

She grateful smiled reply, then thoughtful said,
But not reproachful, only as the thing
Were past the grasping of her gentle mind,—
' It marvels me the Queen can sceptre laws
So cruel and so heartless. You should know
Her well from often converse—is she then
So stern and cold as some do paint her here ? '
' Believe it not,' he urged with eagerness,
' There is no truer woman in the land
Than Mary Tudor ! Only all her life
The wellspring of affection has been dammed,
To burst forth now in torrent. Spain it is
That rules the realm—most woeful rule for us !
His lightest word she worships. All her soul
Giv'n up to love she deems him paragon,
Whose only thought and only God is self.
Unhappy for us all this foreign match !
For right or wrong, within her heart of hearts
The Queen doth lay her mother's wrongs the most
At door of heresy.—Tush, hasty tongue !
The word, dear love, must clang within your ears—
Say then at door of him, the slavish priest
Who when all England's hi'rarch stood aloof,
Did countenance his master in his lust.
Then Primate made, and for the very deed,
Pronounce with cold and callous lips the doom,
The lying doom, that shamed a virtuous queen—

Debased her offspring, and a wanton raised
To royal spousals and her mistress' bed.
Small wonder then, if Spain through mighty love
Should warp at will his injured consort's mind
To serve his own stern purpose. Love is strong
To mould or alter. Not so long ago
I held it duty both to Church and Queen
To stem what then I deemed a deadly tide.
But then to me came vision of a face—
More fair by far than that which doomed Narcisse—
With contact after of so pure a soul,
My own revolted from my former thought,
Now counted folly. Blame not then the Queen
If moved by mem'ry of a cruel wrong,
Done unto her she loved the most on earth,
With often urging of a much loved spouse,
And cleric prompting all for sake of Church,
She stifle down the instincts of her heart
And do a thing may jeopardize her throne.
Blame rather them that having power to say,
The thing shall not—I mean the parliament—
So they may keep their godless spoil, will do
Whate'er the Queen may bid them.
                                        Now forget
If so we may this vampire dread awhile,
Or pray for glad escapement. Agnes, see!
This dial wrought by masterhand. I bought
It late for you and graved thereon your name.
Nay, never deem the gaud beyond your state!
If 'tis, 'tis not for long—whene'er you will,
I dower thee with all I call my own,

Who giv'st to me a thousandfold in turn,
Thy priceless self!'
                            Now touching spring he showed
Her name twice set within the golden case.
Then while she doubtful held the jewelled toy,
Drew forth a scroll from pocket of his vest
And showed her verses bravely set thereon.
'I penned them, Agnes, ere this misery fell.
But that is trespass subject. Fear away!
I'll read the lines, then set them in your breast,
Fair home of gentle fancies.—List you now!

For my true love, that she may know
    How fast Life's moments glide and go,
And gone ungrasped, nor worth nor might,
    Nor pray'r, can e'er recall their flight.

This, dial, say,—' Life is not life,
    But penance, harass, dolour, strife,
Unless Dan Love the moments kiss,
    And quick'ning fan them into bliss.'

So bid her love, lest all too soon
    She wake to find her day at noon,
And vainly know, her morrowing done,
    That love is life and love alone.

Thus if with me, she think aright,
    She'll heed no more, or day or night,
Nor dial need while pulses beat,
    Love's horologe in Love's retreat.

So read the knight.   She blushing, smiling, stood
Her pure eyes pearl set.   Then—' Oh love, my love!
What then am I to be so singled out
From courtly maids and gentle ?   Summer dream
It is for sure, with after waking rude.
But yet most pleasant.'
                                      Round her neck the chain
He twined with eager hand.   " Thus bend I now
This queenly neck to worship.   Fetter fast
With golden gyves this panting heart to mine.'
Then quickly grasped her, yielding, in his arms.
' I love you, yea, I love you !—Ah too cold
And weak the words to speak my passioned soul !
These kisses tell then less delinquent tale
Yet not more truthful.'
                                      Silent now she lay
Her head upon his breast, her lovelit eyes
Full of devotion, while her curly brow,
Her cheek, her lip, and now the little hand
Fast in his own, he kissed a thousand times.
The robin joyous sang.—The sunbeam stole
Through bough and bush and like a blessing lay
Benignant on them.
                                      Heavenly gift of love
That Death can spoil of all his terror-load;
E'en light the vale of shadows, till aghast
Its tyrant flies effulgence, filling all
The crannies of his kingdom with dismay;
Without thee earth at best were prison hold,
And man its dungeoned captive gyved to ill.

IX

The land was deeply moved.   On this side, dread,
Pressed sore on martyr souls, yet ne'er begat,
Or seldom, thought of coward compromise
Or yield of faith for freedom of distress.
On this, again, was joy, fanatic joy,
Exulting them that kept the ancient faith,
And deemed all others enemies to God.
But yet of these, some doubted still if He
Were pleased that Cain, made Christian, should again
His hands embrue in brother's blood ; or she—
Vile traitress acting host with murd'rous thought
Deep set in heart—once more her Judith part
Play under cloke of zeal for holy name.
But not of these De Vere, proud girl, aflame
With jealousy, whose pangs were swoln of hate ;
Born of the knowledge—cruel foe to pride—
That she high born and wealthy, yet was spurned
For lowly maiden.
                        Spring was come and joy
Reigned everywhere in Nature. Man alone
Made sorrow in his kingdom. Arm'd with power
To mar or bless, how misery tracks his step !
His godly gift, how oft Satanic curse
To him and all that hang upon his will !
Sweet was the morn ! The ruddy sun anigh
Its Easter gala, gilded all the grove,
And waked with warmth the nuzzling buds of thorn,
And furze, that thrust them further into day,

Eager to greet dame Flora, late returned
From winter sojourn, where the middle deep
Laves with its balmy waves the Italian shore.
Sweet was the grass with daisies overspread,
Fair Flora's broider-carpet pearl'd with dew.
The lark, cloud-canopied, with bursting throat
Sang as he'd shake the zenith arch with song,
While every bush beneath made undertone
Of melody, in harmony with winds
That softly blew as loath to mar the lay.

At Copt Hall, now of purpose, Catherine Vere,
Withdrawn awhile from Court on subtle plea,
Made sojourn by permission of the Queen.
And rising rathe of sleeplessness, went forth
Through park and warren, till she found a path
Beside a brook that tinkling through the wood,
Now slid through roots that grasped the ashen clay,
And now enraged brawled over snagget stump,
That swelled its fretful volume into lake
Whose afterfall woke all the solitude.

Here sat the maiden down, with Herbert nigh,
And watched the waters where they swirling ran
In foamy riot. Soon she heard a step,
Heavy and falt'ring. Looking sharply round
She saw the crone of Chingford, she that Joyce
Had threatened on the green the day they kept
Blithe holiday for wedding of the Queen.
She coming nearer, Vere rose quickly up,
Her pale face flushed, and made the holy sign

With hasty hand, then spake with quivering lips,
' You keep good meeting, gossip. Say at once
What have you for my purpose.'

       From a poke
The beldam took a parchment. Coming nigh
She laughed a cruel laugh.—' Read, lady, read,
I wot you can. I found it in the hut,
Sir Anselm hardly dead. It tells a tale
Full worth the telling.'

       Vere impetuous now
Brake forth with frown and gesture.—' Peace, hag,
  peace !
I mislike age that waxes garrulous.
Sit you or stand, whiche'er you will, I'll read.'
And reading, soon there overspread her face
A look of exultation.—' Let him plead
Howe'er he may, her grace will never heed
Entreaty, and for daughter of the man
That next to him that wronged her royal dame
She most misliked in girlhood. Cromwell ! He
That first brake down the bulwarks of the faith,
Churl-pander and apostate ! She his child !
'Tis Nemesis, and but a goodly deed !
A rival set aside, and Mother Church
The better for an enemy the less.'
So said she, then the hag addressed again—
' This parchment truly more than answers need.
But more must follow—witnesses to swear
Her out of faith.'

      The beldam chuckled—' Foy !
There's witnesses enow. Myself full oft

Have seen her in the chapel reading books.
Her Lollard carols singing all the day,
She fills the woods with blasphemies—our ears
Are sorely hurt.'
                        At this Vere laughed amain.
'Enough, good Margot! Keep your lying tale
For such time as 'tis needed. Fear you not!
I'll call upon you soon. See then you swear
Enough of truth to bring her to her doom—
Or know yourself in greater peril still.
What else you add, I care not. 'Tis your own!
See, here, your promised largess. Yet a word—
Why hate you thus a harmless maid to you?
Is't contrast of her beauty with your scrag? :
Or is't your devil pastime finds reproof
In things themselves malignant? Lollardy,
Methinks, would rather serve your master's will
Than, adverse, lose him subjects. Well! to me
Your hatred's source is naught, so that its flood
But sweep away this hilding from my path.'

Vere turned, the parchment safely set within
Her bodiced vest, nor bade the hag farewell,
But slowly wended homeward. Full of rage
Awhile suppressed, the beldam saw her go,
Then curst her under breath.
                           'Of both the most
I hate you, mistress. Satan tear the tongue
That blabb'd my deathly secret in your ears
And slaved me to a tigress! Happy day
Some woodbrained swain might crave a philter charm!

I'd brew thee such a potion, dread and fear
Were strangled in the drinking.'   Muttering thus
She scowling left the woodland.   Vere, again
Disturbed in thought, stayed pensive at the stream,
That fickle wand'ring crossed the coppice way.
Against the sinuous rail that kept the bridge,
She leaned and watched the water hurrying by.

' What is it then,' she sighed, ' that curbs me now ?
Why should I halt in purpose, like to child
That sees in reach the tempter fruit, yet dreads
To take and eat for fear of secret guard ?
The girl is beauteous.   So are thousands more
Whose fate is naught, or less than naught to me !
And modest.   So ! that's heirloom of our sex,
Our common ornament, that laughing Love
With eager hand full oft doth disarray.
She loves, and one 'tis crime in her to love.
There's all her fault, yet fault enough for me.
Proud Semele, the godlike sons of earth
Too humble for her mating, scorched at last
In clasp of Jove, like moth in taper flame.—
But he, an' if he love her ?   Can I then
Uncruel prove, yet crush the thing he loves ?
Would he forgive ?   Did e'er the stricken deer
For comfort turn to him that sped the shaft ?
My God ! I love him.   Were this wench's love
A hundredfold beyond what 'tis, mine own
Would still enfold it.
              Henry ! Henry ! name
Deep graven in my heart, and canst thou scorn-

A Vere for mate and strain a cottage chit
Base-born, of upstart churl, to lover breast ?
It shall not be. I'll save thee from the shame
Despite thyself, though hatred be reward
Of lover service ;—hate more fell than death
To me, fond fool, who cannot choose but love ! '

The hot tears springing, dwelled upon her cheek
A moment, then fell down to swell the stream.
Too proud for show of grief, her drooping head
She quickly lifted, haughty glancing round.
But none was nigh to mark her misery
Save Herbert. He with boyish sportiveness,
A mossy log was rolling down the bank
To dam the stream and make a louder roar.
'Ah ! careless child,' she sighed. 'Would I were
    boy
Contented most, when most the world is tost,
And life flows noisiest.' Slowly down the path
She walked and came upon him unaware.
'So ! Chafes the brook too little for your mood,
Dear lad ? ' she said, and wound her trembling hand
Amid his flowing locks. He laughing turned
And courtly made obeisance. 'Lady, yea,
'Tis best when most it rages. Up at Sheen
The river runs too sluggish for my thought,
Too broad and lazy. Here the frothy brook
Beats out a way athwart the wood and frets
Its banks to shelves and caves—makes foamy eyots—
And leaps and fumes and rages.'

                              ' Other tale
You told last Autumn, boy. The pompous barge
And broadly flowing stream were joyous then.
Dost mind how oft you urged us take to boat,
And pretty sang ?
                         ' I'll sing you, an' you'll list,
A better song,' the smiling lad replied,
And shook his locks.—' Nay, Herbert, I am dull.
Your song would rather heighten malaisie.'
A wistful look he cast upon her face,
Then quickly made reply with flashing eyes—
'My own dear lady, I am but a boy
But yet I bear a dag ! If you have need ?
Or any wrong you ? '
                         Smiling sadly now
She made him answer—' Never need have I
But only of a thing you cannot give.
Just now I wished I were a careless boy ;
And now again I would I were a maid
A year below thyself, and sweethearts we.'
He laughed again.   ' I'd guard thee 'gainst the world.'
' Then wert thou traitor, Hab, to fairer maid.
This glistering chain, whence came it ?   Hast for
      got ? '
' Ah no ! ' he said ; ' but I had known you first.
Yet 'tis poor heart that cannot worship more
Than one sweet saint a-time.'
                         Vere bitter laughed.
' Tush, boy, who taught thee such ungallant strain ?
And yet 'tis truth, in man, if not in maid.
Sir Anthon twice was wed within a year.'

Then musing—' So! in that is hope for me.
He may forget, for aye removed the face
That witch-like holds him captive.   Thanks, good lad !
Unconscious, hast thou well resolved my doubt.
I'll win him yet, or striving die.   Ne'er yet
A Vere was conquer'd or in court or field.

X

Within the Owl—a cottage hostelry
That crowned the hill o'erhanging Fairmead plain—
Blithe evening come with rest from woodland toil,
Sat Joyce with hamlet comrades.   Overhead
Were rafters, black with faggot smoke, and beams,
Rough-hewn, of knotty oak.   The latticed panes
Were small and crazy, yielding little light.
But yet enough for idle day, for most
The night brought guests to whom the ingle blaze
Was summer glow, so long the spicy ale
Shone golden as it frothed from jack to horn

Loud rang the inn with laughter, and the din
Of alehorn smiting dull upon the board
Some merry jest at end.

                              ' 'Tis turn and turn.
The call's with you !—Name, neighbour Chilton,
      name ! '
' I name Geoff Joyce,' a burly rustic roared.
' Give's " All atop the Daisies." '   ' Ay ! Ay ! Ay !

His comrades shouted, till the hostel rang ;
While drowsy Hector, blinking at the blaze,
Lift up his head, and shook his lappet ears,
And angry gazed around, until the voice
He loved brake into song, when satisfied,
He sank and worshipped once again the flame.

Song

All atop the daisies,
In the nether dell,
Phyllis—all men's praises.
Me out-running fell.
Tell me, Sir, I prithee ! Tell me what could I,
But lift her, cosset, kiss her ? Yet did Phyllis cry—
Let me go, I say, Sir !
You're so rude at play, Sir !
Phyllis ?—No, Sir ! No, Sir ! Now nor evermore !

All among the brambles
Plucking berries ripe,
Phyllis sudden scrambles,
Screams like startled snipe.
Tell me, Sir, I prithee ! Tell me, what could I,
But cheer her, cosset, kiss her ? Yet did Phyllis cry—
Let me go, I say Sir !
You're so rude at play, Sir !
Phyllis ?—No, Sir ! No, Sir ! Now nor evermore !

Seeing me a-running,
Or in croft or lea,
Phyllis, mortal cunning,
Hides behind a tree.

Tell me, Sir, I prithee! Tell me what can I
But after, chase her, kiss her? Yet doth Phyllis cry—
  Let me go, I say, Sir!
  You're so rude at play, Sir!
Phyllis?—No, Sir! No, Sir! Now nor evermore!

  But upon her finger,
  Golden ringlet set,
  Phyllis now doth linger,
  All her fear forget.
Tell me, Sir, I prithee! Tell me what can I
But, cosset, kiss her, tease her? While she now doth
 cry—
  Welcome now I'll stay, Sir!
  'Tis such pretty play, Sir!
Phyllis?—An' you will, Sir! Now and evermore!

———

'Aye! Aye! There's woundy virtue in a ring,'
A cotter laughed. 'Church blessing and the book
Make wonder change in women. I do mind
When gammer Joan was meek as callow dove.
Shouldst hear her now! Bid parker Tom recall
His rating yestere'en.'
     'God's cross! old Mat,'
A sturdy keeper answered—'True for you.
But still I'll swear her honest!—Hast forgot
An empty stool your ingle-nook beside?
Where's gotten Madge?'—
     Now quickly interposed
For sake of peace the Owl's intent.—'Faith, lads!

There's wisdom in the proverb " tongues were made
To prison truth."   I'll fine you and you brawl.'
' Right, master Langdon !   Fine them both a stoop,'
Said yet another out the chimney seat.
' 'Twill never sate your thirst, my perky chuff,'
Spake Mat and hotly.
                         Here to end the jar
Joyce smote the board, with ' Neighbours ! Neigh-
        bours all !
Why waste good breath a-wrangling ?   Fill your cups
I'll sing no more if thus you loutish rate.
Here's Waltham Will with open mouth.—Good lad,
Toss off your horn and sing us " There's a lass ? "
Canst sing it and with unction.—Half a monk
Thyself and keen to all their coltish tricks.'
Thus urged, the whilom thief made small ado,
But drained his cup and cheerly sang anon.

SONG

There's a lass that I know ! Ho, boys ! and Ho ! Ho !
    Such a lass and such a lass—she for me !
Rosy cheeked and cherry, eyen like the sloe,
    And lips as red as hips on the hawthorn tree.
Then troll, boys, troll to my cossikin and me,
Troll the bowl and troll the bowl and troll it merrily.

There's a monk that I know ! Ho, boys ! and Ho ! Ho !
    Such a monk and such a monk—not for me !
Round as any tun, boys—cheeks and nose aglow
    And twinkling little eyen full of villainie.
Then troll, boys, troll, etc.

There's a miller I know ! Ho, boys ! and Ho ! Ho !
  Such a thief and such a thief—not for me !
Roguish as a pie, boys, ruttish as a roe,
  Rightful prince of millers and of thieves is he !
Then troll, boys, troll, etc.

Say then pretty, maiden—Ho, boys ! and Ho ! Ho !
  Monkling, monkling, monkling, shame on thee !—
Wilt thou in the woodland all awooing go ?
  Never such another for thy mate shall be.
Then troll, boys, troll, etc.

Holy sir, I will, sir !—Ho, boys ! and Ho ! Ho !
  Such a lass, and such a lass, she for me !—
When the day is done, sir, in the dell below
  Where there's none to see, sir, there I'll wait for thee
Then troll, boys, troll, etc.

And should the miller come, sir—Ho, boys ! and Ho
    Ho !
  Cossikin and cossikin, here's to thee !—
Shalt take thine oaken cudgel—like a lover show—
  And trounce him up and down, sir, for his ribaudrie.
Then troll, boys, troll, etc.

Say then, Molly darling !—Ho, boys ! and Ho ! Ho !
  Miller, miller, miller, fie on thee !—
Wilt you in the lofting see the mill-sails go
  Up and down and up and down, whirling merrilie !
Then troll, boys, troll, etc.

Yes, good miller, yes, sir !—Ho, boys ! and Ho ! Ho !
  Mollikin and mollikin's the lass for me !—
But not within the mill, sir,—in the dell below
  When the day is done, sir, there I'll wait for thee.
Then troll, boys, troll, etc.

And if the monk should come, sir—Ho, boys ! and Ho !
    Ho !
  Mollikin and mollikin, my own lass she !—
Shalt give him goodly greeting with buffet and with
    blow
  And crack his shaven crown, sir, for his villainie.
Then troll, boys, troll, etc.

Monk and miller meeting—Ho boys ! and Ho ! Ho !
  Pair o' fools and pair o' fools—all for me
In the dingle dell, boys, waited long I trow
  But never there a token of a maid could see.
Then troll, boys, troll, etc.

Monk, you scurvy shaveling !—Ho, boys ! and Ho ! Ho
  Monkling, monkling, monkling, out on thee !—
Quick, sir, out and off or a beating I'll bestow.
  What ! prowl the woods o' nights, sir, and for
    lecherie !
Then troll, boys, troll, etc.

Miller, you're a thief, sir ! Ho, boys ! and Ho ! Ho !
  Go hang thee on thy wind-sail twirling free !
Now up and down the dell, boys, struggling to and fro
  Monk and miller battling, maul them merrilie.

Then troll, boys, troll to my cossikin and me,
Troll the bowl and troll the bowl and troll it cheerilie.

'Well sung, i' faith! Wert not the lecher friar?
Too crafty thou for that!'—the host began,
When lifting latch came in another guest,
Whose coming woke loud laughter.
                                    'What! Didst hear
The song without, good miller John, and so,
Eavesdropping, catch no favour?'
                                    Geoffrey thus,
And smartly smote the miller on the back,
'No jape breaks bone,' the miller made reply,
'I'll give ye good acquittance for your jest
Before I go, or call me cull at will.
Natheless, needs rinsing down. By'r leave, friend
   Will!
Sith you will sing, I'll drink thee lusty lungs
To cry your wares a-housetop.—Neighbours all!'
This said, he sudden seized the singer's horn,
Drank deep and sat him down at Geoffrey's side.

Now out the chimney corner piped a song
Full thin and reedy.—'List to gaffer Free,
Like bat o' dusk about the gable eaves,
Or wind awooing bulrush. List him now!'

SONG

Lying lovers bragging pain
Fume and fret and fever,

Happy ne'er, whate'er they gain
Discontented ever.
Fret away! Fret away! Fretting's the devil
Let alone! Let alone! Roister and revel!

Maidens buxom, boasting prime,
Love ye! Love's a ranger!
Mate him now, or moan the time
Scorned he went, a stranger!
Love away! Love away! Fretting's the devil!
Let alone! Let alone! Roister and revel!

Parsons, tell your prudent tale,
Fool your flocks and fleece 'em.
Gulls and witlings never fail,
Fleecing does but please 'em.
Prate away! Prate away! Prating's the devil!
Let alone! Let alone! Roister and revel!

Windbag Lawyers wasting breath,
Canting, cozening, cheating,
One day facing Chancellor Death
Vain your plaint and pleading.
Talk away! Talk away! Talking's the devil
Let alone! Let alone! Roister and revel!

Bacchals, ye're the only wise,
Callow care defying,
Till the night-bat homeward hies
Lip to cup applying.
Care away! Care away! Care killed the devil!
Drink away! Drink away! Roister and revel!

The song at end, a dozen voices joined
In cheerful clamour. So a little while,
Till wearying of debate, the miller sang
Reprisal song ; then Joyce ; and then a third.
But then came knapping at the hostel door,
With shout austere—' Intent ! Come open, quick ! '
This done, the inn's low hanging lantern showed
A troop of armèd men, with him that led,
Dismounted at the porch-block. Startled much
All gathered at the door, in front th' Intent
With cap in hand obsequious, next him Joyce,
His heart most strangely fearful.

                         ' Good mine host,
Your ale must needs be strong—more lusty throats
Ne'er lifted burden ! Bring us of your best,
With rosemarie enow, yet not to cheat. ·
Then bid one fetch the village constable,
And presently, we've scanty time to stay.'

So said the sergeant trooper. ' He is here ! '
The host exclaimed, and, zealous, pushed to front
The piping songster. He with quavering voice—
' What would you, masters ? '—' Sirrah, fetch your staff,
And lead where dwells one Mistress Agnes Leigh ! '
Now rose a murmur all about. The clerk
Stood doubtful, then with urging from his mates
Made answer ' Yea, but wherefore ? Harm is none
In Mistress Leigh. Your warrant, let us see't.
I do but ask of duty, an' you please.'

The trooper laughed. ' Right, man ! Canst read ?
   Then see.'
And showed a parchment. ' Needs no mystery.
She is appeached of heresy by one
Joan Savil of your village.'
                  ' God forfend ! '
Cried Joyce in horror, while hot anger showed
Amid his neighbour keepers. ' Devil's dam,
To peril thus our pretty guileless maid !
Shall drown for't sure, the demon-hearted witch ! '
He careless of their murmuring—' Peace, knaves,
   peace !
And you, brave tipstaff, wherefore stand you still,
Agape and speechless ?—Quick, mine host, a can !
And of your best, these miry lanes breed thirst.—
Now, constable, art ready ?—Farewell, host !
How namest thou thine hostelry ?—The Owl !
My faith 'tis neatly cleped. A knowing bird
Asleep by day and wide awake o' nights.—
God keep thee, honest man, from moonbeam thief ;
And God befriend at need Queen Mary's deer !—
We'll pay thee for thy beer when next we pass,
Or send thee soon by royal messenger.'

Now mounting steed, he led his troop adown
The forest lane, the constable in front
To show the way, in rear the angry folk
With Joyce who secret whispered Waltham Will,
And patting Hector sudden sped away.
Soon Will, too, disappeared. 'Twas but to meet
His friend without his cottage. Quickly now

They took them down a rusted sword and pike
That decked the wall, and hastened on in hope
To gain the maiden's cottage ere the troop,
And bear her off from danger.

                      Calm the night
With breeze enow to wake the mellowing leaves,
Or wistful sigh amid the hilltop trees,
That answer made like ocean monody,
Crooned in the twilight. All about, around,
The star worlds glittering, danced them in and out
The gently moving boughs. The roadway brook
Made music in the air, like faëry harps
Attuned for dance, or Elf-land lullaby
To charm the cot-stol'n changeling into sleep,
Astir with half-waked memories of earth.

In silence sped they on ; till solemn—slow—
Far off, but clear, a bell began to toll.
When Geoffrey shudd'ring spake his mate—'What
    bell,
Good lad, is that so long past compline chime ? '

' I know not,' said the outlaw under breath,
' 'Tis eerie work ! There's death abroad to-night !
Say you a paternoster and for both,
If still you purpose that you whisper'd late.
What can we twain against them,—and afoot ? '

' I know ! I know ! 'Tis madness ! Yet may be
The blessèd saints will aid, for love of one
As sweet and clean as Mary-Mother's self.
See ! there's her light.—Christ's curse upon their heads,

How fast they ride towards it !—Would Sir Hal
Were nigh to rescue !—Useless, useless all !
We are prevented, see they near the gate !—
But yet I'll venture all things for her sake.
He set her in my charge, and God forbid
I blench a hair's-breadth at her trouble's call !
We'll wait them yonder where the narrow way,
Abrupt and steep, will give but little space
For horseman prowess. Once within the holt,
If but our sudden onset free the maid,
We're safe.—But yet 'tis deadly emprise, Will,
E'en as you say. So an' you will keep back,
I'll prove the deed alone with Hector here.—
Brave dog, your master stands in evil plight,
And nearer death than life, wilt fail him now ?
Nay, pup, I wrong thee. Were this cursed troop
A whole Castilian squadron, thou wouldst spring,
And do thy best at only beck of me ! '

So said the reeve and laid his ruddy cheek
Against the panting nozzle of his dog.
Here Will with oath brake in—' Good lad, forbear !
I'll do for you—Sir Hal—and mistress Leigh,
What man may do ! Push on and gain the road !
I'll take this side, you t'other. Shout as if
All Lucton were in ambush when they come ! '

Within the copse they waited, crouching low,
Brave men resolved of love to brazen death.
Soon came the troop, with Agnes set behind
The middle guard and holding at his belt.

Now loudly shouting, out their covert sprang
The would-be rescue. Fiercely Hector bayed
And at a word from Geoffrey seized the horse
That bore his oft-time playmate. Geoff the man
Assailed with fury. 'Agnes, slip you down
And hide within the wood,' he cried,—then shrieked
And dying fell, a halbert thrust in eye
From hinder horseman.—Will, a vigorous stroke
Gave back to one that smote him.—Hector, stunned
By cruel blow that shore an ear, fell back
Amid the horses' feet.—'Twas hopeless all!
And over, scarce begun! With bitter cry,
But striking yet another blow, Will turned
And fled amid the thicket.
                                        'On! Push on!'
Now cried the troop. 'Push on for open ground!
Ne'er heed the knave that's fall'n. Good guerdon his
For letting royal writ upon the road!'
But Agnes, weeping, 'Nay, my masters, nay!
I fear he's sorely hurt. For Christ His sake
Attend his ill! Alack, alack that I
Should bring such harmful hap to trusty friend!'

Then whisper'd kindly he with whom she rode—
'Faith! girl, were best to let him lie, his friends,
Be sure, will tend him once we ride away.
If but we take him, surely must he hang
For hindrance of our warrant.' So she prayed,
They hast'ning on, if living, he might live,
And 'scape all after evil;—dead, his soul,
Might find God's pardon and eternal rest.

The evil news fast sped. But hearing shouts
And clash of arms, the village folk alarmed
Held off long time till all again was still.
Then came they fearful.—Dead upon the ground
Their neighbour lay, his wounded hound with oft
And bitter whine, belicking cheek and brow ;
The while from batter'd head his brave blood dript
Upon the face he fondled.—At the sight
Loud lamentation rose, with deadly threat
Against the beldam witch, whose evil tongue
And hellish heart had wrought them such annoy.

Ere long a litter-bier of twisted boughs
They made for him, brave lad, who never more
Should joy at flush of leafing wood ; or smell
The breath of rose, hedgeborn, or sparse woodbine ;
Or wake the glade with song, or pluck the bell
Of hyacinth or cowslip, simple gift
For simple maid ; or twine the windflower cup
Amid her glossy hair !—With sob and tear,
They lift him up and bore him slowly home,
His hound at side, oft stroked of kindly hand
And cheered of broken voice and honest woe.—
' Shalt have good tending, dog, thy hurt composed ;
No cot in Chingford but shall be thy home.'

Now laid upon his pallet in his cot,
At foot and head they set the taper lights,
And on his breast a crucifix, that one
From wreck of Waltham minster treasured up ;
Then fetched the priest to benison his sleep

With prayer and strowing out the holy stoop.
Thus did they, mourning sore their neighbour dead,
And then had sought their homes, but nearing tramp
Of horse fast spurred, awakening question, stayed.

'It is the knight! 'Tis he!' each whispered each,
The saints be praised, he'll save our harmless maid!'
Now coming up with hasty voice he bade
One take the reins. 'And wherefore stand you thus,
Good friends, about your neighbour's cottage door?'
They only pointing in, he entered quick,
And at the sight, cried out in stress of woe—
'And Geoffrey, dead!—Dear friend, dear brother,
dead!
My God, it cannot be!'—Then light broke in
Upon his soul. He knew full well the tale
They eager told, before 'twas told, the while
He knelt beside the corse, and not ashamed
Of manly ruth, bent down and kissed his brow.

'In youth he gave me life, brave lad, what time
The hungry waters lapped me. Now his life
He nothing counts, but gives to keep the charge
I gave him, trading too much on his love.'—
So cried he mournful. Now a grievous whine
Arose beside him.—'Dog, where wert thou then?'—
He stern began, then saw the wounded head
Ear-shorn and clotted o'er with ooze of blood.
'Good hound, good hound, I see! Thou didst thy
best
I need not ask it, yet well mayst thou whine,

The truest heart in England stilled to-night.'
Then laying arm about the creature's neck—
' Bind up his wound, good friends, as best you may,
I take him for my own. Henceforth, none else,
If he but live, shall know such goodly lot.'
So said he tearful. Hector, as he knew
His meaning, licked his hand with mournful look;
Then pawed the pallet, as he would awake
His master out of such unwonted sleep.

A little time first spent in troubled prayer
Sir Henry rose. 'See well now to the hound!
I'll on and swift to London!'
                              Mounting swift,
And followed far by blessings from the crowd,
He rode apace, intent to overtake
The troop before they reached their prison bourne,
And whisper words of comfort and of hope
To Agnes ere he spurred amain to Sheen,
For audience of the Council and the Queen.
But failed in this, for reaching Walthamstow
The troop had turned aside to stay the night,
At ancient convent cell not yet destroyed,
But turned to baser use as hostelry.

Meanwhile the hamlet stormed, and curse and threat
Against the hag grew louder. Needed now
But spark to flame to fury vengeance will.
It came, for she returning home from quest
Of fearsome herb and bent in noisome dell,

Was met by some that Hector led in leash
Unwilling from the cot where lay the dead.
He, fierce'with pain of wound and instinct sense
Of cruel loss, at sight of hated face
Sprang at her furious.

                  'Ah! the devil's dam!
Dost hate her, dog, with reason!'   Thus the cry
'Out, witch! Out, witch!   Shall's prove her in the
    pond?'
One asked and fiercely of the folk that drew
Again together at the hound's wild call.
'Aye, aye!' they shouted, and had ta'en her then
But that her hovel nigh she fled therein
And hasty shut and barred the sturdy door.
They furious, and the more at prey escaped,
Some battered door, some brake the parchment pane,
While others shouted loud above the din—
'Come out and drown, foul witch!   This even's work
Hath damned thee, hag!'

                She safe within her shed,
As so she deemed, cursed loudly in reply,
Nay more, in madness, mimed the angry crowd.
Then upspoke one—'So burn her in her den!
Damned warlock! Fetch a torch and fire the
    thatch!'
'Twas done!   A-sudden flamed the tinder-straw,
While baneful glare uplit the bosky scene.
She direful screaming, now had oped the door
But, self-doomed, could not, all too firmly fast
The cross-bar jammed of blows.   With eager clutch
Her skinny fingers grasped the stubborn wood,

And shook and tugged, but tugged and shook in vain.
Fierce grew the heat !—The burning thatching fell
Within the hut !—She shrieked, but none would aid,
Their blood afire with vengeance-thirst and hate.
But scowling muttered—' Let the warlock burn !
She-devil ! brewing ever poison broth
For man or maid that crossed her demon path.
Let Satan save her, an' he will, or burn ! '

Down sank the blazing roof. A curdling yell
Affrighted night, as struck by rafter beam
The hag lay scorching, wrapt in vengeful flame !
So perished she of righteous doom, whose hate,
Enhanced of fear, gave up to rack and stake
Her neighbour maid unharmful as the day.

XI

Not cruel of malevolence, but moved
Thereto of wounded pride and jealous hate,
Vere had forborne to use her hag-bought power—
Month after month—till vexed beyond restraint
She sped the bolt that laid her quarry low.
Now darkly brooding in her privacy
At Sheen, as maid-attendant on the Queen,
She sat awaiting tidings of her deed.
Anon came Herbert, bearing in his hand
A letter which he proffered on his knee.
The missive read, she sighed and spake the boy—
' 'Tis matter of much moment, needing thought ;

So leave me, Hab, and wait my call without.'
Her bidding done and Hab withdrawn, she sighed—
' Ah ! love, enthralling phrensy—domineer
Most rigorous, of soul and mind and will,
Unhappy they that yield them to thy rule,
Or rather fall beneath thy iron rod !
'Tis said thy splenic stringlets move the world
Of men, as puppets on a market stage.
'Tis true, or wherefore should I sweep a maid,
Who never harmed me, out my fancied way
To lover bliss and rapture ? Even now
I half repent me of my deed.—A word,
One little word soft spoken by the lips
Whose coveted caress—Ah God ! the thought
Stirs all my virgin blood to wild rebel !—
Once set upon mine own, the world, wer't mine
To give, I'd lay it humbly at his feet ! '

Her weary head awhile upon her hand
She rested, then sprang up, and to and fro
Unquiet moved. ' To-day, so these assert,
He hither comes in haste to plead the Queen.
So ! Let him come, to prove unprofit task.
Her pain-drowsed ears are dulled to all beside
The torture-throb and beating of her brain ;
While I the Council have at beck and will.
Ay, let him come ! But let him come to me,
If he would aught !—I have Sir Francis' pledge,
My wish alone his law ! Complacent fool,
To deem a Vere would think a thought of him,
But as her dog to carry and to fetch !

But if he come, what answer shall I make,
My woman heart in league with tempter voice
To cozen hate of purpose—traitor part
Prepared to play, when most my hazard calls
For aid to cope with urgeful plaint and prayer ?
Ah me ! set down in labyrinth of doubt !—
Here moved of love, and here of lover hate—
How shall I steer me forth to haven fair
Of happiness, no clue to guide or lead ?—
This gird of pain and fear, mislike, misdoubt,
Would I might loose its ever-tightening fold
By stroke of sharp resolve !—Let her go free,
And him be happy in his will. Myself
Tear out with headsman hand the strings of love,
And end its mad delusion.—Aye to die !
God pity me ! I could not live and see
Another basking in the summer beam
Of his so sweet devotion !

                        Peace ! Mad boy !
Why jar my soul with mocking lays of love ?
How canst thou sing, thy mistress nigh to weep
The counter to thy ditty ?—Fool ! the lad
Alone doth love thee truly, of the throng
That daily cringe and flatter. Yet canst mar
His harmless mirth with chill of passion spleen !—
So still art merry, Hab,' she said, the lad
Recalled within, ' and wilt thou never tire
Of trolling ballads out thy boyish ken ?
What canst thou know of Love his shafts and bow ? '
So said she kindly, bending o'er the boy,
Who seated at her feet, upgazing, saw

Her sad proud eyes suffused. 'Why marry this,'
He answered warmly, setting to his lips
The dainty hand that careless wooed his cheek,
'To love what lovers me. And so I wed
My lady's hand with kisses, and methinks
I love her more she shows so cold and proud
To all beside.—I, only, know her heart,
As I were goddess priest and privileged
To draw the veil that hides her lovely face,
And catch her whispered secrets.'

                           'Silly boy!
No goddess I, too earthly wrought for that.
Yet love me, Hab, for all I show so cold!
'Tis famed of them that cleave the wat'ry deep,
Hot streams full oft do flow beneath the wave
That all around is gelid, and the home
Of crystal hillocks sailing at their will
'Gainst tempest, wave and current. So, good lad,
The sternest face may be but boggart mask
To hide calentic bosom!—Let it be!
Now troll thy song, and if thou canst, beget
Awhile in me heartease forgetfulness.'

Song

A lordling there was and a lady so fair;
  Dan Cupid, Dan Cupid, thy bow, sir!
They mated would make such compatible pair;
  Dan Cupid, make haste with thy bow, sir!
So Cupid he shot, but he shot all awry,
The knight he was hit, but the lady was shy,
  And left him awearing the willow.

His worship now gat him in gallant attire;
  Dan Cupid, thy bow was but slack, sir!
He languish'd, he ogled, he sighed his desire;
  Dan Cupid, thy skill was but small, sir!
Sweet lady, I love thee! Canst never say nay!
She flouted, she pouted, and turned her away,
  And left him awearing the willow.

His lordship he swore him by this and by that;
  Dan Cupid, thy shafts are but straw, sir!
And wilt thou not wed me, mayst hang thee,—she
  cat!
  Dan Cupid, mayst lay by thy bow, sir!
He fetched him a flagon of sherris and drank,
Here's health to the ship, wert thou in it, that sank,
  For woman I'll never wear willow!

The lady thereafter she waited in vain;
  Dan Cupid, what sulk in thy sleeve, sir!
No lover e'er ogled, or sought her again;
  Dan Cupid, thy craft is at end, sir!
So, maidens, be wary and mate when you can,
What matter for comrade, so't be but a man,
  'Tis better than wearing the willow!

' Tush! boy, you sing you know not what! Who
  penn'd
Such sorry lay ne'er dreamed Love's roseate dream,
Or drank Love's draught, or felt his rankling shaft
Sink deeper all for straining at release.
Yet well for thee, mayst prove the ditty true!

Hist! Hist! I hear a rapping at the door
Of antechamber. Mistress Clarencieux,
Has orders to deny her grace to all;
So go you, Hab, and see who 'tis that knocks.'

'Sir Henry More, it is,' he said returned.
'His errand should be urgent. Scarce he'll take
Denial of her grace, by one or all.
Methought he would have forced him audience.'
Vere laughed. ''Tis well the Spanish rule prevails,
Else had he seen the Queen.' Then under breath—
'Yet were I he and his the need, in truth
Despite them all I would my purpose gain.
But here he comes! Now, Mary, grant me strength!
My heart in tumult, wish and will at strife!—
How stern his look!—But more I love him so
Than all the galliard crew that smirking draw
About our maiden kirtles.'
                              Rising up
She pressed her hand against her throbbing breast,
And stood expectant. Courtesies observed,
The knight spake urgent—'Mistress Vere, good-day!
I crave a word, with hope—if but you will—
Of gentle service.'—Here she interposed—
'Such service as in honour I may yield—
So 'tis not 'gainst myself—Sir Henry More
Need never doubt the granting. Seldom now
He deigns to crave our maiden offices,
So I am surer bonded.'—
                              More the girl
Had said, but fearful tongue should outstrip wit,

Was sudden silent. He was silent too
Awhile, and marking how she flushed and paled,
With all the troubled beating of her breast,
Felt anger and disdain die out his heart
O'ercome of mild compassion. Somewhat nigh
The maid he moved and courteous spake again—
' My knightly word is pledged to one, whose hap
Is grievous and beyond all hope of help,
If not of me. Could I but see her grace,
I doubt not but to move her.'—Quickly here
She made him answer—

         ' Truth her grace is sick,
Incessant racked with deathly pangs, she lies
Scarce conscious e'en of us upon her couch.
So none may now approach her.—Lying so,
She has no part in life.—Affairs of state
Devolve upon the Council. If your need
Affect the realm, 'twere best to parley them.
If self, then patient must you rest, until
Her grace can give you presence.'—So she said
Yet halting somewhat in her speech, too proud
To lie of purpose, e'en to counterfeit
Dull ignorance ashamed.

         He marking well
Her manner and her words made mild reply—
' Both state and self my matter touches, yet
'Twould little aid my purpose to invoke
The council, since of them is all the ill,
While of their number two are open foes.
Yet, Mistress Vere, methinks all lofty souls
Should firm combine to remedy a wrong ;—

Maid fight for maid distressed, not counterwise.'
Imprudent here he added—'Least of all,
Should high-born maiden stoop from vantage seat,
Like hawk on sparrow.'
                                    All her fiery blood
Rushed in her cheeks, her eyes with angry light
Shone baneful.—'Then should hedgeborn sparrow
        keep
To hovel thatch, nor dare the courtly haye.'
Thus she impetuous. Then—'Would God that I
Could cozen—lie—becloke my purpose thought
With gaberdine of words fallacious, sly!
I cannot! Will not!'—Here her troubled gaze
Fell on the lad, who stood astonished by
With wide-spread eyes, attentive. Quelling now
In part her fiery outburst—'Ah! the boy!—
I had forgot,' she murmured. 'Go you, Hab!
I have no present need of service, child!
Go you and walk the pleasance or the maze.'

The lad obeying, spake De Vere again—
'Sir Henry More, I know your errand here.
This girl—this wench of Chingford! Do you well
To prove her cause against the Council's will,
The Court, the Queen, the Parliament, all set
As one, against this plagueful heresy?
What can you of your project but draw down
Upon yourself suspicion, anger, loss
Of royal countenance, with all that springs
From warmth of kingly sunshine. Madman you
To fling away great prospect for a whim!

The Queen doth honour you beyond the most ;
And honouring, doth purpose place and rank.
Bethink you ! Will you turn her royal mind,
Make naught her set intention, and for maid
As much beneath your stoop—forgive the words,
Your own, you used them but of late to me—
As sparrow is to hawk ! The girl's a witch,
And heretic to boot. What has been done
Was done for sake of you.—I could not brook
Sir Henry More should crush the springing bent
Of hon'rable estate with heedless heel !—
Nay, frown not so !—Think yet again, and this,
Are there no maids about the Court as fair
As her you covet ! Be she what she may
However comely, sweet and worthy love,
Unless you seek her only as a toy
To use and cast aside—Ah ! now you flame.
Forgive me ! All too lofty you for that !—
I know it most unhappy !—Yet your wish
Attained, how long would happiness remain
Complaisant tenant of impatient breast ?
Ne'er's lasting love with sense of purchase ! Loss
For ever nigh like dismal Death at feast.'

So said she eager, earnest, scorning still
To hide her deed with coward subterfuge.
He list'ning courteous but with plain constraint,
Now answered coldly—' Sith my word is pledged,
You can advance no argument to shake
My firm-set resolution. What you urge
May be or not, but faith to helpless maid,

Must be, and shall while I am that I am!
But you, why should you labour so for me?'

The hot blood fled her cheek, her piercing eyes
Showed liquid with reproachful grief and love.
Her bosom swelled to bursting—shame alone
Restrained the words her anguished soul conceived.
So stood she silent. He, to anger moved
At injury to her, his harmless love,
Confessed thus boldly, and by sister maid,
Beheld her sternly.
                         Sudden at his feet,
She flung herself with sharp and bitter cry,
Most abject and the more for conquer'd pride,
She proudest of all maidens.
                                    'Ah, forgive!
Forgive me, and have pity!—Look not so!—
Of love alone I did it.'—Here the blood
The hot blood of her shame, rushed back again,
Rich crimsoning veil of innocence that told
The outrage done to virgin modesty,
And worse for self-infliction. Not unmoved,
But all astounded she could thus unbend,
He had no words, but pitying, speechless stood
Till yet again of misery she cried—
'You kill me with your silence!—Better far
Your worst reproach than silent scorn that smites
Like scourge of steel!'
                              Thus urged, now found he speech,
And bending took in his her outstretched hand—
'Rise, Mistress Vere! I would not other eyes

Should see you thus abjected. Pray you, rise !
I do forgive, so you but make amends,
And presently do bring me to the Queen.'
Still crouching down, and clinging to his hand,
She murmured low, so low he scarcely heard—
' Too much, or all too little have I said.
Despair doth drive me—life or death doth hang
Upon a word.—You cannot truly love
One set so much beneath you.—I am rich !
Give me a look of kindness now and then—
A smile—a word so I may hope to win
Sometime your heart !—Can you not promise this ?
For her, I'll snatch her out the Council's hand—
Her grace knows naught—will dow'r her so, a score
Shall eager wed her ! Soon she would forget ! '

No more she said, but laid her burning cheek
Against the hand still held within her own,
Not daring to look up. He were not man,
Whose soul had not been stirred at such appeal,
Nor moved to know himself so much beloved,
Nor tempted by such self-abandonment.
The maid was fair,—high born,—of great estate ;
And in her hand the key to eminence
For him she dowered with gracious gift of self.
And thus for all his fealty to her
His prisoned love, there woke within the knight
A whirl of thought, not yet disloyal, but
Indulged, akin to treach'ry and deceit.

Scarce born the thought, he loathed it, and his soul

Purged from its blight, by instant self-reproach
And sternest condemnation.

                  Quick his hand
He drew away, and spake the prostrate girl
With low but firm remonstrance—'Mistress Vere,
I may not hearken further to your suit.
You urge you know not what. An hour, and this
Our parley—you confronted with yourself—
Will seem but frenzied dream. Beseech you, rise !
Entreative thus at foot of love-pledged knight
To lie, befits not Mistress Catherine Vere.'

'Twas flashing flint at powder. Springing up,
She checked him with a gesture, haughty, wild.
'Enough ! Enough ! Your cold and steely tongue
Jags all my soul to torment, worse than death !
My love you scorn !—Then take relentless hate !
Of all my race, none ever stooped so low
To kings, as I to you. But none such height
Of vengeance e'er attained, as humbled I.
Go now and boast a Vere lay at your feet !
Go brag your will ! 'Tis naught ! I'll wash the stain
Away in such a-wise your coward boast
Like bubble in a torrent shall be lost !
Away ! Away ! I scorn you !—Get you gone ! '

Thus she in storm of passion and despair,
The higher wrought that in his steadfast eyes
She read a wondrous pity. Sinking now
Upon a nearer settle, bursting heart,

And anguish'd face, she hid amid the silks
With long-drawn sigh of unconceived distress.
Now spake he, and more gently, much disturbed—
'Forgive me! and I spake you, Mistress Vere,
With seeming lack of kindness or respect.
Indeed, 'twas not so meant, and never word
Of this our converse shall escape my lips.—
I swear it! e'en to her my other self.—
I pray you hear me. Surely you would scorn—
And justly scorn—the faithless swain who cast
His pledges to the winds, for larger wealth
Or prospect of distinction. Could I break
With my sweet maid—just Heav'n forbid the
        thought!—
Yourself would surely judge me and condemn,
Love's hour of blindness by. You say the power
Is with you to release. Be generous then—
Nay, be yourself—undo a hasty deed,
Set free my love, so innocent of ill,
And both will bless you, honour and forgive.'

No sign of hearing gave she, only lay
With heaving breast close pressed against the couch,
That shook with frequent tremour of her woe.
Again he ventured—'Will you not believe
Your sorrow breeds in me a sore regret?
The keener set, I may not speak—faith pledged—
A word to cheer you out your deep distress.'

Like tigress now she faced him, half upraised—
'You do but probe my wound, with callous words!

The thought of her for ever in your heart,
Its lifespring and its being. What to me
Profession of your pity ? Void of love
Your ruth is degradation. Go ! Begone ! '

So wild her mien, so set her haggard face,
He could but know her far beyond appeal.
So giving o'er his sad but fruitless task,
Obeisance made and left her to her mood.

XII

'Twas morn, and now the glorious lord of earth
Upris'n—nor heedful more of king and lord,
Than serf or churl ; castellan, than of him
Who, dungeoned, draws his fetter'd limbs anigh
His prison grate to bathe his pallid face
In the sweet flood of day's benignant ray—
Hi genial beam ere long on Agnes cast
Asleep within her cell at Walthamstowe
And warm caressing woke her out of sleep.

Dismayed, a moment gazed she all about.
Then recollection, like to summer-flash,
Awaking, swift she rose and knelt her down—
Her face toward the casement and the sun,
That set saint-glory on her head—to pray
For help to face the fortunes of the day.
No coward she, nor void of larger hope

In Him, wise Author both of good and ill,
Yet darksome dungeon, with its loathsome breath
Of rotting straw, and noisome rags, and filth,
For her had double horror—her whose soul
Was wedded close to fresh and waving woods,
Whose thymy depths were storehouse for the gales,
Health messengers that filled the fields with sweets.

Again in thought she stood beside the brook
That gave back smile for smile ; or rippling past,
Made answer to her laughter, as she danced
Her infant charge upon its mossy brink.
Again the arching trees made murmur low
Of welcoming, like minster organ pipes,
Afar off heard, and all their music blent
To one deep mellow strain, that soothingly
Sinks in the ear, and lulls the soul to peace.
Again the birds trilled out their merry songs
Untroubled of her presence, while the deer
Lift up their heads among the bracken tall,
And slowly sought the tangle, as ashamed
Of fear and flight from angel loveliness.
Again, her knightly lover at her side,
She trod the grassy glade ; again she heard
His burning words of love ; again the blush
She felt, that flamed her sunny cheek, when first
His lips had sought her own in blissful kiss.

But now, unhappy change ! came back the sense
Of looming evil. What should be the end
Of this her durance ?—What if moved to wrath—

She, as she must, resisting unto death—
They should adoom her to the deadly rack,
That cracked the thews and sinews of brave men,
And, martyr-resolution oft constrained
Of agony, to passive suppleness, to fill
The air with babblings, lies, confessions false,
To mate the minds of them that hellish turned
The cruel crank ?—And after at the stake ?—
She shudder'd, while her upturned brow was wet
With beads of mortal misery, outwrung
Of anguish.—' Jesu, as Elias rode
Involved in flame, his course at end, to know
The rapture of Thy presence, so to me
May lappet flame be pen innocuous
To imp me up to Thee.'
                              Thus praying slid
Such comfort in her soul, that cheerful song
Brake from her lips, a simple Lollard lay
Of loving trust in Him that keepeth all
Whose minds are stayed on Him in perfect peace.

My Father, though life's tempests rise,
    And fierce about me rage !
All undismayed I lift mine eyes
    To Thee Who canst assuage.

What if the skies show dull and drear,
    No star to cheer the night ;
I dauntless tread, Himself anear
    Who said—' Let there be light ! '

If lions lurk about my way
  With shapes and forms of ill ;
I call—in haste they flee away,
  He bidding—'Peace be still !'

And if my journeying o'er, pale Death
  My faltering steps assail ;
I faint not, hid His wings beneath
  Who, Victor, trod the vale.

In Him I wake, in Him lie down,
  He all is mine I wis ;
He clokes my shame ;—I wear His crown ;
  He stoops—I rise to bliss.

So singing, heard she not the opening door,
Her face toward the loving, bright'ning beam.
Until within her ear rang peevish voice—
'Mad wench, wilt ne'er give o'er thy heresy ?
Why dost not tell thy beads, or pray the saints ?
Best do't I reed thee, else another lay
Thou'lt lollen soon amid the Smithfield flame.
But here's thy fare.'—This not unkindly urged
Her soldier gaoler.
                    Smiling, out his hands
She took the food he brought, with meek reply,
'Good friend, I thank thee, both for reed and fare,
But yet no heresy was that I sang,
Thyself might sing it, never losing faith.'
'Good lack, not I ! Out faith, in faith, such songs
I leave to shaven priests. To each his trade,

I am a soldier, paid to fight at need,
Not sadden air with convent canticles.
Well, wench, my reed is good, I would not see
That pretty face besmirched with faggot smoke!
I have a daughter too. But hist! a step,
God save you! None may speak you, so 'tis writ.'

She making kindly answer undertoned,
He left the cell in haste for fear of blame.
The door fast barred, she sat her down again
Amid the gleaming glory of the pane,
To pray and muse, with frequent sigh and tear,
Not once, nor twice, recalled the cry of pain
When Geoffrey fell, his mad, but brave emprise
At end with life, as she too surely deemed.

So passed the day. At dusk there came again
Her kindly gaoler.—' Marry, girl, but now
There came a messenger, post haste from town!
Your business 'tis I warrant—so I brought
Your fare betimes, and with it sup of wine.
Nay, nay, such praise is all beyond the meed
Of such small charity. Were you but wise
None need bestow it. Prithee, girl, be warned!
I who now tell it, stood at Aldham Green,
When Master Rowland Taylor hung and burned.
'Twas gruesome work! The heat—the reek—the
    stench
Of charring flesh!—I've fought in Flamondry,
And seen a hundred woeful sights and deeds
In field and town, but never like to that—

A brave man, helpless, chained to snaky flames,
With blacken'd hands, that foolish beat the smoke
A little back from splutt'ring gasping lips;
And blistering limbs that quivering rose and fell,
Incessant while the life blood scorching failed.
'Twas awful!—Nay, I did not tell the tale
To make you weep for pity o' the dead,
But rather for yourself! Not one of all
The troop but would the same prefer. 'Tis law!
And so has been these hundred years and more,
Yet none the less distasteful!—Aye he spake
E'en as you say, and cheerly, mid his pain;
But oft thereto he groaned, and after hung
His head in torment.'

        ' Yea, His Will be done,'
She sighing answered. ' 'Tis but passing pain,
Heav'n's royal chamberlain!—But yet full well
As but a timid maid, I dread the doom!
Still He that comraded the blessed three,
In Chaldee cauldron, surely will for me
Assuage the woe, so that I may endure
Ungrudging for His sake!—A soldier you
To do and not to question.—I too march
Beneath the ancient of my Captain, Christ,
Blood-seamed and broider'd! His alone to will,
And mine to do, sans parley or complaint.'

Not long thereafter, down the corridor
There rang the tramp of feet and clang of arms.
At creak of opening door, with set pale face
She rose and waited meekly. ' Mistress Leigh,

My orders are to bear you to the Clink.
Mayst see the warrant newly come from Court.'
So said the captain. She with trembling hand
Received the scroll and slowly read it o'er.
Then gently answer'd—'Doubtless you are bound
By this, but yet to me 'tis incomplete
As lacking still her grace's signature.'

Again to horse, they bore her through the night
O'er stream, and marsh, and heath, to London gate.
Thence through the sleeping town, to wakeful Thames
That broad and clear, lapped onward to the sea,
And softly stirred of breeze and backward tide,
A thousand crystal wavelets upward lift
To greet the queen of night, who, stooping, met
And kissed them into beauty, gleamy flakes
Of silvery light, that flashed like polished mail
On royal warrior's breast.
       Across the bridge,
Their warrant shown, they made their after way
In shade and sheen. Till out by Nonsuch gate,
With witless head of Wyatt set thereon,
They reached the Southwark shore, as midnight tolled
Out Mary Overies tower, deep, dull, and slow,
Like knell for soul called out of mortal cell.

Within the far-thrown shadow of the pile,
Where warriors lie, their turmoil deeds forgot;
With peaceful poets, great, undying souls
That move adown the far succeeding years,
To fire the brain, and prompt the minds of them

That wake the thoughtless throng to goodly aims,
And mould unlovely wills to lofty ends,—
They passed. Hard by, the massy prison walls
Frowned cumbersome and gloomy. Now the gate
Short parley made, 'twas quickly oped, and shut
Behind them, while they waited in the yard.
Now came the warden. Soon the warrant read,
He spake and bade, in harsh unkindly tones,
His underlings the trembling maiden bear
To common lodgment. He that led the troop
As won by Agnes' beauty, or her sweet
And uncomplaining patience, upspake now—
'Soft, master warden. 'Tis no franion wench
To herd with cut-throats, thieves, or common bawds,
But virtuous village lass! I charge you show
The girl what courtesy you may, so you but keep
Her safe against the Council's further will.'
Then lower—'Just a word for private ear!—
There's one in sooth, if all be told, at Court,
Will champion the maid, come weal, come woe!
Of that be sure, so ware you what you do.'

Good fruit the warning bore. For presently,
The troopers gone, the warden's burly wife
Brought Agnes forth the common room, to lie
Apart in gateway cell. A sorry place
It was, and squalid. Yet its window gave,
For all its bars, a glimpse of outer things,—
The moonlit stream—the cumbrous house-topt bridge
That dammed the chafing flood with frequent pier—
The convent church, its tall tow'r glimmering grey

Within the stilly beam—a row of cots
Safe nestling in its precincts—all asleep
And restful, save betimes for half-heard call
Of watchman in the High Street, marking flight
Of night-plumed Time, in laboured monotone.

Here then the woman left her. Much relieved
At freedom both from sounds and sights unclean
The maid rejoiced.—'Far better solitude
Than comradeship of evil!—Blessed light!—
So pure and calm like holy Him, that called
Thee forth, and bade depart primeval gloom—
Fill all my mind with quietude, and be
An angel-ladder, whence my troubled mind
May mount to hallowing heights of heavenly peace.—
But he! Ah he!—Fair radiance, dost thou light
His chamber pane as mine?—Ah me! perchance
He walks distrest, within thy gleam, my hap
Forbidding sleep!—Grieve not! grieve not, dear lord!
Are we not girdled both by self-same arm?
The loving arm of Him that firm upholds
The round world and its creatures.—Gentle beam!
Be messenger of solace. Bid my love
Take comfort, I, so small and weak, am called
To witness somewhat for my God; perhaps
To join His altar martyrs!—cry how long!
How long! O Lord! till gently stilled to rest
By chide of great Archangel.'
                         So the night
Wore slowly by, she set within the gleam,
A-thought, till sleep with kindly hand let down

The fringes of her soul's bright fenesters.
Now, bowed her head against the casement-sill,
She slept awhile, but not unbroken sleep,
The convent bell oft mingling with her dreams
Disturbful. Once, half-waked, she 'Jesu!' sighed,
Then sobbed; and once th' unconscious tears be-
    dewed
Her prayer-crost hands. Yet knew she naught of
    this,
But slept, the pale beams all about her set,
Like angel guard attendant, till the morn,
The busy morn, aroused the sleeping town,
Whose civic clamour waked the weary maid.

XIII

Where moral Gower lies within the aisle
Of Mary Overies lofty cloistral fane,
His laureate head firm pillowed on his books
While prayer for pity paints the fretted wall,
Vere paced impatient. Solemn was the place
And cold and empty, save that in the choir
One kneeled, while Herbert leaned against a pier
And watched his troubled mistress.
                        Two days now
Had passed since Agnes lay within the Clink,
A pris'ner strict by will of them that ruled
The realm in place of anguish-stricken Queen.

The day was done—the stately pile was dull
With gathering gloom; alone one window tall

Shone in the west with failing ray, and flung
A weird wan radiance o'er the poet's tomb.
Within the far recesses, all unseen,
The organs softly playing filled the fane
With dirgeful voicings ; as the many dead,
'Neath brass, and slab, and crocket-monument,
Made orison in concert with the strain.
Full touching was the harmony, and sweet ;
Yet all unheeded fell on her who trod
The cloister pavement restless. Halting now
She mutter'd coldly—

            'Wherefore comes she not ?
Too much beholden she, as not to keep
The parley I demanded. Husband—all
She has, she had of me in fair requite
Of nursemaid service done me when a babe.
Yet better had she slain me at my birth !
Or better still, my tortured soul had ne'er
Shaped into being ! '

            Now her mournful eyes
Again toward the tomb, upon the wall
The prayerful legend shone, and Charitie
With Mercie, Pitie flamed her full in face.

The words sore rankled—'Aye 'twere sorry deed
The girl not out o' faith !—But heretic,
I do but lessen pain. Her fate is sure !
The faggot-stake, forsooth, would rack her more,
Yea, thousandfold, than draught all unsuspect,
That ta'en bids spirit farewell flesh, but not
With torment throe, or pang of parching flame.

And thus 'tis charity. Were mine the hap
I'd bless the friend that brought me such relief.'
Thus Vere salved conscience, madly resolute
To predetermined evil. 'So she comes!'—
She said a little after as there came
A woman swiftly up the shadowy aisle.
'Good-e'en, dame Joan! Sometime the hour has
    passed!
I gave you o'er.'
           The woman curtsied low,—
None other than the prison-keeper's wife,—
And made excuse.
          ' Well, well, sith you are come,
I'll blame not for delay! Now lend your ears,
I have that, dame, that irks me much to tell.—
Will move you greatly. Have you seen of late
Your mother in her cot at Chingford plain?—
You have not. So, then, shalt thou never more!
The dame is dead!—How did she die?—Alas!
She died a cruel death.—Her hut was fired,
No matter how—but fired, and she within
Fast barred from exit.'
           Further question here
The woman groaning made.—' Good nurse, her skill
In ointments, philtres, drugs, had wrought her harm!
Then she, in evil day, did name a maid—
The wench you have in keeping—out of faith,
And so gave fresh offence.—The tale, in short,
Is that she suffer'd cruel death, at hands
Of angry folk for goodly deed. 'Tis right,
Such self-sufficient scorners, should be brought

To book for foul contempt of royal law.
And so your dame did show but loyalty
When she appeached this gillian, at whose door
Must lie her death.'

        Thus Vere with fell intent,
And dagger speech, inflamed the woman's mind
Against her prisoned victim. Seeing now
Her words' effect in flaming eyes, and rage
Restrained alone of reverence for herself,
She urged the plainer.

        'I, too, hate the maid,
And would be glad she had her recompense!
And so would cheerful leave her to her fate,
But that at Court she has a paramour,
Who if may be, will snatch her out our hands
Uninjured. He has favour with the Queen.—
Dost understand?'

        The woman evil smiled,
A cruel light within her greenish eyes.
Then answer'd low, 'You hate her and for love
Of him you speak; I, too, for murdered dam,
And so am doubly bound. Say then your will!
A hundred times I've kissed those sparkling eyes—
That tell such tale of unrequited love—
And soothed you into slumber on my breast.
Think not 'tis all forgot! I'll do your hest!'

De Vere took now a vial from her vest.
'Your mother brewed the potion for a maid
At Court who feared to use it. They that drink,
Drink tasteless death, but certain. Nay, 'tis safe!

L.L.   U

It leaves no trace beyond a sharp surprise,
What time the palsied heart gives o'er its beat.
Once set within her food, and in an hour
Both you and I are vengeanced at a stroke.'

Thus urged, the woman took the proffer'd doom.
But somewhat loathful. 'I had rather see
Her pretty face in frame of faggot smoke;
Flame-pencilled, than bestilled by sharp surprise.'
Vere laughed. 'Good proof your mother's blood is
          yours.
I do not blame you, only if she 'scape—
As 'scape she will, unless I sore mistake
The temper of her lover and his strength—
We lose our vengeance. You reward to boot.
I'll gift you well. Shalt name yourself the price.
I am your foster daughter.'
                              'Aye, and so
I'll do for love of you, and sake of her
That clownish ruffians tortured unto death,
What gold had vain importuned. I have still
The silken cratch that held you when you slept.
I begged it, when, alas! delusive hope
Awoke within me proper babe of mine
Might clamant hail the longed-for pry of day,
And sleep within't, the better you had pressed
Its snowy pillowkins with cheek as soft!—
But I have none!'
                    'I know! I know, good dame!
Yet better never children than to bear
A babe 'neath evil star. My horoscope

Was cast awhile agone. Malefic shone
Red Saturn, foul consumer of his flesh !—
Venus was hid, so never kindly shaft
For me sped out her silv'ry armoury !—
And I was bid beware.—Enough ! But yet
I'll dare the worst. Who bears a fearless soul,
Bears adamantine shield that blunts all darts
Untoward Fortune and unkind may cast !
So I, I'll prove what mortal may to wrest
Good hap from out th' unwilling grasp of Fate.'
Thus Vere, so lovely in her lofty pride,
So royal in her mien, her comrade stood
Amazed, yet most contented. Now she cried
' It cannot be, sweet lady, village wench
Can draw away a lover, and from you !
Were I a man, a thousand would I scorn
Might I but service you. O' night and day
I'd suit you till I drew you to a pass
And sealed the pledge, with sweeter at your lips.
The girl has surely used some witchery—
Has slily given him draught.'—

                                 Impatient here
Vere interposed—' Did Venus' self intreat
Compliance, doubt me, he would say her nay,
So fairly has the giglot won his heart.
No matter how—he loves her ! Hope for me
Is none, she living.'

                           ' Then shall ruddy hope
Be yours, and ere to-morrow's day be done.
You say the drug leaves not a trace ? The more
It will be thought she died of deadly fear.

Such thing has been.—But—hark! the organs cease.
Best not be seen by old Sir John. Right well
I'll service you in this for sake o' past.
Go dream of lover bliss. Sleep, cosset, sleep,
As you were couched in arms of equal love.'

XIV

' Nay, Mistress Finch, it is no vagrant whim!
That were to shame my love, dishonour me!
I pray you set me not with gat-toothed knaves
Who take their villain pleasure and depart,
Unsated, to fresh conquest. She I love,
Pure as the beam that gilds yon twirling vane,
Is worthy royal suit. An' you but love
Sir Edward.—Nay, that frowning look, that blush
So richly red, confederate with me
In tell-tale accusation!—As you love
Your loyal fere, so I my gentle maid!
Her joy is mine, her ill my harm, her hap
My hazard!—Yea, my very soul to hers,
True comrade, leaps at waking, and at night
Withdraws forlorn from loverly embrace!
Thrice now, in vain, I've sought to see the Queen.
Have maids so little love then for a maid,
That mis'ry undeserved has never voice
To thrill their ears neglectful!—Mistress Finch,
Were you but thus bested, my love were first
To aid you and to comfort. Let your heart

This one time fetter prudence. Sure am I
Her grace will ne'er o'erchide such gen'rous suit.'

Sir Henry thus, to Mistress Mary Finch,
The Queen's approved attendant. Lothful she
To break the royal mandate, and disturb
The stricken Queen, to-day a little free
From sickness, and the pang of morbid pain,
With jar of outer world and misery
Of rule, her people pulling thousand-ways.
So somewhile made she, like her comrades, stand
Against the youth's entreaties, till at length
He won upon her by his fervent plaint.

Now gently made she answer—' Good Sir Knight,
'Tis said Dan Orpheus with enchanted lyre
Moved Proserpine to plead his tearful suit,
With Pluto, for his lost Eurydice.
So you with master-touch have tuned my heart
To harmony with yours in grievous plight.
So rest you here. I'll do whate'er I may
To move her grace to see you and anon.
But here's the rub ! Her heart is set to mate
Our comrade Vere with one Sir Henry More.
Good project too, were youthful hearts but clay
To twist and shape at royal potter's will.
Now while I go, call you upon the saints
To aid us, doubtful, in our enterprise.'

So did he till aglow she came again
A little after.—' She is much displeased

But yet will see you. Vere has nothing said—
Too proud I ween for that!—so I more bold
Told all your story! Be you careful now!
Dwell most upon your love! Her hungry heart
Be sure will lover-echo beat to that.
Gloss all the rest!—She calls!—Now go you in,
The guard will pass you—I have told her will.'

Amid the crumpled cushions of a couch,
Sat Mary Tudor weary unto death.
Her pallid face was sharp with often pain,
Her piercing eyes, illumed of fever torch,
Shone like to twin-stars 'neath her knitted brow.
One hand lay pressed against her aching heart,
The other grasped a golden crucifix,
That ever and anon was set against
Her parching lips. Her mien was very stern,
But not withal unkind, the mien of one
Whom Fate had grievous buffeted, but not
Had conquered or dejected. In her look
Was longing, yearning as for joy withheld,
With tale of blighted childhood, wishes, aims,
Deep writ upon her face, as withering storms
Leave trace of desolation.
                              At her feet
The knight knelt lowly, then her outstretched hand
Laid humbly to his lips. Awhile she gazed
Upon him sternly, then with strident voice—
' What is this tale, Sir Henry More, my maid,

Reluctant, brings me ? Love of cottage wench—
And she a heretic ! I thought you wise
Beyond your peers, and purposed many things
In State and Court for you, with one whose wealth
Would fit more lofty station. Is your Queen
So little in your thought, her favour naught,
You stoop to woo a silly village lass,
Contemptuous all of us, our wish or wrath ? '
So Mary coldly. He with studious calm—
' Your grace's wish to me was ever law
Delightful, till Dan Love, with envious hand,
Touched heart and brain to ingrate treachery.
So 'tis your highness' pleasure I will tell
The tale, assured, the Saints be praised ! of judge
Most kind to wrong, conduced alone of love ! '

With careworn smile the Queen made answer—' Tell
Your tale, Sir Knight, but yet be brief. I know
Not, hour from hour, what time my agonies
May deadlier rage for respite unallowed.'

So did he, all the while her searching eyes
Ne'er once removed from his most mobile face.
Not all displeased, the oft recurring flush
Of loyal love, she marked, the kindling eye
Of lover pride, the trembling lips, the tone
Of tender hope, with heartache fearfulness,
For all too constant comrade. Now a sigh
Brake from her lips, a softer light appeared
Within her eyes,—' 'Tis said no advocate
So eloquent as Love ! I knew you not

For orator, but rather deemed somewhile
Your wiser thought would arm superior tongue
With moment-matter.' So she made reply.
And after—'Weigh you well the thing you ask!
Do I accord your suit, what is't you gain,
At best but simple country wench for wife?
What is't you lose? A virtuous well-born maid
As beautiful as this your paragon,
With wealth to mate her virtue. Place at Court
With honour of your Queen, and comradeship
Of minds that overtop the common crowd
As summit-crags the valley. Weigh you then
Your purpose well!—Alas! I plainly see
I lose a lofty friend, who have so few.'

Here as she spake, her face was sudden blanched—
Her eyes grew dim and filmy—woeful pain
Tugged at her heartstrings. 'Twixt her clenching
    teeth
A prayer came gasping—'Jesu, Jesu! aid!'
The torture passed. Anon she spake again—
'Erelong 'twill come again, say then your say,
Decide and quickly.'
                 Thus adjured the knight
With faltering voice made answer, 'I have well
My purpose weighed, your majesty. My faith,
My knightly faith, I still must keep, though life
Itself should crown the edifice of loss.
But yet, your grace, believe me, this alone
I count distressful!—This that I must lose
Your royal favour!—Yet for her I love——'

'Enough,' the Queen now interposed, 'enough,
Love's hunger lights your eyes. Would God that I
Might read such light in eyes oft-searched of me
For spark of kindling tenderness, in vain!
Ah me, ah me! What hope of love on earth
Have I unhappy!—Peace, thou puling heart!
A Queen and yet complain!—Well! Well! I see
Your calenture, good youth, will ne'er abate
Till torch of Hymen lead your leman home,
And lie extinct without your chamber door.
Have then your will, but first make knightly pledge,
To do whate'er you may as loving spouse
To bring the maid again to holy faith.
So shall her soul's weal lie within your hand,
And I be still excused, should royal grace
Endanger subject welfare, when we stand
Together suppliant at th' eternal seat.
And this for me.—If Mary Tudor aught
Can claim for clemency, ne'er yet refused
To them that sought her—when yourself shall be
Again yourself, and lover ardour fail,
Reproach you not the maid 'twas love of her
That wrecked your fortunes. Now God speed you
   both!
Farewell! sith so must be! My bedesman still
Remain you yet, for sake of charity.'

Again he kissed his royal mistress' hand,
Then spake with broken voice his gratitude.
'Farewell, your grace! The mercy shown to me
Just Heav'n repay a thousandfold! I'll pray

So long I live for blessings on your head.
I go! Yet let but shade of danger light
Upon your royal throne, no sword shall leap
So swift its scabbard—never knight nor earl
In all your kingdoms, spur so fast to aid.'
A moment kept she silence, while her eyes,
Her pain-dimmed eyes, devoured him. Then she
   spake—
' Hold you to that, and I am well repaid.
Now wait you with the guard.—My tablets, Finch!
My tablets, quick, my pain comes on apace! '

A little while, and safe within his breast,
There lay the royal ordinance that gave
Th' imprisoned maid her freedom. Yea and gave
Her custody to him that more esteemed
Her safety than his life. In gratitude
To her whose kindness brought him to the Queen
He much had said. But she with woman wit
Put by his words.—' Tis naught! But haste you
   now!
Go, get your wood-dove out the fowler's net,
Ere harm befall it! Power has hundred hands
To work at will; while conscience-mocking gold,
Foul Satan's craftiest spell, doth ever bow
All men this way or that. Right furious she
Who caused the hap, to know her venture marred!
So get you back in haste—nor stay for words.'

XV

With joyous heart, Sir Henry hastened forth
And, quickly mounting, swiftly rode away.
Yet ever lover thought outstript his steed,
For all the brute right willing spurned the road
As conscious of great errand. So ere long
He reached the town, and, well informed of all
That touched his prisoned mistress, turned aside
To Southwark and the Clink.

                   Within, the maid
Sat by the open casement. All unused
To lodgment strait, and sordid prison air,
She, daughter of the woodland, pined for kiss
Of the fresh winds that sucked the sweets of thorn,
Of hyacinth, and woodbine, eglantine,
Or marish mint. Her bonny sunny cheek
Already told its tale of close restraint ;
But still her look retained its calm content,
And still a patient smile uplit her face
Whene'er she spake, or trustful, lift her eyes
In prayer to Him Whose azure firmament
O'ershadowed forest, town and cell alike.

With her, in parley, stood the warden's wife,
The prison fare within her trait'rous hand.—
' Nay, nay, must eat and drink ! See you, the food
I brought you yestereve is all untouched,
And this you would refuse. It will be said
I starved you in your quarters.'

'Good wife, pray
Leave here the plate.   I'll eat sometime when taste
Comes back anew.   Believe me I am sick.'
' And so wilt be and worse, if dost not eat.
I will not go, forsooth, till I have seen
Those pretty lips kiss cup of wholesome broth.'

' Good dame, indeed I have no thought for food,
Its sight brings loathing. Set the basin down.
I thank you, but, this glimpse of yonder sky
So cloudless and so blue, with thought of all
The blessed shapes that cleave its aëry depths
On errands ministrant, is sustenance,
More choice to me than costly dainties served
With lavish hand to palace habiters.'
So Agnes said, yet still the woman urged
Her deadly purpose under kindly words.
Till worn of importunity, the maid,
To get the woman gone, was moved to yield.
Now in her lap the baleful pottage set,
She took the spoon, and dipping 'gan to eat.
But as she raised the instrument of death,
Unconscious, to her lips, a voice without
Brake joyous on her ears. Swift set aside
The porringer, she started up, and clasped
Her trembling hands in mute expectancy.

Again ! And now with thrilling cry of love,
She sprang toward the door, that opening gave
Her lover to her arms. A thousand times—
Unheedful of the woman glowering by

Or rugged-hearted gaoler—on her lips,
Her cheeks, her hair, her eager clasping hands,
He set his kisses—seals of ardent love—
With often call and murmur of her name.
She nestling, moveless, like to wearied dove,
Her head upon his bosom, speech had none
Save in her eyes, that told such wondrous tale,
His heart leapt, thricefold joyous, and the tears
Welled up and overflowing dewed her cheek.

Their transport somewhat past—'My queen! my
    queen!
Didst think thou wert forsaken or forgot?
Sweet love! Sweet love! I've slept nor night nor
    day
Since thou wert taken.—Agnes! every thought
Has been of thee—for thee! and Christ be praised!
Now never more for thee bleak prison cell,
With ruffian guard, but closure of fond arms
In loving wardship. Yea! my life! henceforth
I am thy gaoler-husband—all thy fare
Love kissings and caressings. Sweet! the Queen
Has given thee freedom, set thee in my charge
With urge to wed thee straight.—See, love, the scroll
Writ with her gracious hand!'
                         Here brake a cry
Beside them full of heart-ache misery.
From Vere it came, whose footsteps Fate had led—
Avengeful Fate!—to seek the warden's wife
For knowledge of the deed so dire conceived.
Herself unseen, th' impatient knight she saw

Ride hasty to the gate—heard all the court
Ring to his knocking, while her mournful heart
Foreboding answer made to every blow.
Him following in, within his loyal arms,
She saw the maid unhurt! One questioning look
She gave the woman. Reading in her face
Confession of her failure, madness filled
Both mind and bosom, deepened by despair.

But at the cry, Sir Henry turning quick—
His clinging bride still fast within his clasp—
Beheld and gazed with anger on the girl.
' So well, whate'er thy purpose, Mistress Vere,
Mayst know and see thy schemes and plots at end.
Nor Court, nor Council, aught can now effect
Against the Queen's own royal signature,
Backed by a sword to reach the heart of him
That dares impugn her grace's will, or harm
By word or look, my own life-cherished wife.'

No answer made she, only in her face
Such doomsday tale of agony was writ.
Such deep despair, reproach and misery,
He could not feel but sorrow for her lot
Knock loudly at his heart, compassionate.
But even, while his eyes more gentle look
Assumed, her hand was laid against her lips,
And, fearless, she had drained the draught of death
She purposed Agnes. Loudly shrieking, snatched
The gaolwife at her hand, but only drew

Away an empty vial, while the girl
Smiled mournful.—

    'Nay, 'tis done, good dame, I die !—
The battle lost, and honour, what but death
Is left the beaten captain ?—Lay me down,
For fear I fall a-sudden, like to maid
A-tumbled in the haycocks.'—

      In her arms
The woman clasped her swiftly.—'Fetch a priest !
And quick ! No leech can save her ! '—So she cried,
And bitter weeping laid the maiden down,
To hang above her clam'rous, while the rest
Amazed, drew all around, with frequent prayer
And invocation of the holy saints.

So lay she still awhile.—Then sudden shook
With gathering agony.—A grievous moan
Brake from her, wrung from stress of direful pain.
The spasm past—her troubled eyes unclosed,
And wistful seeking, rested on the knight.
Him beckoning down, with mild imploring look,
She smiled and faintly whispered—'Henry, all
My girlish life I've loved you. Yet no word
Nor smile had I in recompense of love,
But only icy looks that froze my soul,
Which did but flame the fiercer when the fire
Of love had thawed resentment.—Now I die !—
Forgive me all my folly !—Take me now
A moment to your bosom !—Set a kiss,
Dear love, upon my lips, and churlish Death
Shall come a welcome visitant, and thought

Of this, our first and last embrace, sustain
My weary soul through eons of distress! "

Great sorrow dimmed his eyes. A questioning look
He cast on Agnes kneeling weeping by,
Then gently raised the dying girl and laid
Her head against his bosom. 'Nay, but kiss
Me once,' she faintly murmured. So he bent
And kissed her on her lips. She at his touch,
With last brave effort, cast her failing arms
About his neck and sighing—'Love forgive!'
Lay peaceful in his arms, at rest, asleep!

XVI

Miserere! Miserere!
Earth to earth!—his soul with God—
Give we now our brother, weeping;
Leave him restful—leave him sleeping;
Care is not, 'neath grass and clod!
Miserere!

Miserere! Miserere!
Mortal life's but shadowing vain;
Strength, is naught but self-illusion;
Wealth, but golden-winged delusion;
Joy, forerunner swift of pain!
Miserere!

Miserere !   Miserere !
Flush of day, bestirring morn,
Woke he, blithe as lark, that springing
Skyward, shaketh earth a-singing ;
Nether earth, forsook with scorn !
Miserere !

Miserere !   Miserere !
Purple Eve at Night's command
Leading forth the circling seven—
All the thousand lamps of heaven
Lighting up with jewelled hand !
Miserere !

Miserere !   Miserere !
Sullen Death, his dart uplifted !—
Fall'n for aye, whose step was fleetest !—
Stilled for aye, whose song was sweetest !—
Life-spoiled, lay he—all unshrifted !
Miserere !

Thus sang the village choir, brave Geoffrey Joyce
Borne slowly to his rest, within the shade
Of ivied aisle, and sound of holy psalm.

Much people gathered out the hamlets round,
Knelt either hand, as priest and choristers,
With Agnes and her lover, drew anigh.
He, as became his sterner manhood, shed
No tear, although he deeply mourned—but she,
Beside the bier moved weeping, in her hand

A wreath of forest wildings—simple gift!—
But yet had death but speech, the more esteemed
By him, slow borne amid the sorrowing press,
Than aught from garden plat or pleasaunce gay.

Now, sombre, out the belfry swept the knell,
That mournful labouring over mead and hill,
Awoke a hundred echoings in the woods,
Lugubrious. 'Come, weep! come, brothers, weep!'
The buds and bents seemed saying. 'Weep our
    friend,
Who all our haunts forsook, must sleep to-day
In lap of earth, our mother; e'en as we,
Our summer sheen at end, return awhile
To bide within her bosom.'—Thus the bents
Lamented to the breeze, that now began
More urgently to sigh, and through the woods
Distressful wandering, moved the stolid oak
To louder symphony of dirge, with yew
And elm and ivy in the churchyard garth.

And sang the birds, but yet a softer lay,
More sober, as they knew their woodland quire
Should never more be moved to emulate
The jocund strains of master-singer, who
Beneath their leaf-hid habitations, oft
Would sing of things within their ken ;—of love ;
Sweet wishes tender as the breath of Spring ;
Fond greetings, or the flush of wedded joy.

And overhead a cloudlet floating slow—
A fleecy pall, with fringe of silver fret,
And glittering taglets all of burning gold—
Hung somewhile o'er the turret, while the vane
Weird answer made to plaining of the wind
Amid the yew-tree branches. Nature so
In sympathy of sorrow, tribute brought
To honour him, who, simple forester,
Enshrined a royal heart 'neath peasant coat.

And now, within his clay-wrought hermitage,
Laid gently, all his bier bedewed with tears,
The reeve lay sleeping, while the white-robed choir,
The priestly rites at end, brake into song,
More cheerful, hopeful, than their erewhile strain.

Jubilate ! Jubilate !
Brother, rest ! Life's journeying o'er.
Rest ! blithe heart, absolved from sorrow ;
Rest ! nor heed what brings the morrow,
Joy or sorrow, nevermore !
Jubilate !

Jubilate ! Jubilate !
Nevermore canst joy forego !
Sleep, on angel pen for pillow,
Calm and still as bird on billow
Where the halcyon breezes blow !
Jubilate !

XVII

At Bourne, within his ancient moated hall,
Safe dwelled Sir Henry More with Agnes Leigh,
His cherished spouse. Unfailing in their love,
Years did but twine affection's tendrils more
And more about them; while the gracious gift
Of God, in children, closer drew the bond
Of soul to soul. Erelong Queen Mary died,
Heartbroken, glad her troublous days to end.
But for her sake Sir Henry kept the faith
She loved too well for after name and fame.
And often when, in turn, the fiery hand
Of persecution smote the older creed,
Would secret hide the priced and hunted priest,
Whose life was forfeit, dared he in his zeal
Administer to dying wretch the rites
His fearful soul craved trembling. Agnes, too,
Would feed such in their covert, of pure love
For him that hid them, and yet more for Him
Who bade ' Go feed thine enemy affamed,'—
While earshorn Hector, faithful watched o' nights
To bay approach of stranger.
                  So the years
Sped by and fast, fleet-winged of happiness;
Till fell upon all England, dread of chain,
And stake, and lust, at hand of angry Spain
Long threated and prepared. Then Agnes girt
Her husband's sword about him—set a kiss
Upon his lips—embraced her eldest born,

With never tear, but only noble pride.
' Go you, sweet love, for children and for wife !
And you, love's pledge, for mother, sister, faith !
For country, both go battle ; and the God
Of armies guard you, aid you, bring you back
To me, and these that wait upon your weal ! '

So they departed, but, while yet they turned,
A moment wistful at th' embattled gate,
Ere hedge and tree should hide them from her sight,
She lifted up her youngest in her arms,
Who, laughing, cast them kisses, all aglee
At sight of flashing panoply of war.

Now gone, she set the prattler down, to lay
Her head in haste upon her daughter's breast—
A second Agnes woman-grown and like
Her maiden self in doubtful days of old—
In haste to hide the working of her face ;
The too distressful tremour of her breast ;
And holy tears, that still would well for all
Her trustful faith in Him, Whose steadfast love
Had blessed her virgin, spouse, and mother proud
Of goodly children.
            ' Daughter, let us pray '—
She whispered. So they kneeled them where they stood
With all about them. And the Lord of war,
Made answer, when, His hour complete, He bade
His tempest winds leap out their ocean womb,
And scourge the boastful tyrant off the deep !

Then clashed the bells at Bourne and all the folk
Made holiday; and eager at the green,
Who first might greet with manly English cheer
The master, watched impatient!

                             Now they come
And now the bells are drowned in joyous shout
From hundred throats in welcome.—'Follow on,
Good friends to hall, no resting may I make
Till my sweet mate I have again in arm.'—
She at the gate stood trembling—to his breast
He lift her, and so rode, while all the air
Rang jubilant with voice of folk and bell!